The Fiercest Joy

Shana Abé

Five Rabbits, Inc.
Boulder, Colorado

2 5 6 1

www.shanaabe.com

Cover Design: The Midnight Muse, midnightmusedesigns.com
Interior Design for Print and ePub: Dayna Linton with Day Agency
Editor: Anna DeStefano

Library of Congress: Pending

Print ISBN: 978-0-9984702-2-1
e-Pub ISBN: 978-0-9984702-3-8

First Edition: 2017

10 9 8 7 6 5 4 3 2 1

Printed in the United States of America

Books By Shana Abé:

THE SWEETEST DARK SERIES:

The Fiercest Joy
The Deepest Night
The Sweetest Dark

THE DRÁKON SERIES:

The Time Weaver
The Treasure Keeper
Queen of Dragons
The Dream Thief
The Smoke Thief

ALL THE REST:

The Last Mermaid
The Secret Swan
Intimate Enemies
A Kiss at Midnight
The Truelove Bride
The Promise of Rain
A Rose in Winter

BY SHANA SHAHEEN:

Starcaster

The Fiercest Joy

Dedication

To all my readers. This journey would not have happened without you.
I treasure every step we've taken together.

PROLOGUE

I N THE MOST HUSHED, weighted moments of your life—in dark dreams that smother you and leave you breathless; in stark daylight that flays you bare—you realize how dangerously close you skate to magic.

You walk your streets and meet the eyes of a stranger (or brush shoulders at a coffee shop, or catch a fleeting smile from across a room) and understand, even subconsciously, that you've just stumbled across something far beyond *human*. Something that may walk and talk and grin, but was, in the end, only a Thing wearing the construct of a human mask.

There are many kinds of monsters in your world.

You *have* seen this. But likely you don't remember.

I remember, though.

Even back when I was alive, I could remember every instance, because I was magical too.

It made me unique . . . not that I wasn't already. You couldn't survive the enchantment of the stars scorching through your blood without realizing you were unique, at least back in my day. My life as a mortal boy occurred at the soft dying end of an era. Lamplight and telegrams and carriages were fading away. Electricity, telephones, automobiles: that was the future. Technology was the only magic ordinary people desired.

Yet even though they didn't want it, the other kind of magic was still there, simmering beneath the surface of things. Occasionally boiling up.

My human name was Jesse. I dwelled in a cottage in a forest by a cold blue sea, and in all those years leading up to the Great War, I never spoke but to those whom I loved. The fishing folk and villagers nearby thought me a lot less *unique* and a lot more *simple*, but I had reasons for my silence.

I was waiting for her. For my own beloved *drákon* to arrive.

And the instant she did, I *saw* her. I truly saw her for whom and what she was; even she had no notion of her own untapped potential. She didn't know, you see, that she was actually a dragon disguised as a girl. It strikes me as almost funny now, but she didn't know.

She was plain but beautiful. Wounded, but not quite mortally so.

She was all I'd ever wanted.

She was sixteen when we met. I was seventeen. I perished at seventeen, but she lived on. And now, since I'm dead and she's not, I dwell above her. I've embraced my celestial heritage in my afterlife: I burn as a glorious star, illuminating the heavens.

Illuminating her path, I hope.

Illuminating the depths of her heart.

Honestly, what I see there might kill me all over again.

Her human name is Eleanore. Stars, however, have a different language from anything familiar to you mortals below. Up here we call her *fireheart*, or *ours*, or *soon*.

As in, *soon she is ours. soon we cut the thread of her life, and she rises up to us.*

CHAPTER 1

Letter from Dr. V. Becker, Tranquility at Idylling
Recovery Hospital, Wessex

To: Dr. P.F. Scott, Moor Gate Institute for
Socially Afflicted Youth, London

3 September, 1915

Percy,

Trust this finds you in fine health and good
spirits despite the circumstances. Although my
assignment here has barely begun, I've already
discovered how slowly news trickles to us in the
countryside. We've had no word of zeppelin raids
hitting near you of late. Hope it's true.

Matters here progressing apace. Most of the
injured arriving at this point are either beyond
our help or else nearly fit to return to duty.

Tranquility is a sprawling, mad sort of place, and you know I don't use that word lightly. Decent of the Louis family to convert their home into a hospital for our wounded soldiers, but I'm told the entire manor house was designed by the Duke of Idylling in the years before his diagnosis of non compos mentis, and it shows. Halls going to nowhere, chambers left unroofed, stairways leading to stories never built. Still, the parts of the mansion that were finished before the war began are lavish enough. Rather better quarters than my old rooms at Moor Gate, I daresay!

Writing to fill you in on a peculiar bit of business that just occurred. I was working my rounds the other day, hands full but the usual sort of thing: broken bones, burns, shrapnel, gas gangrene. We've nurses everywhere, of course, plus the household staff (maids and such), but as I was leaving the rec room I noticed a girl I hadn't seen before standing in the hall. She wasn't in uniform, so naturally I thought her a visitor, a sweetheart or a sister or something here to see one of the men. Anyway, there was something about this girl that struck me right off. She was tantalizingly familiar—her hair, her walk, her eyes. Haunted eyes, truly unforgettable. I couldn't help but stare until I recognized her. I swear to you, Percy, it was Eleanore Jones.

Eleanore Jones. I know you remember her. All those sessions with the electrical shock machine.

That scruffy, scrawny little girl surviving all those sessions. Who could forget?

I followed her a while to be certain; I don't think she ever noticed. She's older now, obviously. Done up in a decent frock, her hair pinned, proper as you please. She very nearly fooled me, but not quite.

I took it to Aubrey Louis, the Marquess of Sherborne. Not only is he the duke's eldest son and heir but a patient here (Royal Flying Corps/'plane shot down/extensive burns). Couldn't think of a single good reason why Jones would be all the way out here in Wessex. Thought the chap needed to know a former mental patient was walking the grounds of his home.

Told him what's what. And this is what he said to me:

"Eleanore Jones is no more insane than I. She is welcome here whenever she wishes. She can have the run of the whole bloody manor house if she wishes."

That took me aback, I'll tell you! I said, "She's _your_ friend, then, my lord?"

(Can you envision it? A peer of the realm befriending a filthy orphan from St. Giles?)

And he said, "She's not my friend. She's my wife." He paused and thought about it a moment, then added, "_Future_ wife."

I thought he was putting me on, so I laughed. But he was ruddy serious. Nary a smile beneath all those bandages.

Then he said, "If Eleanore Jones wants to toss your lot out of here and raze this place to the ground, I'll let her. She has more right to be here than any of you. Got it?"

Found out from one of the volunteer nurses (a Lady Chloe Pemington; delightful lass! Entrancing and lovely, exactly the sort of girl you'd think a marquess would appreciate!) that Jones is actually a charity pupil at a nearby boarding school, one sponsored by the duke himself. And that somehow she's managed to ensnare not only the marquess, but his younger brother, Lord Armand, as well.

It rather defies the imagination, does it not?

It took 490 volts to stop her heart, remember? The girl was twelve minutes dead. No other patient in the history of Moor Gate withstood that. I recall anew how very sorry I was when Sotheby finally discharged her.

Evidently the Duke of Idylling's madness has been passed down to his sons! Prepare yourself, my friend, for Moor Gate's first genuine duchess!

—Vernon

CHAPTER 2

IN THICK DUSTY BOOKS no one else ever reads, in ancient sagas no longer recited and labyrinthine riddles never solved, I have found the recorded history of my kind. I learned what humans thought of us, how they feared us, and why:

That we are made of fire or gemstones. That we drink mortal blood like wine, or poison fertile lands with our breath. That with our ungodly beauty we turn men into stone and women into swooning morons. That we live in the bowels of forbidden mountains, sleep atop piles of pilfered treasure, and spend our days and nights plotting ways to steal more, more, more.

Rubbish.

I lived in a castle. I slept in a bed. It was an actual medieval castle, true, but I didn't own it. I was merely passing through. The bed was, frankly, narrow and full of lumps, but I imagine still more comfortable than a heap of coins or emeralds or whatnot.

My breath is fine, thank you very much, and the only blood I've ever tasted is my own, usually from biting my tongue.

I admit to stealing, but only food. Very well—*mostly* food.

I've never turned anyone into anything.

But those legends, those creaky old tales arising from the mists of human memory . . . they nearly got one thing right.

I'm not made of fire, but I *am* made of smoke.

And golden scales. And fearsome wings.

And (all the rest of the time) white skin and lavenderish gray eyes and hair of no particular color.

As a human schoolgirl, I was ordinary as could be. If there's such a thing as *less* than ordinary, I was that. I was an orphaned scholarship student fortunate enough (so I was told, over and over) to be attending the most ludicrously posh finishing school in England. That's where the castle comes in, of course: Iverson Castle, home to the venerable Iverson School for Girls. It was situated on its very own island off the southern coast, a dollop of land composed of salty wind and woods and overly polished young ladies.

In the autumn of 1915, I was somewhere around sixteen or seventeen years old. I was one of only three *drákon* I knew to exist.

The other two were boys. Brothers.

One owed me his life.

The other, I had given my own life for.

᚛ ⚜ ᚜

THERE WAS JESSE TOO, of course. Jesse, who had surrendered his life for all of us.

‍❧⬗❧

ONCE UPON A TIME, I had been alone. Not just alone, but abandoned. I had grown up without my name or memory in a London orphanage so decrepit it had been blown to dust near the beginning of the war (and believe me, that was an improvement). I was called Eleanore Jones because that was the name assigned to me on my first day at the Blisshaven Foundling Home—exactly like the frayed pinafore and pair of shabby brown boots I donned every day after that had been assigned to me.

I was ten years old, and I remembered nothing of any of the days of my life before that one. I didn't know what I was, or where I had come from. I didn't know why I heard things no one else did: tinkling songs from metals and stones, secret voices. Why I saw things, sensed things, that no one else could. And I certainly didn't know not to speak of any of it to the adults around me. Not at first.

I learned, though, after they committed me to the insane asylum. I learned very quickly to shut up.

I wasn't mad, but I *was* trapped.

Until magic intervened. Destiny, fate, whatever you wish to call it. The war let loose, and the German airships bombed us, and all the

London orphans were evacuated from the city. Of our thousands, I was the only one sent to Iverson.

It was bloody miserable at first, I can tell you that. *You* try being a penniless nobody forced to cohabitate with the most blue-blooded daughters of the Empire.

But I realize now that magic is more powerful than the petty machinations of mortal men. It is more powerful than coolly vicious classmates, or even war. Magic is eternal, and magic always wins.

I was sent to Iverson so that my life could truly begin.

"LADIES! WELCOME BACK TO our first day of classes! Welcome to you all!"

Miss Swanston, our Arts professor, sent us a wide, handsome smile from her place in the center of our circle of easels. The morning light falling from the glass dome above us picked out the sneaky few strands of silver threading her brown hair, and revealed rather more clearly the charcoal smudge on her shirtwaist from all the pencils jammed into her pocket.

"I trust you enjoyed your summer holiday?"

"Yes, Miss Swanston," we chorused back to her. There were seventeen of us in this class—the eldest two years of students combined. And even though most of the girls spoke in a bored, *we-shall-acknowledge-you-if-we-must* tone, we all recognized our verbal cue.

"How quickly the days slipped by! I'm so pleased to see you again."

I doubted that. Despite the silver in her hair, Miss Swanston was young enough to feel the sting of the slipping days. She had a suitor in the village, our local doctor, but there was no ring on her hand. Since marriage was considered the height of a young woman's ambitions (and an unequivocal requirement of an Iverson Girl), I fancied it wasn't too pleasant to face yet another year of teaching sniffy females barely a decade younger than you, who were bound to wed dukes and earls and watery-eyed blokes with Hapsburg lisps.

But Miss Swanston was nearly always smiling, so maybe she was just a better person than I.

Art Instruction was one of my favorite classes, mostly because it didn't involve taking notes. Our schoolroom was the castle conservatory: a large, humid chamber crowded with potted trees and bamboo and an actual pond in its middle that was home to koi with fiery, flashing tails. They seemed forever agitated, those koi. Darting madly about, flitting beneath lily pads only to race away again.

I realized suddenly, frowning at them, that it was likely because of me.

Even fish recognized a predator in their midst.

"As a fond farewell to our holiday, your very first assignment is to depict something of significance regarding your summer. A location, an event. A person. Whatever you choose."

"But, Miss Swanston," broke in a girl from my year (Malinda Ashland, clearly alarmed). "That's a terribly *vague* assignment, isn't it? I mean, however are we supposed to *decide*? I really do think you need to tell us what you expect. It's only fair. We couldn't possibly figure it for ourselves."

"I *have* told you what I expect, Miss Ashland. Something from your summer. Perhaps a dinner party. A dance. A flawless rose from a beau's bouquet."

"But summer was *months* long!" Malinda moaned. "There were *heaps* of parties and dances and roses!"

Miss Swanston's smile never wavered. "Then you shall have a lovely variety of subjects from which to choose, shan't you?"

"Ooh!" squealed a younger girl to my left, gushing to her friend. "I'll draw my new set of rubies! The ones Papa gave me for my birthday! The earrings are divine!"

Lady Sophia Pemington, at the easel to my right, leaned close.

"What delicious image springs to mind from *your* summer, Eleanore? Something a tad more interesting than rubies and roses, I'd wager. How about . . . Armand in nothing but his bathing costume, teaching you to swim? Armand slipping out to meet you in the gardens? Armand whispering sweet nothings in your ear? Armand . . . in bed?"

"Yes," I fired back, sarcastic. "They're all so tempting. However am I supposed to *decide*?"

"I vote for in bed. I've always wondered—"

"Lady Sophia. Miss Jones." Miss Swanston stood directly in front of us; we sprung apart like repelled magnets. "No doubt you are conferring on which medium is best to begin your assignment. May I suggest the pencils?"

"Thank you, Miss Swanston," replied Sophia and I together, as pitch-perfect as if we'd rehearsed it. We didn't look at each other again.

Believe it or not, Sophia Pemington was my sole friend at Iverson, a matter none of the other girls from our class understood or embraced. But since she was their leader, they usually tolerated it.

Perhaps *friend* was too strong a word.

Ally.

Slightly menacing confederate.

Her minions were Mittie, Beatrice, Stella, Lillian, Caroline and Malinda. Imagine the snottiest, vilest girl you know and multiply her by centuries of upper-crust breeding and wealth. Tack on the unshakable belief that she is superior to you in every way, shape, and conceivable form, and you have an inkling of my charming classmates.

Sophia was well-suited as their queen. She was flaxen-haired and pretty and about as cold inside as the sea-washed winter looming upon our horizon. The only reason she dabbled with me at all was because it enraged her stepsister, Lady Chloe, so very much.

Chloe loved Armand Louis, you see. And Sophia and all the other students and even Armand himself believed that he loved *me*.

And I . . .

I didn't know whom to love. Or how. Or even if it was wise to try.

I stared at the blank sheet of paper pinned to its board in front of me and considered the many images from my summer that I would never draw.

Armand and me drowning beneath the slick gray froth of the English Channel.

My hands over his, trying to show him how to play the piano.

The midnight curve of the planet below us, as I took him up on my back into the clouds.

Armand as smoke.

Jesse as a star.

Aubrey, Armand's older brother, moribund on his cot in that Prussian prison camp, smiling at me in the bone-white moonlight.

The military hospital in France, all those shattered men.

And yes, Armand in bed—not mine. My pretend husband at that beachside hotel, telling me that he'd wait for me. He'd always wait.

Armand and Aubrey were the other two *drákon* left in the world. Even though I was the only one of us (so far) who could complete the Turn into an actual dragon, I counted them as my own. As kin.

Nearly everyone thought I'd spent my summer at the Tranquility at Idylling Recovery Hospital, being a good girl who rolled bandages and cleaned up messes and fetched games for the wounded soldiers.

Sophia thought I'd spent it sneaking about the countryside with Armand, the pair of us illicit lovers (which would make me the opposite of a good girl, something I suspected Sophia secretly admired).

No one but me and the Louis brothers knew what I'd really done: wormed my way deep into enemy territory. Dodged mortars and aeroplanes and Huns.

Carried two souls out of darkness and back into the fine English sun.

In the end, I drew a stacked pyramid of bandages. I'd rolled enough of them during my time at Tranquility to get the swirl of their middles, the tiny tufts of linen poking out from their weave, exactly right.

CHAPTER 3

AGES PAST, IVERSON CASTLE had been nothing more than a plain limestone fortress set upon its solitary isle. Centuries of reaping wealth from the land and sea, however, had enabled its masters to indulge their passions for crenulated towers and filigreed buttresses and acres of stained-glass windows. Both the castle and the island technically still belonged to the successor of those men, the Duke of Idylling. But years ago he had lent it all to the school, and now Iverson was ruled by a woman far more iron-fisted (I was certain) than any of those ancient warlords had dared to dream.

Mrs. Westcliffe, our headmistress, had a ramrod spine and ebony hair and lips that could pinch off her words with such knife-edged clarity you wondered that you didn't bleed to death from a mere, "Good morning."

I'd missed her over the summer. It seemed unfathomable, yet it was true. She was the only adult I'd ever known who'd granted me a second—and third, and fourth—chance to prove that I wasn't the conniving street urchin everyone else thought me to be.

Don't misunderstand. I *was* a conniving street urchin. But I appreciated her efforts.

It was possible, I supposed, that her patience had more to do with the fact that the duke required the school to host at least one charity student per semester, and less to do with any particular, personal faith in me. It was possible that the thought of having yet another version of Eleanore Jones residing at Iverson was enough to keep alive the hope that I'd somehow miraculously transform into a real debutante.

Whatever the case, I was there, she was there, and my first day of school had nearly concluded without me having garnered a single freezing black glance.

Surely it was a positive sign.

"Good evening."

Mrs. Westcliffe's voice was not quite as knife-edged as it should have been to conquer the expanse of the great hall dining chamber; her greeting barely dented the commotion of nearly one hundred princesses gossiping at their tables. Besides the ballroom, the great hall was the castle's largest chamber. It was tall and stony, and it amplified sound on any given day. But tonight it was positively cacophonous with the chatter of students who acted as if they'd not seen each other in years, instead of just weeks.

"Good evening, ladies!"

The headmistress stood behind the staff table on its dais, looking stern. She always looked stern. Even her smile looked stern, and—at this moment—definitely strained.

She reached for the handbell next to her punch glass and gave it a hard, firm shake.

Ding-DING!

Like hounds responding to a trainer's signal, the many princesses settled.

As was the custom in the dining hall, we students were seated by age. The previous year everyone in my class had been assigned to a table near the back, pressed against the solid chill of the northern wall. This year we were the eldest pupils, and so had advanced to the traditional table of the eleventh-years. It was placed uncomfortably near to the dais, within ready view of the scorching gazes of our professors.

You cannot possibly think of graduating Miss Jones, Headmistress. Haven't you noticed how she is a perfect cowhand with her soup?

Westcliffe screwed her stern smile back into place; a few of the smallest girls shrank down in their chairs.

"Good evening, ladies. How agreeable it is to see you all here at our famous First Night Banquet! For those of you returning to Iverson, I am glad to bid you welcome to yet another outstanding academic year. For those of you just embarking upon your exciting journey through the rigors of our curricula—"

Sophia coughed into her napkin. The *rigors of our curricula* consisted mostly of learning to say in French things such as, "Dear sir, how kind of you to bring flowers for my mother," and of how to manage a deep curtsy without toppling over.

"—we are delighted to have you join our Iverson family. You are the newest ambassadors of our revered school. As Iverson Girls, your gentleness and modesty will set the example for generations to come."

The new girls, none of them older than seven, squirmed and goggled and tugged at the enormous black Iverson bows in their hair.

"No doubt we are all eager to begin our meal. But before we do, I would like to take this opportunity to express my sincere belief that this will be a year defined by you all as the very *best* students, on your very *best* behavior, as together we stroll forward into a future endowed with dignity and grace . . ."

My stomach growled; I pressed my fist against it. Were all the First Night Banquets like this? Were they famous, perhaps, for being so bloody slow to start?

I'd joined the school only months before classes had ended last spring, so I genuinely didn't know.

What I did know was that all the tables were impeccably dressed in miles of white damask, shining with polished silver and gleaming with imported glass and china, and there was not an ounce of food upon any of them. Only our water goblets had been filled, and I'd already drained mine.

The aroma of roasted lamb and mint sauce wafted in from the hallway, where the trolleys holding our meal waited. I tried to ignore it, but the scent was so delectable it nearly brought tears to my eyes. All of my senses were heightened beyond human perception, including smell, which meant that from my chair I could already discern exactly what the First Night menu was going to include.

That lamb and mint. Tomato cream soup and rosemary rolls. Savory sauces, broiled asparagus and onions and peas and crumbled bacon, breaded chicken and potatoes and gravy and by God, I was nearly delirious with hunger.

Drákon senses, *drákon* appetite. I was permanently hungry. Given the chance, I truly would eat like a cowhand. At least *they* didn't have to listen to droning speeches before being allowed to dine.

" . . . sacrifices," Westcliffe was saying. "As such, I am confident you will all understand why, after tonight, we shall no longer be serving meat on any days but Sundays and special occasions."

What was that? I broke off my longing stare toward the hall. A shocked murmur was wending its way through the tables. Mrs. Westcliffe kept her smile.

"Wheat, I fear, is also being more strictly rationed, and we shall adjust accordingly. Now, now," she said against the rising whispers, raising a hand. "I know we are all loyal subjects of His Majesty. And we are all eager to do our part to support the war."

"Outrageous," muttered Lillian, two seats down from me.

"Honestly!" agreed Stella, slightly louder.

"Father shall be hearing about this," huffed Caroline, who must have forgotten how close we were to the dais now.

"Lady Caroline," snapped the headmistress, bristling. "I am certain neither you nor your father would be so ungenerous as to deny a loaf of bread to a hungry soldier in a trench. Nor would you wish him to go without his weekly allotment of cold tinned beef, even as he is risking his life for the survival of our country. Or have I been very much mistaken in your character?"

If Westcliffe had thought that Caroline would forgo any portion of her charmed world without a fuss, then yes, I'd say she had been.

Caroline ducked her head.

"No, Headmistress," she mumbled.

Into the absolute silence that followed my stomach released another gurgle, loud as an elephant's. Westcliffe's gaze flicked instantly to me.

"And you, Miss Jones?"

And me what? I pressed my lips shut and imitated Caroline, staring down at my lap.

"No, Headmistress," I echoed, hoping it was the right response.

So much for getting through my first day unscathed.

A draft pushed through the elegant chandeliers above us, sending crystal ropes and beads tapping, *tink, tink.* Down at the other end of our table, I heard Sophia choking back a laugh.

"Very well," said Westcliffe at last. "Begin the Banquet."

� ⊰✦⊱ ⟞

THERE ARE MANY SACRED rules regarding the art of social dining, as I'm sure you're aware.

At Blisshaven, the orphanage, we had only one: *grab what you can, while you can, and eat it up as quick as you can.*

Blisshaven had served one meal a day. I had not been the only child starving.

But at Iverson, there were meals upon meals, and there was no grabbing of anything. Before you could even touch your food, you had to determine which utensil went with it. God forbid you used the escargot fork on your lobster, or the chocolate muddling spoon for your iced tea.

You had to know precisely how to unfold your napkin. When to use the fingerbowls. Where to put your gloves.

You had to take teeny little bites. Tiny little sips. You had to converse happily and insincerely with your neighbor—no matter how much you despised her, or she you—about cuisine, fashion, or the weather (the only acceptable topics allowed a young woman).

And no matter how famished you felt, you were not to finish the food on your plate. English ladies, you see, were dainty creatures, and apparently required hardly any nourishment at all to survive.

Perhaps that was why all my classmates were so foul-tempered.

Malinda was my neighbor at our table, and the only time we'd ever conversed about anything so civilized as the weather was under the nose of Mrs. Westcliffe during etiquette lessons. Tonight, beneath the clattery din of a hundred forks and knives meeting china, she felt free to ignore me entirely.

Almost entirely.

"Did you hear her?" She nudged Lillian with her elbow, tipping her head toward me. "Did you hear her *bodily fluids*? So crass!"

"A perfect cowhand," agreed Lillian, smirking as she slurped up her soup.

The chandelier directly above us released another ripple of chimes. I lifted my eyes and watched, unsurprised, as the blue-gray smoke above the burning candles twisted into coils that danced and drifted and never quite dispersed.

Mittie tittered; I could always count on her to join in the fun of skewering me. "Well, what do you expect? You can dress up the slum girl all you want, but inside she's still a vulgar slum girl."

"Speaking of that," Stella said, "what on earth happened to her uniform? Have you noticed? She looks positively ready to burst!"

This, unfortunately, was true. All Iverson Girls wore matching uniforms on schooldays, and it appeared that I was still stuck in the same garments I'd been allotted last year. My shirtwaist stretched so tightly across my bosom, the buttons strained at the seams. It was white and plain and supposed to drape modestly loose, but one deep breath and I'd likely pepper the table with bone-button bullets.

My plum-colored skirt wasn't any seemlier. It was meant to be constricting, the better to hobble us into ladylike steps. But I was beyond hobbled; I practically had to hop.

I tried the soup, wondering how much of the feast I could put away before the stitching at my waist split apart.

"Perhaps it's the style in Cheapside," said Mittie, helping herself to another roll. "Perhaps it's the way girls wear things there, the better to lure the drunkards."

Beatrice patted her lips with her napkin. "And did anyone else glimpse that frightful new frock she arrived in? She looked like a dressmaker dummy escaped from some tawdry village shop!"

The chandelier began, very subtly, to sway.

"Oh, I don't know," drawled Stella. "Even ready-made dresses are an improvement upon what she wore last year. Remember those dreadful brown rags?"

"Haute couture from the poorhouse!"

"Quite!"

"Haven't you heard?" I said to the table, my voice low and pleasant. "I've taken Lord Armand as my lover. He purchased all my new clothing."

Sophia lowered her spoon and arched her brows at me. Everyone else simply froze.

I leaned forward and whispered conspiratorially, "*Even my bloomers.*"

I really wasn't very good at following rules. Besides, I wasn't even *from* Cheapside.

Caroline sputtered, "That is—that couldn't possibly be—"

"Ask Sophia, if you don't believe me."

They swiveled as one back to her.

It didn't take her long to regain her composure. She gave a shrug, although her cheeks were turning pink. "It's true."

"Good *heavens*—"

"Are you actually *admitting*—"

"I can't believe she—"

"I *told* you she was a tart—"

"I *know*, but—"

"Eleventh-years!"

Mrs. Westcliffe had arisen from the shadows before us, sudden and glaring. "The level of conversation at your table is approaching stridence. Is this how I've taught you to comport yourselves during meals?"

"Headmistress!" Mittie was all but bouncing in her chair with joy; she had always hated me the most. "Eleanore has just confessed to—"

"To finding the most *divine* shawl in the village," Sophia said over her, very bright. "We're all *dying* to see it. She says it's Irish lace."

"From nuns," I added, into the hush.

Mittie shook her head. "That isn't—"

"Likely in such a remote village, I know!" Sophia wasn't going to lose, especially to a minion. "But apparently Mrs. Forth's shop is *so* much more fashionable than it used to be. It sounds *ever* so promising. I do hope, Headmistress, that you'll allow us a free day to go to the mainland next week so that we might find out for ourselves."

She shot a frigid smile down the table that had all the underlings cringing. I realized anew how much I really did like her.

Westcliffe had missed the smile. "Free days are predetermined for the semester, as you are well aware, Lady Sophia. Should you wish to walk to the village as a group for one of them, perhaps an arrangement might be made. But only as a reward for *proper* behavior, which I have yet to witness from this table this evening."

"Yes, Headmistress," answered Sophia, abruptly, properly meek. "Thank you, Headmistress."

Westcliffe studied us a moment longer, then clipped off. Mittie looked at Sophia, looked at me, and straightened her spine.

"I don't know why we should bother protecting *her*," she sneered.

"Because I wish it," Sophia replied.

"But she's nobody!"

"Now. But who knows? Perhaps someday she'll marry Armand. Then she'll rank higher than you, won't she?"

"Even Armand Louis has better taste than that," Mittie said stiffly.

A taper from the chandelier tumbled from its crystal cup. It landed squarely in Mittie's soup, spattering her with tomato cream.

I had to credit Sophia: it turned out to be much more difficult than I'd expected to choke back laughter.

CHAPTER 4

As befitting my outlander status at the school, I lived by myself in one of Iverson's isolated towers, which suited me beautifully.

As clusters of the other students retired to their own luxurious wing, I walked just behind them, and then past them, to the lonely stairwell that wound upward to my room. Oil lamps burning in alcoves lit all the main passageways—the island had no electricity—but if I wished for illumination, I had to carry my own candle up the stairs. Conveniently, I was handed one by Almeda, the chatelaine, as I was leaving the great hall after the banquet.

"I thought we were allowed only two candles per month," I said, surprised. I'd left both of mine in my room. These upper-class girls weren't above pinching any little extras they could find.

"Aye, that's still the rule. But oil's become dear. Since this wretched war began, a great many things have become dear, I'm sorry to say! We'll not be lighting your way to the tower. Doesn't make sense for just one lass."

I didn't point out that they'd never actually lit the stairs. I was used to traveling them in the dark.

"Very generous of you," I said, accepting the candle.

Almeda gave a nod. She was plump and gruff, but not unkind. "Well. No one wants you breaking your head, do they?"

I imagined quite a few people would be happy if I broke my head (Mittie at the very least, scowling at me with her tomato-soup face), but again, I said nothing.

It was three flights up to my door. The air took on its particular chill as I climbed; the castle was always cold but the towers especially so. The pewter holder for the candle soon ringed my finger in ice.

But the flame I carried was golden and flickering. It offered the illusion of warmth, spreading light that danced along the pits and lines of the limestone walls before vanishing into the shadows that lingered soft above my head.

I kept my pace measured. I kept the candle close. I touched my hand to the knob of my door and turned it without hurry, because I already knew what I'd find inside my little round room.

Who, rather.

He waited for me upon my bed. To be fair, there wasn't anywhere else to sit; my chamber contained a bed, a bureau, and an armoire. That was it. That was all that would fit, frankly, but he looked right at home on the bed, relaxed and smiling. He'd gathered a few of my quilts around him, because the room was quite as chilly as the stairwell, and beneath the quilts he would be wearing no clothes.

Here was Lord Armand Louis, second son of a duke:

Brown-haired, very deep brown and glossy. Always slightly ruffled and too long for fashion.

Blue-eyed, intensely blue. Cobalt oceans, infinite nights, surrounded by thick jet lashes. Girls of a certain ilk were known to swoon over those lashes.

Ivory skin as pale as mine.

Arrogance in the cut of his jaw, the curve of his lips.

Strength in the cords of his neck, his shoulders. All the rest of him.

Beauty, sharp-edged and dangerous.

Magic beneath and above all that. Magic like mine, invisible power that hummed through him and changed him and blessed him, even though Armand certainly needed no further blessings in his life.

About a year older than I, he had come into his Gifts later than I had. Yet it seemed to me that his were already more obvious. Whenever I'd seen him lately, I couldn't believe I was the only one to notice how he shimmered now. How he shone like nothing else alive, like the blade of a sword freshly whetted to draw blood, to slice through tangled destinies and claim forbidden crowns.

Armand was rich, handsome, and irrevocably focused on me. Always me.

He had no idea that just over a month ago, I'd promised the stars my mortal life in exchange for sparing his.

I had no intention of telling him. I had the uneasy feeling that *drákon* love was far darker and deeper than anything human, and this dragon loved me. What I felt for him was less crystalline, but I did know, with my entire being, that I couldn't bear to break him. So I would never tell.

Someday, I supposed, I'd just . . . be taken. And then I'd never have to see him break.

I was a coward, because I was glad about that.

"What a lot of sour little prigs," he said genially. "Blimey, who knew?"

"Shhh." I closed my door. "It's very quiet up here. Voices carry."

"No one's around, waif."

He would hear them as well as I. He would sense them as well as I. Heartbeats. Respiration. Sweat.

I placed the candle upon my bureau. The small looking glass behind it caught the flame, cast it back at me in doubled gold.

I tried for a severe tone. "You shouldn't be here. I'll get tossed out."

"Do you think they'll catch me in your bed?"

"They'd bloody well better not."

He cocked his head. "What have we to hide? Haven't you taken me as your lover?"

I couldn't help it; I started to laugh, so I pressed my fingers over my mouth to hold it in. "That was so . . . Did you see their faces?"

"I did."

I let my smile break through. "That was worth every bit of it."

Armand slanted back against my pillows. "I don't know what they were going on about. You look rather smashing in that uniform."

"If only I could breathe."

"Breathing," he said, with a wicked smile of his own, "can be entirely overrated. Aren't you cold over there, all by yourself? I've warmed the blankets quite nicely, you know."

"I meant it, Mandy. You shouldn't have come. I'm a schoolgirl again, a ruddy respectable one."

"Really?" he asked, still genial. "Then why did you leave your window open, schoolgirl, if you didn't want me to come?"

Despite what I'd told everyone, and despite his own wishes (and what a good many people had already assumed), Armand was not my lover. Not entirely. But ever since last August, we had been sleeping beside each other nearly every night. It wasn't as scandalous as it sounded—all right, it *was*, but at least there had been no silly sneaking about the darkened halls of Tranquility in our robes, skulking from room to room in the middle of the night like characters in a very bad farce.

When you could Turn to smoke, you needed neither robes nor darkness to pass by unnoticed. All you needed was a sliver of space—a crack beneath a door, an empty keyhole, an open window—and you could find yourself wherever you wished.

I liked sleeping beside him. He was lean and comfortable and scented of spice and clouds and woods. And although I'd never admit it out loud, I rested better when he was near.

I worked at the buttons on my boots until I could kick them off, unfastened the top of my skirt, then climbed into bed. I was wrapped instantly in quilts and arms.

"You can't stay," I whispered, closing my eyes.

"No, I know." He turned his face to mine. His lips brushed my forehead.

That was all he did, and I knew that was all he would ask of me tonight. Even with the unpredictable heat of *drákon* in his blood, Armand Louis was a gentleman. So it had to be me who inched closer, who tilted her chin in invitation and waited, waited, until he shifted to find my lips.

I sighed a little against him, my breath warming his skin. His hand lifted, his palm skimming my shirtwaist, up my corset to my shoulder. His fingers curved firm around my arm.

Whenever Jesse and I had kissed, I'd felt bliss. There's no better word for it, just bliss. It had been bright and shattering. But when I kissed Armand, it was different. I never felt blissful, exactly. I felt ravenous. Like I'd never get enough; I'd always want more and more. And it was getting harder and harder to stop at mere kisses.

If the end of my life was a precipice approaching, I teetered at its brink. I would not go over it without taking more from him, I knew.

So I was selfish *and* a coward.

But I wouldn't take more tonight, because even though his lips were velvet, and even though his body was strong and familiar, and even though his fragrance filled me and intoxicated me—better than wine or champagne or gin—tonight was not our night. Somewhere inside me, in a deep and still place, I knew that.

I thought perhaps that he did, as well.

He gave a ragged exhalation and eased away. He stroked my shoulder, restless strokes, as our pulses calmed and the shadow-thick night began to reclaim us.

Beyond the bed and him, the air held the tang of autumn. The

Channel surf struck echoes against the shore. A breeze slipped in past the window, a soundless breath pushed from the sea to the candle, and the flame guttered out.

"Well done with that taper," I said sleepily, after a moment.

"Thank you," Armand replied, very soft. "But I was aiming for her head."

$$\text{\textasciitilde}\,\text{\textbf{+}}\,\text{\textasciitilde}$$

I DREAMED OF A song. It was a small song at first, barely a skip of sound against the low steady rush of my heartbeat over Armand's. But it was persistent, a tinkling, pretty thing with a hint of urgency about it, a scale of melody that grew louder and then quieter and then louder. It rose and fell like the waves that scored the coast, up and down, up and down, on and on . . .

I opened my eyes. The song remained, sliding through the dark.

Armand took a heavier breath, lifting half of me with him.

"I hear it, too," he said.

I sat up. I pushed a few sticky strands of hair from my cheeks and looked toward my room's lone window.

The song was coming from somewhere beyond it.

It wasn't a star-song. Even from the bed, I could see the dense gray fog that concealed the sky. The stars would be singing above that, of course, but if I wanted to hear them I'd have to fly up to them.

It wasn't a stone-song, either. It was too tiny and chiming for that.

It was from something metal. Something made of gold.

The castle, needless to say, had many objects of gold within it. Most of the students had cases and cases of fine jewelry because on the weekends, out of uniform, they were allowed to show it all off. Even our professors sported modest rings or bangles or earbobs. I had become accustomed to those sorts of songs, which nearly always sounded lethargic or downright aloof.

I myself owned a golden brooch and a golden cuff, but the cuff was on my wrist, and the brooch still tucked in the bureau.

This song was new. And although it had no words, it felt like it . . . knew me.

Was trying to summon me.

I padded to the window. It was tall and composed of diamond-shaped panes and typically opened only just enough for me to stick my head through. I placed my hands on the glass and pushed, and the hinges squeaked and gave a whit more.

Were it not for the fog, I would have seen my usual view of the lawn that smoothed the land before the castle, plus a few of the eerie animal-shaped hedges that seemed poised to wander about. A portion of the rose gardens. The beginnings of the woods. I would have also seen the bridge that connected the island to the mainland, a spindly wooden toothpick nearly a mile long, Iverson's sole link to the rest of the world.

But there *was* fog tonight, damp and thick and salty. So that was all that I saw.

The song sparkled through it, beckoning.

I glanced back at Armand. He was watching me, his mouth turned down. He gave a short, quick shake of his head.

I smiled and shook my head back at him. Then I Turned to smoke, letting my too-small clothes and the cuff and my hairpins and everything that was not me fall to the floor. I flowed out the window and went to answer that summons.

≻━━❄━━≺

GOING TO SMOKE IS just as it sounds. You lose your human body, all its human weight and human problems. You become something both more and less than what you were, because now you are the sinuous, mystical vapor of *drákon*, and you soar where you want to, and you see and hear and even feel a very little—but not much.

Dragon smoke, sheer and twisting. Swifter than birds, wilder than the wind. All that may ever catch you now is yet another dragon.

≻━━❄━━≺

THE BEACH WAS MOSTLY pebbles beneath my bare feet, but the fog bothered me more; it felt as if I had been slathered in a layer of cold, wet dew. A few paces away, the sea chattered against the rocks, un-concerned with the girl who'd just materialized from haze into flesh and was standing naked and alone nearby.

By midmorning the sea would be gone, leaving only sand and stone all the way to the mainland: for a few hours each day it gave up the island and retreated into the deeper pockets of the Channel. Then slowly it would change its mind and steal back, and Iverson would be bounded by waves once more.

But tonight the seawater still splashed close. Iverson lurked nearby too, but I couldn't see any of it, only a world of smoky dark gray.

Then I was no longer alone. Armand Turned to boy beside me, quite as naked as I. He kept his weight mostly on one leg. The other had been broken over the summer, and he'd only just gotten the cast off.

I looked away and clasped my arms over my chest. I was abruptly glad for the fog, after all.

"It's here," I said, not looking at him again. "Out here."

"I know."

He bent down, and I followed. We were both digging through the pebbles and sand, but it was I who found it: a starfish no bigger than a shilling, rigid and solid gold, wedged between two stones. It was cold, like everything else. Heavy, for something so small. I brushed the sand from it with one finger and listened to its song and felt my heart grow heavy too.

This had been the beach where Jesse had died. Jesse, who'd had the power to turn any living thing into gold. This had been the spot of his last stand, when he'd used his powers to save the school and me and Armand and everyone else.

This little starfish had been alive that night. Now, just like Jesse, it wasn't.

Out of nowhere, I saw his face, tanned and smiling. I saw his eyes, green as summer. I heard his voice, his laughter. Felt his touch—

"It must have been caught in the spell," Armand said. "Out in the water all this while. Probably washed up only tonight."

"Yes."

It would have grieved him, I knew. The loss of even this slight life would have grieved him. Jesse'd never wanted to harm a thing.

I clenched my fingers around the star, let it poke hard into my palm.

"There'll be more, Lora." Very gently, Armand cupped his hands around mine. I kept my gaze fixed on our fingers, on the tendrils of gray that floated between us and wiped away all our clear edges. "Fish. Clams. Kelp. Anything small like this will start to turn up more and more, especially with the winter waves coming."

"Then this is about to become the most popular beach in the world," I said bitterly.

"No, it won't." He tugged at my hand until my fingers opened. He took the starfish from my palm and rose to his feet. "I won't let it."

I knew what he was going to do and didn't try to stop him, even though a part of me—the worst part, the most wretched part, the part that grew up without enough food or coal or a coat—was thinking, *No, no, it's still valuable—*

But I only watched as Armand drew back his arm and flung the starfish into the sea.

I heard it strike the water. Then its song vanished, drowned once more.

━ ✦✦✦ ━

THE TRUTH WAS, I had enough gold of my own already. Thanks to Jesse, I had a whole treasure chest of it safely buried in the island woods. If I was ever really worried about money, all I had to do was remind myself about that secret chest.

And it had to remain secret, at least as long as I was at Iverson. Years ago, I had been found an impoverished orphan; months from now, I would be graduating an impoverished orphan. About a second after that, I was going to become someone shiny new. Someone with grace, and wealth, and magic. And I was going to live like that until the stars decided to claim me.

I wasn't certain of anything else. But that was enough.

Armand or not, Jesse or not, Aubrey or not—that was enough.

Wasn't it?

CHAPTER 5

DRAGONS MAY COMMUNICATE WITH stars. Stars may answer. It's a powerful Gift, but the stars tend to have the better end of it, since they're mysterious and all-knowing and right about everything.

Jesse had ascended to the heavens after the death of his human body. He'd surrendered to his celestial heritage to burn entirely as a star. Armand could hear him; Aubrey could hear him. Even their father, the duke, was visited by Jesse in his dreams. But I'd had very little luck finding Jesse as a star, and I wondered if it was a punishment of some sort, or a test, or just a rule (stars have *many* rules) that blazing new souls are forbidden to linger with those left behind. Those they loved the most.

I wanted to believe it was that last possibility. I wanted it to be that he loved me most.

Still, sometimes he did appear in the vast dark vault of heaven, and we could touch thoughts again. It wasn't the same as when he'd been a living boy at my side; he was more distant now, more distant in every way, as if the impossible stretch of space between us had permeated his spirit and cooled his passion, if not his heart.

He spoke to me less as Jesse Holms, child of the earth, and more as Star-of-Jesse, wise and calmly inscrutable. While I'd been left behind to subsist (surviving in seconds, in mundane tick-tocking moments), he'd been unfurling. Bigger, bigger, bigger than I would ever be.

❦

So, AFTER ARMAND RETURNED home later that night, this was my conversation with Star-of-Jesse. I'd lifted as smoke above the fog to hunt him, a glint of green and gold pinned low against the horizon:

Jesse?
lora, beloved.
How much time have I left here?
time?
How much longer will you let me live?
i'm not the one claiming you, dragon-girl.
No—but—the stars. The other stars. We struck a bargain. When do they plan to kill me?

No response.

I only want to know how long. I'm not complaining. I only

want to know.

i cannot sing of these matters.

What?

these matters cannot be sung.

Why not?

there are laws, beloved. there are fates yet unsealed. there are matters sung, and matters unsung.

I don't understand!

i know. i'm sorry. fly well, my lora-of-the-moon. fly well and fly soon.

CHAPTER 6

THE SECOND DAY OF the new school term commenced much as the first had, with me waking alone in the quiet of my tower. I opened my eyes, my body warm and my nose icy, and was instantly overtaken by one of those heart-stuttering, *where-am-I?* moments that arrived sometimes with the light of dawn.

Am I hiding in Germany?

Am I at the prison camp?

The dormitory at Blisshaven?

My cell at Moor Gate?

But then the tower came into focus. Concave ceiling. Shadows. A few spiders among the eaves, curled small and waiting at the corners of their webs. On sunny days those webs would glisten, but I'd neglected to close my window after I'd returned last night, and the fog had crept in. This morning they were ghost webs, barely visible.

My heart calmed; I rubbed a hand across my eyes. The faint aroma of sardines and buttered toast wafted over the briny sharpness of the mist. It was enough to get me out of bed and over to the wardrobe.

My door opened just as I was struggling with the last button of my shirtwaist.

"Good morning, miss," said Gladys, the maid assigned to me and my room. She slammed the basin of water she carried onto my bureau with a *thunk*, exactly as she did every morning. The water sloshed over the rim and onto the floor, exactly as it did every morning.

Gladys appreciated my presence at Iverson about as much as my classmates did. That is to say, if I happened to stumble off a cliff in front of them all, I was sure she'd clap just as enthusiastically.

"Good morning," I said, turning to her. "Dearest Gladys, I wonder if you might lend me your opinion, as I value it so highly. Tell me, how does this shirtwaist look?"

"It looks very fine, miss," she lied, right to my face.

"Truly?"

She offered an unpleasant smile. "Aye."

"I fear this is someone else's clothing," I said. "An elf's, perhaps. I thought we were to be fitted for new uniforms at the beginning of every year?"

"Mayhap you should try eating less, miss."

"Mayhap I should ask Mrs. Westcliffe what she thinks of my figure in the attire you've provided me. It seems I've got rather a lot to show her, don't you think?"

We locked eyes, both of us now unpleasant and smiling.

"Or possibly you might see fit to take my measurements and procure me new garments," I said. "I mean, if you wouldn't mind."

"Of course not, miss. Why should I mind?"

She stepped carefully around the water puddle and left.

I knew I'd just earned myself an afternoon of bloodletting by pins. But honestly, if I had to keep wearing what I had, I might pass out and fall off a cliff, after all.

⊱ ✶✦✶ ⊰

I'D SCARCELY ENTERED THE great hall before I was intercepted by Sophia. She looped her arm through mine and grinned, and I knew something terrible was about to happen.

"What is it?" I asked, halting near the first-years' table.

Her eyes grew round. "What is what?"

"Why are you being so chummy?"

"Because we are chums, silly!" She tossed a sparkling laugh to the little girls at the table, all of whom gaped at her open-mouthed over their breakfast plates, enthralled.

I sighed. "Just tell me."

Sophia began to move us along. "Well, since we *are* such chums, and since Westcliffe had to trot off to some appointment or another, she asked me to give you this."

She handed me an envelope with a broken wax seal. I unlinked our arms and pulled out the folded sheet of paper within.

My Dear Miss Jones,

You are cordially invited to tea at Tranquility today, to discuss matters pertaining to your scholarship. A car shall be sent 'round at half three.

Yours etc.,

Aubrey, M. of S.

"Chums invite their chums along for tea," Sophia said. "And Westcliffe already told me you could go."

I snorted. "I can't invite you. I'm not the hostess."

"Tea at Tranquility. It's quite impressive, as you'll recall. Cakes. Puddings."

"We have those things here," I pointed out.

We had stopped again, this time in the middle of the dining hall. A pair of tenth-years pushed past us with a muttered *really!* Sophia shoved back at the nearest one, and they both hurried on.

"Yes," she agreed, taking my arm once more. "But we don't have *men* here, do we? All the cakes under the sun don't make up for that."

"And Chloe," I added, dry. "She's still volunteering at the hospital. I'm sure that has nothing to do with you wanting to go."

"If we *happen* to see her, and she *happens* to notice we're off to a private tea with the Marquess of Sherborne, well, that's just gravy, isn't it?"

"I can't simply—"

"You owe me a favor, Eleanore, do you not?"

I did. Months ago I'd been forced to confess that I was going off with Armand during the summer. And although she didn't know the truth of where we'd gone or what we'd done, the price of Sophia's silence had been a promised future favor from us each.

We'd reached our table. Platters of broiled sardines and scrambled eggs and toast were already laid out, steam curling up like crooked fingers, inviting me closer.

Sophia kept her arm locked firmly around mine. I wasn't going anywhere without giving her an answer.

I should acquiesce, I knew. I'd been anticipating she'd demand something much more outrageous, like having me break into song during class, or publically declaring my love for our doddering old history professor.

God knew what she was going to ask of Armand.

"All right," I said. "Tea at Tranquility, if that's what you want."

"Wonderful. Wear something nice, won't you?"

"Aubrey is used to seeing me in my tawdry dressmaker frocks, I assure you."

"Is he indeed?" she asked, bright-eyed. "How interesting."

A gossipy buzz was rising behind us, louder and louder. We turned together to see what was happening.

A student lingered by the main doors to the hall, her hands behind her back. She was rosy-haired and slender, and I could see from all the way across the chamber that she was blushing furiously, even with her chin tucked to her chest.

Mrs. Westcliffe stood beside her, surveying us all with cold, unblinking eyes until the buzzing subsided. She then put a palm to the girl's back and propelled her into the room. They wound their way to the very end of the hall, where the tenth-years awaited.

"New girl," announced Malinda, coming to stand beside Sophia. "New *charity* girl," clarified Mittie, with a malicious glance at me. I gave a shrug and found my seat. There was no point in feeling sorry for the girl. I knew well enough what her first day here would be like, but I found the warm sardines and toast more interesting by far.

DESPITE THE FACT THAT I had ridden in automobiles several times before, I still found the experience to be only somewhat less harrowing than confronting an enemy airship—at least when Armand was driving. But as Sophia and I walked across Iverson's graveled driveway to the auto sent for us (for me, really), I was relieved to see the duke's chauffeur holding open the rear door.

Armand must not have found out about the tea in time to take his place.

We slid in, Sophia smiling and me not, because even though I'd changed into one of my own dresses (pale blue muslin woven with pale peach peonies; everything appropriate for young ladies was pale pale pale), I still felt too tight in my skin. Chafed by the leather seats, chafed by my corset and silk stockings and the various steel pins in my hair that hummed tunelessly against my scalp.

It meant only one thing. I was going to have to Turn to dragon soon. If I tried to hold it back, the Turn would overtake me anyway, whether I wanted it to or not. And wouldn't *that* be a sight for my schoolmates?

Headmistress! Headmistress! There is a dragon in the hall!

Then we must walk away from it with decorum. Remember, a lady never *runs.*

I hadn't taken my secret shape in nearly a month. At my best, I wasn't very good at controlling it; all my powers were still more or less beyond me. I didn't know if I'd ever get better at any of it, and I didn't have a more experienced *drákon* to ask. Armand and Aubrey knew exactly as much as I did about our species.

I hoped I'd get better. Having to be so careful all the time was bloody aggravating.

I was a beast of glitter and gold, but I had to stay hidden. I ached to fly, but I mustn't be spotted. Even out here in Wessex, there were U-boats and soldiers with guns and watchmen stationed all along the cliffs, and I waited for moonless nights with all the keen longing of a child waiting for Christmas morning.

Each Turn was precious to me. Each second I'd spent in the air was sketched in song across my heart.

And each time I became a dragon now, I knew it would be one time less before my life was done.

fly well, Jesse had told me. *fly well and fly soon.*

I didn't know if that was a command or merely advice. Either way, it looked as though I'd not have a choice about it. Which made me even more aggravated.

"Sophia," I said.

"Yes?"

"I want to talk to you about Aubrey. About his condition."

She sent me a silent, sideways look.

"Have you seen him since he's been back?" I asked. "Back from the front, I mean?"

Sophia had known both Aubrey and Armand for years longer than I; practically her entire life. There were only so many stinking rich aristocratic families milling about London, I supposed, and since they tended to socialize strictly with each other, it must have made for a very small pool of tennis partners. For a short while over the summer she'd tried her hand at being a nurse with me at Tranquility, but that was before Aubrey had returned home. Sophia had abandoned her career in nursing after only a few weeks, not long after I'd vanished myself.

I'd had no further word from her. For all I knew, she'd spent the remainder of her holiday playing skittles with the king.

I said, "If you shame Aubrey at all—if you hurt him or embarrass him because of how he looks now—I'll ensure you regret it."

She tilted her head. "Gracious, you sound so serious. I almost believe you mean it."

"I am very serious. And I do mean it."

"How touching. The mudlark has a heart."

I only gazed at her. The motorcar grumbled up a hill, pressing us back into the leather. The cab filled with the smell of oil and hot grinding gears. Mist stroked the windows in great feathery curls.

Sophia faced forward again. "You needn't concern yourself. I've visited since he was transferred to Tranquility. I popped in to pay my respects right before school started."

"Oh. So you know."

"Yes." She glanced out the window. "Yes, I do."

"Well, then."

"Yes."

The road leveled out, and the oil-gear smell subsided. Past the fog I began to glimpse listing fence posts protecting meadows and dark-leafed hedgerows, shadowed trunks of trees—ordinary sights that, in this auto, in this moment, slipped by like visions from a dream.

"He's no worse than some of the other soldiers we've seen," she said suddenly. "The other patients at the hospital. He's no worse than some of those."

"True," I said softly, and we both knew it was a lie.

She reached over to pat me on the knee. "Oh, let's cheer up. Listen, I'm not going to dog your heels the entire visit. I have plans of my own, you know."

That got my attention. "What?"

"I wouldn't dare interfere with the marquess's interrogation of you. *Matters pertaining to your scholarship*, indeed! How frightfully boring! We'll walk in together and make our greetings to whomever matters, and then I'll find a convenient moment to nip off. And you won't say a thing, will you?"

The car rounded a hard bend in the road. I grabbed the doorstrap to keep from sliding onto her lap. "What are you planning?"

"What do you care?"

"We're *chums*," I said, caustic. "And I don't fancy getting into trouble because of you."

"How amusing, coming from *you*." She pretended to examine her nails, which were pink and perfect. "Don't worry. I'm very good at this. We'll both enjoy a lovely visit and then safely retreat back to our pile of rocks by the sea. I promise."

"Sophia . . ."

"Eleanore."

She lifted her eyes to give me that long, glacial stare that worked so well on everyone from the minions to the housemaids. I held it, but the road was bumpy and I was beginning to feel nauseated on top of everything else, so in the end, I gave up.

"As you wish. Don't get caught."

She returned to admiring her fingernails. "I never do."

🙥 ✦🙢🙣✦ 🙠

TRANQUILITY LAY ONLY A few miles inland, so it didn't take long to reach the edges of the estate. By then the sun had burned a silver hole in the sky, and the fog had begun to lift. As we approached, the entire manor house appeared to be steaming: a hellish, brimstone assortment of towers and wings and spires, all slashed through with black glassed windows. For years it had been the home of just Armand and his brother and father (and their army of servants, of course), which was ridiculous enough, given its sprawl.

Now there was an actual army housed within its walls, and still all the rooms weren't taken. They couldn't be, because they had been designed by the mad duke, and so had been left unsafe or half-done.

Even with all the new people in it, Tranquility looked haunted to me. Like it was hungry for its lost soul, and would never, ever find it.

The auto rolled grandly up the crushed shell drive. In finer weather, there would be convalescing soldiers and their nurses crisscrossing the grounds. This afternoon, however, there was only a lonely line of fellows parked on a bench beneath an oak, silently watching us drive by.

Sophia waved. I sat back and drummed my fingers against my thighs, then pressed my palms flat. I didn't like it here. I never had. But this was where my family lived—all that I knew of my family, at least. And so, when bidden, I would come.

No doubt Aubrey had a good reason to formally send for me. He might have just given a message to Armand instead.

Tranquility's butler was at the front doors to greet us. He didn't bat an eye at the sight of Sophia emerging from the auto behind me, only intoned, "Miss Jones. Lady Sophia," in his rich baritone voice, bowing his head as we came near.

Sophia sailed past him without pause, but it still felt strange to me, having an adult treat me with deference. I smiled at him but he didn't smile back, only waited for me to pass.

I had spent my childhood either invisible to grown-ups or scorned by them. I would never become used to this odd, in-between place, where I was watched by adults who would not meet my eyes, and fed and dressed and followed by people not even allowed to speak my given name.

Sophia and I entered the cool darkness of the atrium. A pair of doctors stood a few feet away, talking quietly with their hands shoved into their pockets. A nurse in starched white hurried by, her heels clacking against the marble tiles—not Chloe, I was relieved to see.

The nurse swung open the doors to the induction room. For a brief, piercing moment, the atrium was flooded with conversation and the smell of iodine and rubbing alcohol and rotting flesh. Then the nurse went through and closed the doors, and everything calmed.

Most of the soldiers at the hospital stayed either in that room (it used to be the front parlor) or else shared the series of private chambers that made up the remainder of the main floor. Aubrey, however, had been placed back in his old bedchamber, the same one he'd had here as a boy. It seemed that being the acting head of the household had its perks.

Not that he didn't deserve it. In my opinion, Aubrey Louis deserved all manner of special treatment. But he would have never demanded it for himself. I knew without asking that Armand had arranged everything for him.

We were led slowly up a set of back stairs (the elegant marble ones in the atrium climbed to nowhere, since they'd never been completed) to the second floor, obediently tailing a footman even though I knew the way, and I'd bet Sophia did, too.

The footman rapped on Aubrey's door.

"Your visitors, my lord."

"Thank you, Philip."

Aubrey's room was the nicest I'd seen at Tranquility, and by that, I mean the least unnerving. All the furniture matched; all the patterns in the curtains matched; the colors were masculine bronze and sage and brown and russet; all the paintings were ordinary scenes of lakes and ships and horses. The view from his windows revealed a sliver of the sea in the distance, a flat platinum dagger shimmering with the vanishing fog.

Aubrey sat in a wheelchair before the windows. Daylight behind him bounced a glow off the bandages swathing his head and hands.

"Miss Jones. And Lady Sophia. How . . . nice to see you both."

Sophia waited until the footman was gone. "Don't fret. I'm not staying."

Aubrey couldn't quite hide his relief. "Oh?"

"As long as you keep my secret, my lord. I've already got Eleanore's promise not to tell."

He smiled. "If it's good enough . . . for Eleanore, it's good enough for me."

"Don't be so sure," I warned him.

"Tosh," responded Sophia lightly, angling back toward the door. "You two have a marvelous tea. We'll catch up another day, Lord Sherborne."

"What about when it's time to leave?" I asked, exasperated.

"I'll find you."

"You'd better."

She was already past the threshold. "Don't be so pettish, Eleanore, you'll give yourself frown lines. Ta!"

I turned back to Aubrey, who was still smiling. He was fair-haired and gray-eyed, and it was the sort of smile that had probably gained him all manner of sweethearts before the war, a smile designed to melt hearts: tender and mild, kind and knowing. And if the war had rendered his face no longer as attractive as that smile, my heart was nonetheless not immune.

"She'll land us both in the soup," I said tartly, because he was older and Mandy's brother, and I wasn't entirely comfortable with the warm, slushy feeling he could invoke in me.

"We'll deny we . . . even know her. Never seen the gel before."

"That might be difficult, since about a dozen people witnessed us arriving in your motorcar."

"We'll say she stole it."

"*That* people might believe."

I glanced around for the nearest chair. There was no tea service set out anywhere (I sincerely hoped that hadn't been just something he'd invented to get me out of school), so I dragged a filigreed armchair over to him and plunked down in a rectangle of that hazy, silvery sun.

"I've brought something for you," I told him.

"Have you? Splendid. Let's have a look."

I opened my handbag. I owned only two, and I'd had to bring the larger one, which was ruby velvet and clashed rather violently with my dress. But the stack of letters hadn't fit in my daintier white one.

"These are . . ." I began, and trailed off.

These are the letters of a dead woman.

These are the letters of a dead drákon.

These are the letters of your ancestress.

These are the only proof in the world that we were not always so alone.

"These are for you," I said eventually, and handed them over.

They were very old and very brittle. They'd been stored in Jesse's cabin in the woods for all the summer, hidden beneath the coal bin. None of the original envelopes had survived the years, but the writing covering the sheets was still clear enough to make out.

I watched as Aubrey cupped them in his ravaged hands. I watched without moving or offering to help as he laid the letters on his lap and attempted to unfold the one on top, melted fingers and pristine bleached linen trembling against the worn yellowed paper.

He managed it. He lifted the sheet and scanned it quickly, his gaze lingering on the signature near the bottom.

"'Rue, M. of L.'," he read aloud, and looked up at me. "Who is that?"

"That is your great, great—I don't know how many greats—grandmother. I think. All the letters are addressed to the same girl, and are dated from over a century ago. We weren't able to work out exactly how many generations it's been."

"'M. of L.' That's short for . . . marchioness of something, surely?"

"That's what Armand thought," I agreed glumly. "But we haven't had any luck at all finding her. These letters were stashed in your mother's chamber," I added, "back at the castle. She'd concealed them there before she—before she died."

Before she'd killed herself. Before you and Armand and the duke had abandoned Iverson forever. Before our own stormy lives had ever entangled.

He nodded, reading again, lost in the words I knew practically by heart:

You're sixteen. I've counted the years until this day, felt them pass in my marrow, each minute creeping, each second a fresh bleeding ache. How I long to be with you during this time. You've no idea what's to come . . . .

Listen to the gemstones; celebrate their music. Imagine how it will feel to stretch your wings for the first time. To taste the clouds. To hunt the moon.

I've hidden you well. I hid your entire line from the Council and the tribe, and of all my many notorious accomplishments—I am not so modest as to deny they are many—the secret of your life and that of your progenitors is my greatest.

I closed my eyes. I let the sunlight paint me with its dull heat and listened to the sound of Aubrey's breathing in the quiet. The slight, dire hiss that still sliced through his lungs.

"A grand mystery indeed," he murmured, after a while. "Why don't we . . . ask the stars who she is?"

I shifted irritably, my conversation with Jesse replaying in my mind. "Because the stars aren't always especially interested in providing answers. They're rather more interested in presenting riddles than not. But go ahead and ask. Perhaps they'll be more forthcoming with you."

"Lora," Aubrey said, and I opened my eyes, squinting at the light. "Are you hungry?"

"Yes."

"Tea's on the way. Ah . . . did you think I'd forgotten?" The tender smile returned. "Never fear. I asked for scones and chocolate mousse. Salmon salad. Those absurd cucumber sandwiches without . . . the crusts. I asked for everything . . . they could scrape up. Should be here soon. But first . . ."

He wheeled his chair to his writing desk, reaching for a drawer. He pulled out a smallish box bound by a jade-green ribbon.

"It happens that I . . . have something for you, as well."

"Oh!" I accepted it gingerly. The ends of the ribbon brushed smooth against my skin. I tugged it free and lifted the lid and said, "Oh," again, but this time much more hushed.

Inside the box was a dragon.

It was a miniature dragon, no longer than the span of my hand, and I knew without even touching it yet that it was made of gold. The tips of its tail and wings and ears had been enameled in purple. Even its eyes, a pair of polished amethysts, were ringed in purple.

It was me.

"Do you remember the illustrations of you in . . . the German broadsheets?" Aubrey asked.

I could hardly forget them. I'd been seen over there, seen several times, and drawings of a monstrous mechanical dragon attacking Hun soldiers had been splashed across the papers.

"I described you to the goldsmith in detail. Not *you*, of course. The design I wanted. The dream I had. That's all he thought it was, a dream. But . . . this is what you actually look like, Lora."

I bit my lip, wordless. The little dragon was beautiful. Exquisite.

"Really?" I finally whispered.

"Really, truly."

I picked it up, only now noticing the clever hinges along the body that gave it slinky movement. Every inch was perfect: perfectly etched scales, perfect sharp bones defining the wings, perfect curving claws. Even perfect eyelashes.

"I—" I swallowed. "I don't know what to say. Thank you, I guess." I took a breath. "I mean, yes, of course. Thank you. I've never seen its like."

"I have," the marquess said, soft.

A knock sounded on the door.

Thank God. Tea was here.

But Aubrey didn't acknowledge the knock or even look away from me. Instead, he began quickly to speak. "Listen, there's something else. I didn't ask you here just for this. Something's . . . *happened*, and I didn't want to write it out in a note—"

"My lord?" The door opened. A man in a white coat stepped through.

He had brown hair and a thin brown moustache. He had pudgy cheeks with a shadow of pox and sparse brown eyebrows. He had the most commonplace face in the world, and all I could do was stare at him from the trap of my chair, my throat locked up and my mind a void and a single word ricocheting through me, a word so small and terrified it scarcely registered; a word so huge it ballooned into every cell of my being.

No.

It's funny how your life can come apart in an instant. How you can feel safe and satisfied one moment, and the next you're dangling over an abyss, no warning, no quarter. You're absolutely about to fall.

That's what happened to me, because I was staring into the eyes of the man who had murdered me.

And right behind him, smiling her gorgeous smile, was Chloe Pemington, the person who despised me most on this earth.

CHAPTER 7

WHY, MISS JONES," SAID my killer with an awful, civilized cheer. "What a jolly surprise to see you again."

I was standing. I still couldn't speak, but I was on my feet, ready to run.

Because I was fourteen again and imprisoned in the stink of that London madhouse, and every single time I'd seen this man, this doctor, had meant hours of horror, of being strapped to The Machine and electrified and electrified until my hands and feet were slick with blood because the restraints never gave way, and my body became a thing beyond my hope or control, unable to stop bucking—

"Doctor Becker." Aubrey's voice reached me from a distance. It had gone very cold.

"Lord Sherborne. Yes. I've come by with the lists for—"

"This is not the time. I am busy, as you see."

"Of course." Those cheerful eyes bored into mine. "I say, Miss Jones, you are looking well. Rather a sea change from the days we first met! We certainly patched you up, young lady, didn't we?"

My mouth opened but my lungs were empty. I made no sound. Chloe had drifted into the room with her smile and her comely face and her body poised like a snake, seconds from its final lunge.

No.

"Aubbie," she was saying in her breathy, childish voice, still watching me, "I've come by to say hello! Oh, Eleanore, how pale you are! Have you seen a ghost?"

No.

The animal in me rose up, white hot fury beneath my skin. The dragon in me swelled and swelled, frantic for oxygen, frantic to break free. And once more my body became a thing beyond my control.

I was dimly aware of someone else at the door. Armand, limping into the room. An ebony cane. Sharp eyes on me.

"What's happening?" he asked, much too calm.

I will eat this man. I will rip him into pieces and dance in his blood. I will destroy the man who destroyed me—

Aubrey wheeled close. "They're leaving. Both of them."

Armand said, "Good idea."

I am older and stronger now, and I will not be bound. I will not be terrorized by you ever again, butcher of children—

"Come get some air." Armand had me by the arm.

I blinked, and I was by a window. Armand was struggling with the latch. Aubrey was saying, "You will not enter my chamber uninvited again, Becker," and I curled my fingers into a fist and smashed it through the nearest pane.

And then I was smoke, and I was gone.

THERE IS A FIERCE joy to letting loose, to cutting yourself free from all the countless mundane threads of restraint that fix you in your place, that tighten so gradually day by day that you do not even realize how bowed you are until you're quit of them.

That was how I felt as I soared away from Tranquility.

Unbowed. Stretching free beneath the sun.

I stayed smoke at first but couldn't hold it; the fury in me burned hotter than my will. I Turned to dragon without looking down, without caring a jot about who might see and point and exclaim. I lifted my chin to the heavens and climbed and climbed, and soon I was a mere speck against the atmosphere. A spark, an illusion.

I snapped at the wind. I tore into it with my wings, dug channels into it with my talons. I would have roared if I had a voice, but since I did not, I only clawed my way higher, and the world below me became insignificant.

All the world but this—sky, clouds, air—became insignificant.

I was *drákon*.

I would devour the sun.

"BY GOD. THAT WAS a near thing," Aubrey said.

Armand turned away from the window, where the sky had become a bright blinding canvas of silver and blue, and Lora was nowhere to be found.

"Did they see?" he asked.

"Don't think so. I was shutting the door on them right . . . as she broke the glass."

"That's something," he said, genuinely relieved.

"Yes."

Mandy lifted a hand to rub his eyes, still sorting out the moment. Lora and Chloe. The fleshy doctor. Aubrey.

Even though it'd been weeks, it was still a shock at times to discover his brother like this. Always seated, always bandaged and too thin and reeking of ointment. Mandy would come across a stranger in Aubrey's room, in Aubrey's bed, and think, mildly startled, *Who is that?* And then he'd remember.

Oh, yes. That's the Marquess of Sherborne. That's what's left of the hero pilot who flew like the devil until the devil shot him down. Who used his bare hands to free himself from a burning, shattered aeroplane, and somehow didn't die in a ditch in France.

The last time he'd seen the old Aubrey had been at Christmas two years past. Aubrey'd been strutting then, laughing. Employing his considerable charm to deflect their father's temper away from Armand, because Aubrey was the golden son and Mandy was not, and deflection was easy for him.

Mandy sometimes thought that everything he'd struggled with

in his life—the duke, making friends, bearing the unhappy weight of his title—had always come so easily to Aubrey. As though good fairies had blessed his birth and used up all their magical dust on this firstborn Louis.

Then the shame would flush through him. Because the second-born still had his skin, and the second-born could still walk.

Christmas had always smelled of holly and cedar ashes. Now Armand could add *regret* to that short list. Regret that he hadn't appreciated the old version of his brother as well as he should have. That he hadn't answered the letter Aubrey'd sent explaining why he'd signed up for the RFC against their father's wishes. Regret that they'd only waved their goodbyes that Christmas, that they hadn't shaken hands that one last time, since Aubrey wasn't ever going to shake hands again.

Regret smelled like that damned ointment, Mandy thought.

He looked back at the broken pane. A wet line of crimson defined a single edge; he smeared the blood thin with the tip of his finger. "What the hell happened, anyway?"

"Bastard spotted Lora last week. Came to me about it. Knew he'd be trouble."

"Why?"

Aubrey, in his casual golden way, shrugged. "Bastard, like I said. You can see it in his eyes."

"*Why* does he matter to Lora? What is she to him?"

"Becker was at Moor Gate before he came here."

Moor Gate, the insane asylum. Of course.

Now it made sense, the scene he'd walked into. The man in the wheelchair and the man standing and Chloe practically rubbing her hands together in delight. Lora gone to glass, stark and awful to see.

Every hair on his body had stood on end when he'd met her eyes. He'd been certain, *certain*, she was going to Turn to dragon right there and cut down the fleshy man.

And the beast in Armand, soul-locked to hers, had been screaming, *Yes, do it, yes!*

He bent down to gather up her frock. It felt cool in his grip, as if there hadn't been a living girl inside it just seconds past. At his feet lay her corset and chemise and garters and stockings, everything topped with a sprinkling of hairpins, but he didn't think he should touch any of those.

He draped the dress over the back of the nearest chair, carefully straightening the sleeves.

"Her eyes didn't flash, did they?"

Because sometimes they did when she was upset or angry or— once that he had seen—when she was very happy. Flashed luminescent, bright as diamonds: a dragon's trick; very clearly nothing human. She'd told him that she couldn't control it.

Mandy possessed the same trick, although it had happened only a handful of times as far as he knew. He couldn't control it, either.

"No," Aubrey replied. "They would have made . . . more of a fuss."

"That's something," he said again. He eased down into the chair with her dress on it and considered going after her.

"Wouldn't," said his brother, reading his expression. "Let her work things through."

That seemed an excellent suggestion. She could Turn to dragon, and he still couldn't. She might be halfway to the moon by now.

Maybe. He honestly didn't know how high or far their kind could fly.

It occurred to him that it was a very rudimentary sort of thing not to know. Peculiar. Like being unable to count all of one's fingers and toes.

Someone tapped on the door. Mandy rose instantly to his feet, but Aubrey looked at him and said, "Tea," and the beast inside him relaxed.

His cane was on the floor across the room, where he'd dropped it. So he limped his way to the door, accepting the tray from the footman before the bloke could get a good look into the bedchamber that contained two brothers and a dress on a chair, and no visible girl.

He placed the tray on a blanket chest. He lifted the lid nearest him and stared perplexedly at the platter of square, chocolate-covered-somethings topped with iced flowers and grated nuts. Looked like pistachios.

He should go after her.

He pondered how hard it would be to find her. If she'd be smoke, or something significantly more substantial.

As he was moving from the chest, a hard glint stabbed his eye. For a second it confused him, because he'd been thinking of Lora in her dragon shape, and there she was, right there on the floor: a pocket-sized version of her lying on her side against the Persian rug, an amethyst eye looking back at him, a golden wing arched over her body in a sleek, feminine curve.

"What's all this?" he murmured, and then stilled, because he knew what it was.

He picked up the mini-Eleanore. He held it in his palm and did not look again at his brother.

Only at the unmistakable offering his brother had given to the girl Armand loved.

From behind him, Aubrey said, "She's returned."

⊱ ✦ ⊰

I DRESSED BEHIND THE chair, ensuring they had their backs to me, even though they'd both seen me without a stitch on an embarrassing number of times.

I stuck the last pin through my chignon, my fingers feeling for snarls.

"Is there a mirror?" I asked, and they turned about.

The chamber had grown cooler and darker in my absence; the rectangles of light shone shorter across the sage-and-brown rug. I didn't know how much time had passed since I'd left, but the shadows seemed heavier too, dense enough to slice.

The tea service had arrived while I was gone. Steam from the pot twisted up whispery pale, perfuming the room with a wet, flowery scent. From somewhere inside the mansion women broke into laughter, a distant sound at odds with the darkness all around.

I should apologize for my behavior. It would be polite, and they were my friends and perhaps they'd expect it. They were aristocrats and bound to a realm of rules as I was not. A well-bred girl would apologize.

Lady Chloe would apologize.

Sorry for losing control. Sorry for breaking your window. Sorry for being such a mess inside.

Except she'd never say any of that. She'd purse her lips and say something like, *I've been such a goose! How lovely you are to forgive me!*

A presumption of forgiveness, not an actual apology. And it would work, too, because she was beautiful and beauty always mattered, even when it masked ugliness.

I realized my right hand hurt. There was a gash across my knuckles, the blood smeared and drying.

"No mirror," said Aubrey.

Of course not. Why would anyone so scarred want to look into a mirror? I stared ferociously at the blood marking my skin. On top of everything else, I'd done precisely what I'd warned Sophia not to do.

Sorry for being such a dolt.

Aubrey said, "Let us . . . be mirrors. You look . . ."

I waited. I licked the thumb of my good hand and rubbed at the blood.

"Terrible," declared Armand. "Dreadful. Absolutely appalling."

"I was going to say *enchanting*." Aubrey rolled into the light; he was smiling. "Two different mirrors, I suppose."

I glanced at the broken pane, thinking very seriously of going to smoke again.

"Becker," said Aubrey.

I forced myself to meet his eyes.

"Let's kill him," he said.

My mind waited for the jest, counted out *One, two, three*—

"Now, there's an idea." Armand crossed to the tray and took hold of the teapot, but he didn't move otherwise, only stood there staring down at it.

"Why not?" Aubrey was still gazing at me. "He did it to you."

I said, "He—he—"

Stop stuttering.

Breathe.

I exhaled, and Armand finally poured. Aubrey accepted the cup offered to him with both hands. "Couldn't wait to . . . tell me about it. Gleeful. Ghoulish. Called you a 'specimen'."

Beneath his fine day coat, Armand's shoulders were stiff. "Did he?"

"'A first-rate specimen,' to be . . . exact."

Armand replaced the teapot upon the tray but did not release it. The steam twirled up and up and unraveled by his chin.

"Everyone would know it was us," I said—the first thought that popped into my head, even though it was likely untrue.

Aubrey raised a brow. It meant *Really?*, but he only tried some of the tea.

"We're not him," I reasoned. "We're not like him."

Armand remained motionless, staring straight into the shadows;

once I noticed, I found myself unable to look away. In the ticking passage of just these few seconds, he seemed changed. His edges had gone sharper, but his gaze more unfocused. Full of storms.

Armand, with the Gift of fire in his lungs, a Gift I did not have. Armand, who could not yet match me as an actual dragon, but who could become smoke with a thought, and summon flame with a thought. Who had agreed with me once when I'd said out loud that I hoped all the doctors from Moor Gate had been blown to hell by German bombs.

"We do not kill for glee," I said.

"How about just good . . . old-fashioned revenge?" Aubrey suggested.

I wanted out of this conversation. I couldn't tell how serious it was, if this was Aubrey appeasing me, or Armand truly about to splinter. The idea of appeasement made me feel vaguely insulted. But the idea of Armand coming undone made me feel anxious.

Afraid.

And the thought that Aubrey might somehow actually dispatch Becker . . .

If anyone was going to kill that son of a bitch, it was going to be me.

I said, "I'd rather murder Chloe, anyway," but neither of them smiled. So I flicked my hand through the air, waving away all the possibilities. I did it quickly, grandly, the way I imagined Mrs. Westcliffe might do.

"Are those petit fours I see? I hope so. The school doesn't

serve them."

Armand unclenched his fingers. Aubrey raised the other brow.

I walked to the tray, grabbed the entire dish, and returned to the filigreed chair. I sat back and ate all the cakes, one after another, until the silver platter held only a cluster of empty paper doilies and a few chocolate smears.

Mrs. Westcliffe, whom I imagined would have approved of my wave, would have subsequently blacked out in mortification.

Neither of the Louis brothers said another word for the rest of the tea.

$\longleftarrow \Longleftarrow \Longrightarrow$

IN THE AUTOMOBILE DURING our drive back to Iverson, I asked Sophia, "So, who is he? The man you were sneaking off to see?"

"Armand, of course."

I looked at her swiftly, my heart in my throat.

She tossed back her head and gave a frosty laugh. "Whom *do* you love, little Eleanore? You know you can't have them both."

CHAPTER 8

THIS IS WHAT I'VE been seeing lately at the edge of the Unseen, that horizon known only to stars and gods:

A collision of Future and Past, seared into Present. A truth that spreads like a bloodstain, like a thundercloud, secret names trapped within it.

And Lora, my dragon-girl. Her face is sketched into that cloud as well, looking back at me blindly.

This Truth belongs to her, and it is coming for her, although I would spare her from it if I could.

My spells do nothing. My wishes mean nothing. My heart, that long-dead thing buried in the soil with my mortal body—

My heart bleeds for her.

And I wonder at that; that I can still feel the pain of bleeding, when stars have no blood.

CHAPTER 9

I T TOOK TWO DAYS for the rumors to reach the school.

Two days of classes. Two days of breakfasts and teas and dinners. Two days; two nights.

It was during that second night that I was seated in the castle library, staring morosely at the book of prose opened before me. It was English prose by some long-dead English author, and I was to pick a piece to recite in Literature class. I didn't like standing and speaking in class under the best of circumstances. It always made me ill to my stomach, and I couldn't imagine what useful good would come of it in my life.

Dear people of the grocer's market, allow me now to recite the list of sundries I require on this day!

But to make matters worse, every single piece in the book assigned to me ranted on about the Joys of Family, a topic I knew absolutely nothing about.

Behold the tender cheek, roses yet in bloom;
Behold the tender hand, faith in her grasp;
Behold the soul, the blessed heart, her unshaken love.
Cruelty cannot frame her.
Misgiving cannot plague her.
Mater *is her whole and all.*

Lamplight flickered across the page, scrambling the letters. The library smelled of beeswax and my chair of musty horsehair, and my nose would not stop itching.

I rubbed at it, then flipped a few pages ahead. Surely there was something in here less nauseatingly mawkish.

O Daughter, that thou hast blossomed so well!
How we smile at thy gentle grace!
How we celebrate thy gentle heart!
Never do we doubt thy virtue!
Never do we hear a cross word!
For thou art surely the finest of all creatures,
Humble and faithful, a boon to our lives!

I slapped the book closed. I sighed and slouched back and glared at the bookshelf ahead of me.

Would my parents have felt that way about me, had they lived?

Not bloody likely. I wasn't especially graceful, and there wasn't anything remotely gentle about my heart. I had a dragon's heart, savage and quick. It had served me well so far but was a wild distance from gentle.

I knew little of virtue (beyond that it was applauded most by those who seemed to lack it most) and nothing about humbleness.

I supposed I was faithful, in my own fashion. Faithful to myself. To my ideals. To . . . trying to discover what mattered in the world. To honoring whatever I found.

A movement caught my eye. It was the new scholarship student, seated alone at a table before the bookshelf, directly within my line of vision. I realized I'd been staring at her without seeing her, and that now she was blushing again and ducking from my gaze. She hunched lower in her chair and buried her nose in her own book, pretending not to notice me.

I was used to the other students pretending not to notice me. What seemed odd was that *this* student, this fellow nobody, would join their ranks.

Perhaps she was shy. Perhaps I should make an effort to say hello. I didn't have a gentle heart, but I needn't have a merciless one, either.

I tried to remember her name. I'd heard it a few times in the idle gossip of the hallways—Hope or Prudence or Charity, something like that. A good poor girl's name.

I straightened and pushed the book of prose away from me. I was preparing to stand when I finally became aware of the whispers, and only then because they broke off as I moved, and started up again as I fell still.

So I sat there and listened.

Mad girl, did you hear? Locked up, lunatic, mad place, mad.

Mad girl. Without a doubt.

⊱ ✦ ⊰

ONE MOONLESS NIGHT, MONTHS and months ago, I had saved the lives of these very schoolgirls as they'd slept. None of them knew it, true. But I doubted it would have made a difference to them anyway.

Once an Iverson Girl tasted the blood of a scandal, the only possible outcome was a frenzy.

⊱ ✦ ⊰

HISTORY CLASS WAS ACCEPTABLE.

Literature was barely tolerable.

Luncheon was painful.

By the time I entered the ballroom where Music Instruction was held, Iverson had become unbearable.

"Miss Jones, *s'il vous plaît.*"

Monsieur Vachon waved his hand at me to take my place before the grand piano. He was tall and French and sighed very loudly when I didn't rise quickly enough from my chair against the wall. But the ballroom had sunken into chill, and so had I. I'd been bracing myself for so many hours, my joints felt stiffened into rust.

"Please, do take your time," the monsieur said with exaggerated courtesy, and all the other girls snickered.

Some people believe French accents to be the most attractive of them all. If nasally sarcasm qualified as *attractive*, I might concur.

I sat. I placed my fingers upon the keys. Usually they felt like *me*, like another natural way to think or speak, but today they resisted me, slick and foreign. I looked at the sheet music in front of me and closed my eyes on an inner groan.

Vachon had been attempting to teach me to read music ever since my first day in his class. I'd told him that it was hopeless, although I'd never told him why: that the brass-and-crystal chandeliers in the ballroom were more alive with sound to me than any dots and dashes scribbled across a page could ever be. That when the stones and metals sang, I was helpless to ignore them. Their music swelled through me like a river overflowing into an empty valley; all else became swept away. The only way to free myself was to let the music flood outward again from my hands to the keyboard.

I'd been Vachon's pupil both last year and this, and I still didn't know how to play the piano. Only the dragon in me did.

My left middle finger tested a soft, solitary note.

"The music *before* you, Miss Jones," interrupted Vachon, cutting me off before the second note.

I opened my eyes. The pages of sheet music seemed both crisp and dull; someone else's soul, not my own, forced down to paper.

The snickering grew louder.

"Is there a problem, Miss Jones?"

"Perhaps they didn't let her practice enough in the madhouse," whispered Mittie to Stella.

"Perhaps it makes her *insane* to try!" Stella whispered back.

Vachon stood beside me, rapping the wand he always carried into the cup of his hand. His hair sprouted unkempt and bushy even plastered with pomade; his eyes were hidden behind the flash of his spectacles. "May I remind you that our class lasts a scant sixty minutes? We await your performance with bated breath."

"I am unwell," I said.

He expelled air through his teeth. "Is that so?"

"Yes, it is so. Please excuse me."

The wand pressed hard atop my shoulder, preventing me from rising. "You are not excused. I wonder if you think that because in the past I have occasionally allowed you to play as you wished, you will dictate the lessons from now on. Nothing could be further from the truth, I assure you. Play the music I have assigned you."

I stared at the sheets, my face growing hot.

"Despite your modicum of talent, *mademoiselle*, you are no more special than any other student in this room. Indeed, you are less special, because the other students arrive prepared as you do not. So hear me well, Miss Jones. I am your professor. No longer shall I tolerate this laziness. You will obey me. Play the music."

"I merely want to—"

"Play the music."

"If you would only—"

"Play the music!"

"I won't!" I surged upward with such force the bench flew back, squealing against the wooden floor. Vachon jumped, and all the girls gasped.

For an everlasting moment, there was no other sound at all. No whispers. No chandelier-song. Only the silence of my impending doom.

Vachon stood staring, his mouth a peculiar twist. Sophia looked caught between rapture and astonishment, a hand pressed to her chest. I was cold and feverish and dizzy with what I'd done.

"I am unwell," I said again. The words felt fat and strange in my mouth. "Excuse me."

I walked away. No one attempted to stop me this time, not my professor, certainly not any of my classmates.

Lunatic, rose the jubilant hiss from behind me.

Perchance they were right.

I HID IN MY room and skipped dinner. It was very hard at first; I could smell the battered cod and apple salad, even the custard for dessert. I listened to the muffled chatter that filtered up from the dining hall and told myself that after everyone else was asleep I'd steal down to the kitchens and raid the larder as much as I wished.

But I knew I wouldn't. I wanted only to hide.

Night crept close to blacken my window. My lamp was out of oil already, so I'd lit one of the candles to give me something to watch. I lay on my side atop the bed, my pillow warm beneath my cheek. The yellow flame bowed to me, straightened. Bowed.

Tomorrow I would have to return downstairs. Tomorrow I'd have to go through it all anew. I was going to have to look everyone in the eye and sneer at their sneers, and I wondered, really and deeply wondered, what in heaven's name I was still doing at the school. Why I'd wanted to come back so badly. I didn't like most of my courses, I was never going to dip a curtsy to the king like all the other girls, and I had no plans to become anything but what I already was. Surely I could make a home somewhere else.

Maybe the last of Jesse's magic was binding me in place. He was the one who'd summoned me to Iverson last spring; maybe his spell wasn't ready to let me go. It felt that way sometimes, like the gravity here was miraculously increased, holding me down even though I could fly.

"Miss Jones?" called a voice beyond my door.

Without waiting for a reply, Mrs. Westcliffe entered skirts first, a mass of raspberry silk that rustled and slipped against the stones. In her hands was a tray holding a glass of milk and a covered dish. The dish smelled of boiled oats, and my stomach burbled.

"Good evening," she said.

"Good evening." I sat up, then quickly stood. But there wasn't really space for us both and we faced each other awkwardly, the tray a hard line between us, until she turned and placed it upon the bureau.

"Have you come to expel me?" I asked, and then couldn't believe I'd said it aloud.

She shot me an unreadable look. "No, I have not. Have you done something worthy of expulsion?"

I hate it here. I hate everyone here. I hate that I am so different. I love it here and I want to belong and I know that I never will.

"I disobeyed Monsieur Vachon," I said. "I left his class today without permission."

"So I heard."

I slumped a little.

"Posture, Miss Jones. Thank you. I am here to speak with you about Professor Vachon, in fact. Please, sit."

She gestured to the bed. I sank back down, trying to keep close enough to the edge so that my feet still met the floor. Mrs. West-cliffe remained standing, lustrous raspberry and strict black hair. Everything about her was smoothly planned and contained, except her perfume. It reminded me of the flowers in the deep woods, of the masses of snowdrops and buttercups that bloomed wherever the sun touched.

"Were you truly unwell, Eleanore?"

"Yes."

"I am sorry to hear it. I hope that a bowl of warm porridge will aid in your recovery. Almeda seems to think it will. I usually rely upon her in these matters."

"Thank you."

"She also suggested a dose of cod-liver oil. Do you feel it necessary?"

"No!" I cleared my throat. "I mean, no, thank you."

She nodded, staring at a spot on the wall above my head. "I wish for you to understand something about today. Something that may elucidate your experience in class. Professor Vachon received some rather grave news this morning. Some very bad news."

Was it that the entire school had found out he'd been confined to a lunatic asylum?

"His family's château in La Fère was bombed by the Huns last month. Both his mother and father were killed, along with a younger sister."

"Oh," I said, very small.

"He had attempted to evacuate them near the beginning of the war, but—" Her hand swept the air in a gesture that seemed both firm and forlorn. "Well. It was too late. The invasion began and civilian movement ceased. Even the Duke of Idylling could do nothing. We *did* try."

I stared at the glass of milk on the tray. I thought about how bombs sounded when they were above you, how they whistled through the air but seemed to suck it away from you at the same time, and your legs always wanted to run but your brain knew that your existence had become purely a matter of predetermined math and trajectory and detonation. Running likely wouldn't help.

"I tell you this because I trust in your discretion, Eleanore. You've proven to be someone with the ability to . . . keep secrets, as it were."

My eyes went to hers.

"And I want you to know something else," she said slowly, holding my gaze. "Neither I nor my staff have mentioned your time at the Moor Gate Institute to anyone else at the school. Ever. I give you my word on that."

"No." I tried to smile but my lips felt too tight. "There's a new doctor at Tranquility who—who knew me then. And Chloe was there," I added, dark.

"Aha."

The candle flame dipped and bowed. Outside, a seal started to bark, harsh and impatient. The cliffs cast it back in a long, broken echo.

"Cowering will solve nothing," the headmistress said. "You must accept all that you are, and that includes the path which has led you here. No one will honor you otherwise."

"No one honors me anyway."

"Self-pity is the least likely approach to win them over."

"I can't *win them over*," I cried, chagrined. "I'll never win them over! Don't you see?"

"Then I suggest you simply win, instead," she replied. "Good night, Miss Jones."

And she was gone.

CHAPTER 10

ARMAND HAD NOT YET **come.**

I lay in my bed and tried not to miss him, to miss the entire experience of him. I wanted to feel the shape of him beside me. I wanted him to touch my hair. To kiss me, long and velvety slow. I wanted to tell him everything that had happened since the tea, and have him murmur, *It will be all right, Fireheart. It will all be fine, you'll see.*

But he wasn't here. And he hadn't been for the past two nights. I might have gone to him instead but . . . but I hadn't. I told myself that if he didn't want to see me, if his time at Tranquility (Chloe) was so very important, then I didn't want to see him either.

Pride, intoned Westcliffe's voice inside my head. *Pride, on top of cowardice.*

The night spread an even deeper black beyond my window than it had a few hours before, when the headmistress had been here. The stars glittered stark against it. Due west hung the moon, a gaunt blue sickle, too starved to throw light.

Boom. Boom-boom-boom.

I rolled over, pulling my quilts higher. I squeezed my eyes closed.

Boom. Boom.

I covered my ear with my hand.

Booooom.

It might have been thunder, but it wasn't. It was the Germans. Apparently the moon had waned thin enough for them, and the airships were out tonight dropping their bombs along the coast.

It wasn't anywhere near. Even with my dragon hearing, these were more like ricochets of sounds than the sounds themselves. The airships were sluggish and clumsy and had ventured as far west as Wessex only once; it hadn't gone well for them. Ever since they'd stuck to targets closer to their path of retreat, places like London and Brighton and Dover.

Boom-boom-booooom!

I sat up. I walked to my window. Clouds pushed by, tall as mountains, flat bottoms the color of gunmetal. The stars kept watch beyond them.

fireheart, come out.

I pressed a palm against the diamond glass, testing its cold. Feeling my blood quicken.

war beast, beast of war. they hunt. come find them.

Isn't it far? Won't they be gone by the time I get there?

not for you, the stars sang. *not tonight.*

It felt like permission, although I refused to believe I required permission to fly.

Still, it was all I needed to hear.

I KEPT AS SMOKE along the coast. It would have been quicker to Turn and travel as a dragon, but as I said, there were soldiers and farmers with guns, and I'd already been shot enough.

The edge of England ribboned from sand to cliffs and back to sand. The breaking surf was a constant against it, ruffled lines that would have been white or silver given more light, but tonight were more noise and suggestion than anything else.

Sea gusts pushed me faster. Dots of villages slipped by, lights from windows shining lemony warm. Lone farmhouses nestled in square fields. Shepherds' huts in rolling hills. Smells of sheep or cows or spicy autumn leafsmoke drifting up to mingle with me and the wind.

Boom. Boom!

I was definitely getting closer. There was a decidedly more *human* scent to the air now, and all the window lights had vanished. Beneath the human scent came that of gaslights extinguished, and dogs panting, fish markets and butcher shops and bathwater and panic, because the bombs were exploding near enough now for everyone to hear. I'd flown far and time had slipped by, and now the bombs were *near*.

And as soon as I thought that, I spotted the fires. There was a town up ahead; I didn't know which one. From above, civilization looked remarkably the same, lumpy collections of roofs and lanes, treetops and steeples; nearly always sparser inland but thicker as you moved closer to shore. The most exceptional aspect of this particular town was its illumination: many of the trees lining the lanes burned like upright torches; the rooftops and steeples were alive with flames. I could very clearly see the townsfolk running, some toward the fires, some away.

The other exceptional aspect was the zeppelin suspended high above it all, humming with death.

The stars had been right. It hadn't left yet. Shots fired from the ground couldn't reach its altitude, only bullets from aeroplanes could. But there were no aeroplanes anywhere in view, so although the zeppelin was heading east again, it was moving leisurely. There was still plenty of time to kill things.

I heard a *click* and *whrrr* and another bomb dropped from its back bay, whistling to the ground. A building that was probably a warehouse exploded into rubble and fire and dust.

I hoped it had been a warehouse. Not a school. Not a tenement building.

As with heat, sound rises. Flames crackled, people screamed. Liquid fountained upward from a street in a great sputtering gush; the bomb had destroyed the water main.

I tore through the smoke and grit. I swept up and up until I was hugging the curve of the balloon itself, diaphanous against its hard leathery shape. The stroke of its propellers pulsed through its skin. The girders composing its skeleton thrummed *ba-BUM-ba-BUM-ba*: monster bones holding all the gas bags inside, keeping it afloat.

Had I been a girl instead of smoke, my own skin would have

been crawling. Everything about the airship felt alive, but in a twisted, all-wrong sort of way. It felt soulless and reptilian and parched for blood.

Stop it. That doesn't help.

I had done this before. I knew that if even one of my talons scraped a girder, even just for a moment, there would be sparks. The gas in the bags was hydrogen; the airship would ignite like tissue paper tossed into a bonfire, and perhaps me with it. Were we over the Channel, that would be an acceptable risk. But the ship hovered over the edge of town still, and I couldn't let it crash in flames. There were too many fires already.

I spiraled up its side to its top. I formed a cloud above the center of the balloon.

I hated this part.

they hunt! chorused the stars.

Finish it, I told myself.

I Turned into dragon, sank my claws into the skin and yanked back.

What I expected was that the tears I'd created would rip wide with the pressure of the escaping gas, and the ship would begin to sink. I expected that I'd have to hold my breath against the hydrogen and leap backward to avoid falling into the gaps, because the zeppelin was still moving and the wind was still blowing and I was a very small force compared to all of that.

What I did not expect was to see a face rising up over the curving surface of the balloon as I finished, a face that was perfectly visible even with the rushing gas warping the night between us.

It wasn't human. It wasn't even a monster, which at least would have made sense, given how the ship spooked me.

The face belonged to another dragon, a real one, gazing at me and grinning, all its teeth exposed.

CHAPTER 11

I WENT INSTANTLY TO SMOKE. I didn't pause to think about it; it simply happened. I was a dragon, and then I wasn't.

The airship shuddered, and the other dragon—*The other! The other!* my mind chanted—pranced closer across the balloon, still grinning, serpentine and beautiful and horrifying all at once. It was much, much larger than I. It leapt over the holes I'd torn like they were nothing, like they weren't the ruin of the ship listing beneath us.

Its body shimmered black and green and red. Its eyes glowed yellow, bright as harvest moons. They remained fixed exactly on me even though I was only smoke, recoiling as swiftly as I could. But somehow the dragon was faster. It skipped nearer, its feet eating up the distance, its tail whipping left and right and its teeth gleaming in the dark.

I thought, frantic, *My God, is that what I'm like? It's terrifying.*

I Turned to girl, scraped down hard against the side of the balloon and plummeted toward the ground.

Not on purpose.

Again, it just happened.

I was too frightened to scream. Everything had shifted so quickly that my mind still hadn't caught up; only my body understood my peril. I flailed and cartwheeled toward the red fire town, hot air, *scorching* air, tears smearing my eyes, and right as I was about to become impaled on the charcoal remains of one of the steeples, my body decided to save me.

I Turned to smoke. I smashed against the timbers and fragmented, tendrils shooting in every direction.

It's much worse than it sounds. Imagine being torn limb from limb, but it doesn't kill you. It just makes you feel as if it does.

For a while—I'm not certain how long—I only hung above the soot and ashes, embers popping through me, a haunt of smoke above a haunt of a town.

The zeppelin gradually descended and crashed against the ground.

The other dragon did not reappear.

As soon as my nausea dissipated, I fled.

I FLEW STRAIGHT TO Tranquility. I went to Aubrey's room first; he slept alone in the giant coffin of his bed, rawboned, swaddled in bandages. A fire muttered azure and orange in his hearth. Faint light burnished the heavy crescents of his eyelashes, the only part of his face, it seemed, left untouched by the hand of war.

Sssss. Sssss. His breathing rattled slow and shaky. In slumber, his lungs worked harder than ever to keep death at bay.

The other dragon hadn't been him.

Armand wasn't in his room. I Turned to girl and stood quiet in its unbroken gloom. No fire. Unrumpled bed. The fragrance of him unmistakably lingering, wrapping around me like a promise.

Chloe's room, whispered a nasty little voice inside me. *Go on. Check.*

He wouldn't be there. I knew that he wouldn't. Armand loved me. He'd already known about Moor Gate, so that wouldn't be the reason he was staying away. It had to be something else.

And if it *had* been him atop the zeppelin, I think I would have known it. I would not have been so deeply, instinctively afraid.

I walked to one of the windows and pushed apart the curtains. Dawn was streaking the sky in violent bright smears, scarlet and copper and teal. The last of the stars had faded to pinpricks against the distant blue.

They sang without words. One by one, they flickered out.

I scrubbed a hand across my face, trying to wipe away the fatigue. I'd have to go soon. I couldn't let Gladys walk into an empty tower at sunup.

It was only then that I realized I wasn't as fully alone in the bedroom as I'd first thought. I was still the only *living* thing here, but . . .

I found it in his bureau. I opened the top drawer and pushed my fingers through the silk ties and ascots sorted so carefully by color and kind, and all the way in the back was the box.

I pulled it out, returned to the window for the light. I opened the lid and gazed down at the ring inside.

It was a diamond set in platinum, the stone square and slightly modest by human standards. But it *blazed*, just like the sun breaking over the sea. And it sang like nothing I'd ever heard before. Honeyed and delicate, an aria so deliberately swooning I felt almost lightheaded trying to follow it.

I closed the lid. I ran to the bureau, shoved the box back inside the drawer, and straightened the ascots as best as I could.

I knew what that ring meant.

What I didn't know was what I was going to do about it.

THE NEXT DAY WAS Saturday, and I spent nearly all of it sleepwalking. Iverson held no lessons over the weekends, but since there was nowhere else for any of us to go, students crowded the hallways and parlors and gardens. Seeing them out of class was even worse than seeing them in. Their eyes darted to me wherever I went. Their giggles grated off the walls. A pair of eighth-years found it vastly amusing to cringe and feign terror whenever I came into view, as if my madness might somehow rub from my flesh onto theirs.

So eventually I gave up. I went to smoke and vanished down into the bowels of the isle.

Beneath the castle, far beneath, was a natural hollow in the island stone. It formed a grotto that hardly anyone ever thought about, and no one but me, it seemed, ever visited. There were two ways to get there: either by the secret tunnels in the castle walls (which only Armand and I knew existed), or else the cavern opening that allowed in the sea.

Since Iverson Girls were much too prissy to swim, I was able to retire to the grotto in peace.

But it was September cold and I was naked, so that only worked for so long.

I went to smoke again. I slithered out of the cavern and wound my way to the center of the island woods—another place no proper young lady would go. I slipped into Jesse's cottage through a cracked windowpane and Turned to girl by his empty table. Time had settled a fine, hazy blanket of dust over everything in sight.

My footprints marked a path to his bedroom. Ivy spread over his windows in a netted jumble, tinting the shadows amber and green. The taste of dust and drying leaves coated my tongue.

The pane hadn't been cracked the last time I'd been here. The dust hadn't been so powdery thick. I might wonder that no one thought to reclaim this little home from the woods, except that it had belonged to Jesse. Perhaps even the humans sensed the sacred nature of that.

I snapped clean the sheets still covering his bed. I crawled between them, closed my eyes, and slept.

SUNDAY. VISITORS' DAY. THE only day of the week outsiders were invited into the school's hallowed halls. Also, I suddenly remembered, the only day of the week we were to be served meat.

The front parlor was ready for formal tea, all the chairs and tables glassy with polish, all the windows and mirrors blinding clear. Dust would not dare invade here. Iverson stood a distance from most of the families who'd exiled their Little Darlings to our island, yet occasionally some did show up, and Mrs. Westcliffe was not going to leave them any room to criticize. The rugs were the most modern and expensive to be found, with sheared, sinuous woolen loops of vines and butterflies that curled off into the corners. The furniture was mahogany; the curtains were lace. The serving pieces were all sterling, and the china so translucent I wondered how it could have possibly been made by mortal hands. It was rather a test of endurance to deal with that china. I frequently found myself tempted to *squeeze*, just enough, until my teacup cracked like an eggshell between my palms.

But I never did.

I perched uncomfortably in my usual chair. Unlike the rest of the furnishings, it was a fussy, Victorian piece; for as long as I had been attending these teas, it had squatted alone, banished to the shadows. I told myself that was fine. The fewer eyes observing me, the more I could eat.

In theory, at least. The truth was, even set apart as I was, everyone was still staring. Since there was a mix of adults in attendance, nearly everyone was pretending not to, but the attention crawled across my nerves and stiffened the hairs along my nape. Were it not for the array of curried chicken tea sandwiches on my plate, I'd have left.

I took another bite instead. I chewed. I swallowed. Inch by inch, the little sandwiches were disappearing, but I remained hollow inside.

I considered how many more I could serve myself from the sideboard before the whispers roughened into laughter.

Mrs. Westcliffe chatted amicably with a gentleman with muttonchop whiskers and a huge gray moustache. He was approximately as out of fashion as my chair, but no one was banishing *him* to the shadows.

She felt my gaze; her eyes went to mine. She neither smiled at me nor frowned, only continued her conversation with the muttonchops man. But I felt as if I'd gained something by meeting her look.

Cowering will solve nothing.

I picked up another sandwich. I resisted the urge to gulp it down in one bite.

Someone new came through the parlor doors, and a fresh rustle of interest took the room.

"Lord Armand," greeted one of the mothers eagerly, but he only nodded to her and kept winding his way toward me, his cane tapping.

"Miss Jones." He gave a short bow.

"My lord." I glowered down at my plate. After missing him so viciously, it felt awkward to meet up here, caught in this theatre of unrelenting scrutiny. "So sorry. It seems there are no nearby seats available."

"Nonsense." He glanced around. "Murray, old sport! I say, are you done with that chair?"

The young man to whom he'd spoken looked startled, especially since he was plainly about to sit down with a refilled cup of tea.

"Well, I—"

"Excellent. Thank you. Won't have it but a minute."

Armand hooked his cane over his arm and dragged the chair to me, its wooden feet scraping long, dark grooves across the rug. He sat down and regarded me a moment, then leaned close and took the last sandwich from my plate.

I sighed. "What are you doing here?"

"Courting you. Isn't it obvious? Hmm. Chicken's a bit dry, isn't it?"

"Courting me," I repeated, cautious.

He lowered his voice. "Come to Tranquility later tonight. We'll have a feast."

"I *have* been to Tranquility," I answered, just as low. "Several nights now, in fact. And yet *you're* never there. You've certainly not bothered to come here. But now you're *courting* me?"

"Are you angry at me, Fireheart?"

"I'm not angry. I'm—" *Hurt. Lonely. Scared. I missed you and I killed a zeppelin and I faced a dragon all alone, and now you've bought a ring.* I shook my head; this wasn't the place. "I'm baffled."

His lashes lowered. His mouth lost its hint of smile.

"I'm here now," he said.

One of the girls released a shrill laugh. She stifled it at once with a hand over her lips, but spoiled the show by peeping back at me, her cheeks a merry red. The woman seated beside her made a shushing noise. Beneath the brim of her net-and-feather hat, she was watching me as well.

Armand sent them both a lazy look. Just as in Aubrey's room days past, he'd shifted into something different than one second before, into menace and whetted edges. He clicked a nail against the silver rabbit head topping his cane.

"I'm sure the joke is most amusing, yet I fear it escapes me. Eleanore?"

"Doctor Becker," I said. "And Chloe Pemington."

Astonishingly, his expression lightened. He relaxed back into the chair.

"Is that all?" he asked, and the betrayal felt like a punch to my stomach.

"Remember how it was when your father told everyone in the War Department you were mad so you couldn't sign up?" I whispered, vehement. "Didn't you care then?"

"But neither of us are mad, and we know it. You're beyond them, Lora. Beyond all comprehension. On some unspoken level, they realize it. They're so trifling they're trying to shrink you to their own size to feel better about themselves."

"It must be working," I grumbled.

He placed his hand over mine. "Only if you let it, love."

From across the room, the headmistress gave a delicate cough. Armand stroked his fingers across my skin—*heat, want*—then sat back again.

"They're ants to us. They'll never dream of the taste of clouds. They'll never chase the moon."

I was warm where he'd touched me. I was warm where he looked.

I felt all the secrets I'd kept shoved deep inside me welling up, ready to spill, because he was here at last and I'd *missed* him. And waiting suddenly seemed like the worst thing I could do.

I began, "Look, there's more. I have to tell you about the other night—"

But I didn't go on, because it was clear that Armand was no longer listening. He had turned his head away from me to stare at the new scholarship girl angling into the room.

She walked practically sideways, trying to remain unnoticed. She wore a drab dingy gown that blended with the shadows; she kept her shoulders rounded and avoided all the mirrors on the walls. None of the people she passed spared her a second glance.

Only Armand seemed transfixed. His hands had clenched white around the arms of his chair.

"Lora," he said, very composed.

"What?" I was irritated. She wasn't even that pretty.

"Do you recall that night last July back in the hunting lodge, when I told you I'd glimpsed a redheaded girl among the villagers we were trying to save? A girl who'd appeared only for an instant and then vanished, and I thought she was *drákon*?"

Now I was the one staring.

"That's her," he said. "I'm sure of it."

CHAPTER 12

I T HAD BEEN ONE single, extraordinary moment in a summer composed of them, and I hadn't been there for it. He'd told me about it hours and hours later, when we weren't even in the same country any longer.

He'd been counseling a huddle of frightened Belgian villagers, trying to explain to them that the Germans were going to kill them all should they be found. They'd been hiding in a forest (while I myself was off handling those very Germans), and at some point, Armand's eyes had flashed.

Dragon flash. My own eyes light silvery purple when it happens, but Mandy's become an eerie, otherworldly blue.

So he'd confessed to the villagers that we were dragons. He'd said it in French (his is much better than mine), but explained to me that exactly then, this one particular girl—a naked girl, he'd thought, though she'd been at the back of the crowd and he hadn't been certain—had gasped out the word "*drákon.*"

Then she'd disappeared. No smoke or anything. She was simply gone.

He'd been struck on the head right after that. Later that night when he recounted the entire tale to me, I'd honestly believed he'd been hallucinating. Since then, I hadn't given his story a second thought.

But as I looked at the shabby, pasty-skinned girl seated alone in Iverson's front parlor, as unequivocally isolated in this miniature sea of bejeweled and sniggering humanity as I had always been, I saw her hands begin to tremble.

I saw her lips press pale.

I saw her eyes flick to mine, deep satiny blue, far more distinctive than the rest of her.

And I saw how stupid I had been.

CHAPTER 13

MANDY STOPPED ME BEFORE I could finish rising from my chair, his hand clamped hard around my wrist.

"Think," he said urgently, beneath a charming smile. "She *vanishes*, remember?"

I dropped back against the cushions; he removed his hand. The chatter in the parlor, which had breathlessly suspended, gradually resumed.

I didn't care. I felt light and quick with my discovery, keen as a blade. My blood pounded in my ears.

Drákon, this creature named Faith or Charity had said. *Drákon.* Because, somehow, she really had been there in the summer woods. And she would know.

"Stop gawking at her," Mandy instructed, still smiling. He had his profile to her again, his feet crossed at the ankles, casual as could be. "Just tell me what she's doing."

"Surreptitiously watching us, the same as everyone else. No, wait.

Now it's her lap. I can't not look at her and still tell you what she's doing, lordling."

His smile narrowed. "You think she knows?"

I watched the girl get up from her chair, place her unfinished cup of tea upon the sideboard, and hasten from the room.

"Yes," I said. "She knows."

WE COULDN'T BOTH FOLLOW at the same time. Thanks to Armand, we'd already caused enough of a scene. Westcliffe had moved from the muttonchops man to a matron draped in ropes of pearls, but when I caught her gaze there was a hard, new glint to her eye that warned, *Act unwisely at your peril.*

So I left before Mandy did, attempting to move quickly yet nonchalantly through the clusters of people heating up the room. I kept my chin high and ignored the whispering, the constant damned whispering, telling myself, *This is a hunt. You are the hunter. Concentrate.*

But I couldn't find her. I couldn't even sense her. The castle was particularly pungent with perfume and cologne today; if the girl had left a scent apart from that, it eluded me. Apparently the latest fashion in fragrance was honeysuckle over musk. Whenever I inhaled too deeply, I nearly gagged.

I peered into the library, but it was deserted. I walked briefly outside to the front drive, but there were only motorcars and chauffeurs and clouds of cigarette smoke being blown into tangles by the breeze.

I even went as far as the wing that housed all the other students, but if she had retreated to her own room, I wouldn't easily flush her out. There were over fifty chambers set aside for Iverson's pupils covering three entire stories, and I could hardly go knocking from door to door.

Perhaps she *had* vanished. She might as well have done.

"Loitering?" inquired someone from behind me.

I turned. Sophia leaned against the nearest wall, her arms crossed over her stomach.

"Do you know which room belongs to the new girl?" I asked.

She rolled her eyes. "Heavens. Does it seem as if I should?"

"Surely you must know something. I'd wager whoever shares a room with her is complaining about it. Don't you know?"

"It may shock you to discover that I don't actually care a speck about the new girl. Or the hapless soul condemned to share space with her."

Queen Sophia. Always so compassionate.

"Fine." I walked past. She caught my arm; I shook myself free. "Careful. You don't want to catch my insanity, do you?"

"So it's true?" Her expression was a mask.

"That it's catching? Certainly. Enjoy your upcoming incarceration."

"Eleanore, honestly. I just wanted to know. One hears so *many* mad stories these days."

I was sick of playacting that I was normal. I was sick of the ogling, the snickering, the lies. "*My* mad story is true. Yes. I was locked up for a year. I—" My throat closed. I forced myself to finish. "I was a child. I had no say."

She nodded, thoughtful.

"And you're better now?"

I laughed, thinking of the black dragon with the yellow eyes. Of the zeppelin tilting beneath me. Of the girl who looked at me and trembled. "Not really."

"Armand wants to marry you, you know." Her words slipped cool and serene through the stony air. "Are you willing to risk that, to pass along this thing inside you into the line of the duke?"

"The duke's line," said Armand, emerging from the dark, "already has *this thing* within it. Or did you forget that my father currently resides in an asylum? Oh, and thank you so bloody much, Sophia, for bringing up marriage when you specifically said you wouldn't."

"I only *said* I wouldn't. I never promised."

"What are you two talking about?" I asked.

"He's picked out a ring for you," she said. "It's really rather fetching."

"You showed it to *her*?" I demanded, facing him.

"Sophia. Curse it." He grimaced. "I, er, wanted a feminine opinion of it. That's all."

Sophia smiled at me, still so cool. "I *told* you the man I was sneaking off to see was Armand."

I closed my eyes, shutting them both out. I conjured the drab gray figure of Prudence or Hope or whatever her name was, and commanded myself, *Hunt!*

But instead, all I felt was the leaden cold of the castle around me, and all I could imagine was Armand holding that ring, and Sophia looking at it and saying *fetching*, and Aubrey handing me the little golden dragon and whispering that I was its like.

"Well?" drawled Sophia, shattering my reverie. "Are you?"

I opened my eyes. "Am I what?"

"Going to marry him?"

Even for Sophia, it was beyond the pale.

I looked at them both, turned on my heel and stalked away.

HE CAUGHT UP WITH her nearly at once.

She'd let him, he could tell. If she'd truly wanted to leave him behind, Armand had no doubts about the probability of her success.

"Don't apologize," Lora snapped, before he could speak.

"All right."

They walked back toward the main doors of the keep, their footsteps measuring out the silence: hers constant; his with the barest hitch still, no matter how he compensated for it.

He considered all the true things he could say that might help defuse her temper, or might not. That Sophia was a brat. That marriage was his wish, not a given. That his brother might make a better husband, because he was a better man, but not a better dragon.

That Armand loved her, he loved her, he loved her to the point he could barely think straight without her. And that he thought (sometimes) that his love for her might actually be a sort of poison within him, barbarous and unyielding, because this lavender-eyed girl—who granted him sidelong smiles, and languorous touches, and soft, luscious kisses—consumed him as nothing else ever had. That his heart beat for her, his skin burned for her. He would kindle to ash without her.

That he didn't even care about the new *drákon* girl. Not really. Whoever she was, let her live and fly on to other fortunes. Let the mystery of their dragon magic remain unsolved; that would be easiest. All Armand wanted already walked beside him, and nothing was as important to him as that.

He'd loved only three people before Eleanore, but it felt as if, in one way or another, they'd all managed to subtract from him. His lost mother, his drunk father. Even Aubrey. Armand had always heard that love expanded, that it was a gift that gave in return. Yet the price of loving his broken family was that it had shaved away at him, bit by bit, rendering him less instead of more. Before Lora had come, he'd been a witness to his own life, a shade who watched from the margins and wondered when he'd become so insubstantial.

Eleanore, however . . . she was his *more*.

They stepped out into the day beyond the castle. He brought a hand to his eyes to shield himself from the bald blue sky and the flickering rust-yellow-rust of the trees. Lora paused, then took them both toward the rose gardens, a careful maze of stems and thorns. Another young couple was strolling a few paths over, but Mandy didn't know either of them.

The boy looked around slyly, then took the girl's hand. She twirled the parasol resting atop her shoulder and beamed up at him.

"I'll return tonight," Mandy said at last, hoping it was what Lora wanted to hear. "I'll help you find her."

She was also watching the other couple. "You can't be here all the time. You're not good at holding your form yet. And you might spook her."

"*I* might? Have you seen yourself lately?"

She scowled. The sunlight along her hair shifted from honey into fawn. Faint pink beneath.

"Fireheart." Like the bloke ahead, he dared for her hand. Unlike the other girl, Eleanore did not smile—but her fingers wrapped around his. "When you wish it, you are . . . formidable."

She made a sound like a huff.

"You are, love. You could scorch someone to death with a glance."

"That's *your* specialty, as I recall."

"It's not a glance," he said, very dignified. "It's my fiery fresh breath."

Just as he'd hoped, her lips curved. He felt a hard combination of relief and disappointment that they weren't going to talk about marriage or the ring.

He kicked at a lump of mulch on the path. It broke into scent and wooden splinters across his shoe.

"I encountered another dragon," Lora said to him.

"The new girl."

"No, another. Male, I think. Large."

His heart stopped. "What?"

JESSE HAD ONCE TOLD me that the universe worked in the simplest of ways. That we magical beings were brought together from our far-away corners because grouping us together was natural, and keeping us together was easiest. The path of least resistance.

I thought about that later that night as I stood over the other dragon-girl, fast asleep in her bed.

Like is drawn to like.

Jesse'd also said that.

I studied her face, a pale disk in the dark, her hair a plait flipped over her pillow, ragged at the ends. She didn't seem very like me or Armand. She seemed nothing at all like the grinning black dragon. I looked at her and felt no trace of the kinship or connection I'd had with Mandy and his brother from the very first. She seemed merely—ordinary.

But she wasn't. She couldn't be.

It had taken less than a half hour to find her. I'd finally convinced Armand to go back to Tranquility. I'd had to lie very smoothly (which I'm good at), until he believed me when I said I wouldn't go searching for her without him. It took a bit more effort to convince him that I didn't think the girl was the grinning dragon, which was funny, since it wasn't a lie. I didn't tell him how I knew: that the black dragon had struck a knell of cold fear through me, reflexive and bone deep.

This girl, though . . . she left me empty. She was blank to me, a promise of something like revelation, but not anything to fear.

"Besides," I'd said to Mandy before he'd left. "How do you ensure a girl who can vanish into thin air is right where you need her, when you need her?"

He'd looked at me, waiting.

"You invite her to tea at your mansion," I'd said. "To discuss matters pertaining to her scholarship. As soon as possible."

In the cool belly of the night, I'd become a slip of smoke. I'd combed from room to room, in and out before I'd scarcely done more than register scent and faces and the inevitable hodgepodge of rich-girl trinkets that bedecked each chamber.

Now here she was. Second story, eighth door down. One rich girl tucked into a bed against a wall; one poor girl in the opposite bed.

The poor girl wore a nightgown that was curiously old-fashioned. It had a high, tight collar that buttoned up her throat and looked as if it should choke her. The ruffles at her wrists were short and tattered.

She slept deep. I wouldn't have, in her position. I remembered the flash of dread in her eyes as she'd looked at me from over her teacup, and knew I wouldn't have slept.

I turned away from the bed, moving softly to the bureau nearby. For all that she was poor, Charity-Faith-Prudence had the same Iverson furniture as everyone but me, rosewood and teak and mother-of-pearl inlay. Glass-globe lamps, beveled prisms dangling.

Needlepoint chairs. A lace coverlet draping her bed, rumpled now; her hands small, helpless shapes against it.

I opened the first drawer of the bureau. Empty.

So was the second. And the third.

In the bottom drawer I found two pairs of stockings (the toes heavily darned), an unadorned cotton chemise, and a shirtwaist that looked gray in the night, but might have been any other color instead. Her armoire contained the same uniforms we all wore, plus a tweed skirt and that dress she'd worn to the tea.

That was it. No jewelry, no letters, no ribbons, no trinkets. Nothing personal to speak of her character or even her real name.

I rubbed the hem of the skirt between two fingers. The tweed was coarse; it would itch against her skin. It smelled thinly of smoke and grime.

Factory smoke, not dragon smoke.

I considered what I knew about her. I'd assumed she was an orphan like me, but now I realized that the poor girl might have a poor family somewhere in a city. A distant family of *drákon*, waiting for her return.

Then the impact of it hit me, and my breath caught. A *family* of dragons.

A peculiar feeling swept me then, one I couldn't even name. It was yearning and envy and suspicion and elation all muddled together. It was a strange harrowing hope, sharp and bright.

I gave a final glance to the sleeping girl, then Turned to smoke, silent and gone.

CHAPTER 14

THIS TRUTH, THIS UPCOMING collision from the Unseen, is my fault.

I pulled at threads of destiny I should have left unpulled.

I made knots of them so intricate even I cannot unravel their hearts.

I drew these skeins together, these slender red glitter lines of lives, casting spells of hope into their union. Spells for strength, spells about fates, all braided into a single, stronger strand.

Dragon. Dragon. Dragon. Dragon.

Now they're a tangle, Past and Present combined. These threads can never shine alone again.

I've told myself that I did it for Fireheart. To give her the answers she craves before she rises to join me here in the heavens.

But I pulled the threads too hard. I made the knots too tight. In doing this, I distorted the tension of the air, the rind of the earth, and I awoke the attention of those I'd hoped would never rouse to find her.

But they *have* roused, and now they hunt. They whisper riddles and set their eyes westward, and they know what must be done to win. Their dreams are of ice and blood.

Oh, God, Lora. I can't stop them.

They hunt.

CHAPTER 15

IARRIVED EARLY ENOUGH TO **Art Instruction** that I was able to lull the dragon-girl into thinking I'd be content remaining at the opposite side of our circle of easels, the koi pond safely between us. But as Miss Swanston entered the conservatory, I picked up my watercolor paints and brushes and marched across the chamber.

"Shove off," I told the tenth-year next to the *drákon*, and the human girl gave me a haughty, affronted look.

I thought she might have been the roommate, but who could tell? Most of these young bluebloods had the same face: doughy and supple and untested by anything but a safe, comfortable life.

I took a step closer and leaned in, summoning my most dire tone. "Shove. Off."

She blinked, took up her own paints, and fled.

Prudence-Faith stood tense before her easel, her gaze averted as if she could erase me by not looking at me. In contrast to her peers, nothing about her was doughy or untested. I marveled that I'd not noticed it before, her fine angles, the blue-milk cast of her complexion. Even the unusual color of her hair. *Comfortable* would be the last word I'd use to describe her.

Alien was more accurate. *Apart.*

She was me from last spring. The me who'd been funneled to this school via mystical means, who'd arrived with no friends and few answers, but countless wild questions.

Or, I amended to myself while watching her, she was a *version* of me, with *different* answers. And I was going to get them from her, one way or another.

Her right hand reached out, picked up a fistful of brushes from the tray below her easel. Her gaze darted around the circle, searching for any other empty spot.

"I wouldn't," I said, low. "Class is starting. You don't want to make a scene. All these society girls staring at you, talking about you. No one likes an outsider."

She froze, then slowly released the brushes. She turned her head and looked at me with those strange dark eyes. The light from the dome above us cast shadows down her cheeks.

"I'm not afraid of you," she said. Her voice was milder than her face. She had a slight accent I didn't recognize, almost lilting.

"Really? Because I can smell your fear from here."

Her nostrils flared; perhaps she was testing the air herself.

"How's Belgium?" I asked her. "Still occupied by the Huns?"

"I don't know what you mean."

"Oh, spare me. You know precisely what I—"

"Miss Jones? Why are you out of position?"

I pivoted instantly to Miss Swanston and offered an apologetic smile. "I beg your pardon, ma'am. I'm afraid I have something of a migraine, and I found the light too blinding in my usual location. It's better here, though. The other girl didn't mind switching places for today. Is that all right?"

Unlike my other instructors, Miss Swanston had always gone out of her way to be kind to me. I wish I could say I felt badly about deceiving her, but I didn't.

"I see." She patted me on the arm. "Very well. It's fine for today, but if you're not feeling better soon, Eleanore, you must go rest."

"Yes, ma'am, I shall. Thank you."

She gave me an extra pat, and moved off.

The dragon-girl and I exchanged another lingering look, but Miss Swanston had begun the hour, so we didn't speak again.

We were to paint a scene from fantasy. It might be as fanciful as we wished: a dashing knight from a fairytale, an enchanted wood filled with pixies, a crook-backed witch over a cauldron—as long as it sprung purely from our imaginations.

I smirked at the *drákon* girl. She regarded me dourly, then angled away.

It was surprisingly difficult to get the black dragon right. I thought I'd captured the sinewy tension of his body, the blank yellow of his eyes, fairly well. Even the red and green glints down his wings and back. Yet his face eluded me. It was odd, because in my mind I could see him so clearly. I could *feel* how he made me feel so vividly.

But even after I carefully added shadow to the points of his fangs, it seemed that something was missing.

The mirth, maybe. The sinister delight behind his grin as he'd pranced toward me.

New Girl was painting nothing so ominous. I made no secret of the fact that I was observing her, but she never looked at me again, instead concentrating fervently upon her work.

She'd created a mountain, a jaggedy tall one, without trees or anything green to soften it. There were stark white patches that I thought were meant to be snow, and a twisty line that was likely a road winding toward its top. But anchored to the side of the mountain was a castle, a truly fantastical one. It stuck out like a flag over the slope, rectangular white stones and skinny long windows, far fiercer looking, somehow, than the fortress we currently stood in.

The girl began to paint violet night all around it, with lemon-drop stars.

"Miss Smith," said Miss Swanston, and I realized she was talking to the *drákon* girl. "How very clever. Is it the castle of a princess?"

Miss Smith rubbed at a brownish smear on the back of her hand. "No. It's the castle of a prince." She hesitated, then added, "It's a castle made of tears and ice."

"Not a very good one," sniped Beatrice, at my other side. She'd painted a fairy queen of sorts, a stub-nosed, curly-haired creature in a fluffy orange dress and a crown. "There's nothing but open air beneath it. It would never stay in place."

"It's fixed to the edge of the mountain by the bones of the dead monsters who built it."

Miss Swanston's eyebrows raised, but all she said was, "Ah."

I asked, "Does the prince live there alone?"

The girl glanced at me, shook her head.

"And is he a monster too?" inquired Miss Swanston lightly. "A prince by day, a beast by night, perchance?"

Miss Smith smiled. It was a shy, gradual smile that transformed her face from wan and alien into something close to splendid.

"Of course," she said.

That was when I knew that we had both been cheating the assignment. Neither of us had imagined a thing.

As class was ending. Mrs. Westcliffe appeared in the open archway of the conservatory bearing a letter with a broken wax seal. She began to walk toward Miss Smith.

I added a final bit of green to my dragon, then packed up my paints.

Tea at Tranquility beckoned.

I ARRIVED FIRST. IT wasn't difficult; I was a wisp floating above the motorcar that carried Miss Smith, very high above it. Then I was a wisp floating down a chimney (the pane I'd broken in Aubrey's room had already been repaired), and then I was a wisp Turned to girl behind the curtains of Aubrey's bed.

"Hullo," he said. He was seated in his wheelchair by the windows again, one hand lifted to cover his eyes. His lips were smiling. "Look on the bed."

He'd laid out a robe for me. It was a man's robe, the kind that wealthy men wore in private to smoke and drink and think wealthy thoughts, all satin and paisley and shiny thick cording along the edges.

The cuffs flopped over my fingers. The bottom of it puddled around my feet. I realized that I'd never seen Aubrey standing up. He must be very tall.

"Thank you," I said quietly, because I didn't know how many seconds away Miss Smith was from the other side of his door.

"Exciting," he said, lowering his hand, and for an instant I thought he meant *me*, in the robe. Which made me blush a little. But then he added, "Another one of us. Unbelievable luck."

"Yes. Unbelievable."

The tea service was already in place, cups and pots and scones and jams and clotted cream, everything scrumptious and perfect. It looked nothing at all like an ambush.

In retrospect, I'm still not certain how everything went so wrong so quickly.

There was a knock on the door, and I faded back behind the

curtains of the bed. Aubrey said, "Come in," and the door opened, and the footman announced her, and then I heard the dragon-girl edging into the chamber.

I waited to breathe until the door closed again. I'm sure of that. But then Aubrey was saying "Miss Smith," in his friendly way, and I had moved a half-step to see and the girl flew, swift as a sparrow, to the tea service. To the knife that had been placed beside the fine china plates to cut the butter, because the butter would be ice-cold still—this was Tranquility, after all—and the blade would be sharp.

And then she was behind Aubrey with the knife to his neck. And she was looking at me, and her eyes were feral and calm both.

"I will kill him," she said, in her mild, lilting way.

I shifted clear of the bed. "That would be a catastrophic mistake."

Aubrey was immobile, his eyes also on me. The blade was pressed hard against a sliver of skin showing through his bandages. It was pressed to his right side, the side without his jugular vein, I knew. But if she wanted, she could slice deep enough to end his life anyway.

His body was so fragile. *He* was so fragile, and in some blood way—in every way that mattered—he belonged to *me*.

The dragon in me sizzled beneath my skin.

I said, "I could break your neck before the next pulse of your heart."

"Try," she taunted, and the knife pressed deeper.

"Lora." Aubrey twitched a hand. "She's only afraid."

"She should be."

"All I want," said the girl, "is to go home. That's all."

"And where is home?" asked Armand, because he had just slipped through the crack of the bedroom door. He moved unhurriedly, almost languidly, but his eyes blazed luminescent.

She glared at him, then back at me. I could see her mind working, words and actions considered, discarded, considered again.

"Belgium?" he offered, and his tone was as peaceful as his eyes were not. "The woods?"

"No, not Belgium. Why do you all keep saying that?"

"Spain," said Aubrey suddenly. "Yes?"

She jerked, and I was smoke right as Armand lunged. We reached her together, a jumble of bodies and the wheelchair tipping to its side. There was the soft *thump* of Aubrey hitting the rug (*fragile!*), but I won. I was on top of her, one arm braced against her throat and the other hand pinning her wrist. My lips were pulled back into a snarl; my hair framed both our faces.

"I'll do it," I breathed, my nose an inch from hers. "I will."

Someone was saying my name. Someone was tugging at my shoulder, but there was only the girl beneath me, her eyes glued to mine, blue like a bruise, ebony pupils, fathomless. I felt a pull of something new—not the hold at my shoulder, but something larger than that. Colossal. It enveloped me entirely, a sensation of ice and hunger and an airless blackness without end.

I could not move. I could not Turn. I knew that whatever this was, it was coming from the girl.

I began to dissolve within it.

Then it released me, snapping back like a rubber band. I returned to the cozy light of the bedroom and Mandy beside me, saying *It's fine, she's disarmed, let her go*, and Aubrey wheezing very near.

Miss Smith stared up at me, her complexion gone to chalk. I released her throat and leapt to my feet, and Mandy had me in his arms.

Aubrey had pulled himself upright beside the toppled wheelchair. I felt his hand press against the top of my foot, reassuring.

"The next time you threaten one of mine," I rasped, "I *will* kill you first, no matter who or what tries to stop me. I swear it."

No one moved. The dragon-girl lay prone in a square of light; the sun glimmered prettily along the red-gold of her hair.

I tugged free of Armand. "Go home, then. Vanish again. No one's preventing you."

A spasm of emotion crossed her face, anger or despair or frustration, I couldn't tell. She sat up carefully, curling her legs beneath her. "Where are the rest of you?"

Armand glanced at me, then made a circle with his hand, encompassing the three of us.

"Small family," he said.

The girl's gaze kept returning to me, then away. Her cheeks were coloring, and I remembered I'd left the robe on the floor from my Turn. I made a sound of disgust—she'd just tried to cold-bloodedly poke a knife through Aubrey and probably attempted to murder me as well, but my nudity embarrassed her?—yet I gathered up the robe. As soon as I had it on, I noticed that both Aubrey's and Armand's shoulders lost a fraction of their tension.

"I meant," she said, "where is your tribe?"

I frowned. It was a queer word to use, but familiar too. I couldn't remember why.

"Where is yours?" I countered, unwilling to give answers without receiving any.

"Spain," said Aubrey again, nodding. "Served with a . . . wingman who'd spent . . . years there as a boy. Sounded almost exactly like you. Mandy, old chap. Help me up, will you?"

We both did, me righting the wheelchair, Armand tending to his brother, trying not to move him too quickly or grasp him too tightly. When Aubrey gave a short, stifled gasp of pain as his hip connected with the seat, it cut through me like a sword. Even Miss Smith winced.

"No," I said coldly, and pointed a finger at her. "You don't get to feel bad about that. You caused it, you're to blame, and I want you to either go back to Spain or wherever your home is *right now* and never trouble us again, or else start talking."

She flinched small in her beam of light. "I . . ."

"You *what?*"

"I can't go back," the girl cried. "I've tried and tried. I've been stuck here forever and I can't get back, and I thought that perhaps, just now—with you—"

"Wait," I said. "Do you mean—are you saying that you were trying to Turn *with* me somehow? To take me with you back to ruddy Spain?" I goggled at her. "Were you attempting to *kidnap* me?"

"Don't be preposterous." She found her feet. Both Armand and I moved instantly to stand in front of Aubrey, but she didn't seem to notice. "I wasn't trying to take you with me. I don't think it's even possible. But this was the first time in months I've felt the Weave come near. Nothing would have happened to you."

"Weave?" Aubrey asked, just as Armand said, "Just now with Lora *what?*"

Miss Smith drew herself very straight. She looked remarkably regal, even with her hair poking out like bits of straw from its pins.

"Are you, or are you not, the English *drákon?*" she asked.

"Well," said Aubrey easily. "Rather obviously, we are."

"Are you the Alpha?"

Armand and I exchanged a look.

"Righto," agreed Aubrey, still in that easy tone, though I'd wager he didn't know what that meant any more than Mandy or I did.

The girl lifted her palms to us, white fingers cupping the empty air. "Are there truly only three of you left?"

"Left?" I repeated, my mind suddenly working, working—

"*Tribe,*" burst out Armand, excited. "Tribe! Of course. That's the word that Rue used in her letters, remember?"

"Rue?" Miss Smith flinched again, sidling out of the light. "The marchioness?"

The power of words is not like that of guns or bombs. But it can transform the world just as effectively.

Three little words from this redheaded chit, and our world was altered forever.

CHAPTER 16

THE PROBLEM, MANDY THOUGHT, was that he had no experience in dealing with situations like this. He knew inane, useless things, like the best way to sneak out of Eton late at night, or the right sorts of compliments to impress women of a certain age, or which haberdasher in the Burlington Arcade sold the best felt hats and which the best straw.

He knew a very few useful things as well, such as how to destroy a prison camp, or when to push back against the military machine that had taken over his home at his own suggestion, or how to change field dressings with a minimum amount of fuss.

Of late, and thanks to Lora, he knew how to listen, and he knew how to steal, and he knew how to love.

He did not, however, know what to do about the circumstances surrounding him now: the improbable fact of not one but two magical girls, one in sun, one in shade; his brother caught thin and hunched in his chair nearby, visibly in pain but at the same time alight with something else.

Something that might *also* be love, Mandy realized, his heart sinking.

Alpha, the other girl had said, and Aubrey had claimed that title as naturally and unthinkingly as he had all the others.

"Talk," ordered Lora. She was still staring hard at the other girl, who had gone from unfriendly and calm to unfriendly and teary-eyed. It was a strange enough transition that he was goaded to act; Mandy pointed to the chair closest to the girl, a silent invitation. He didn't think it wise to approach her yet.

She wiped at her eyes and shuffled toward the chair. Lora had taken command of the butter knife. As she watched the girl sit, she spun it slowly back and forth between her index finger and her thumb. It seemed like something she might have learned in her other life, the one that involved moldering orphanages and madhouses with evil doctors and barred doors.

Mandy realized he didn't know the new girl's name. It seemed a good enough place to start.

"Refreshment?" he said. "Miss . . . ?"

"Smith," Lora finished for the girl, a sneer in her tone.

"I'm Armand," Mandy said, deciding to ignore the sneer. "My brother, Aubrey. You know Lora, of course. What's your name?"

Both he and the girl looked back at Lora, but she didn't jump in this time. She only kept twirling the knife.

"Honor," said the girl finally, her mouth small and pinched, like she was giving up secrets. "Honor Smith."

"All right, Honor Smith, how do you do? And why did you attempt to kill my brother?"

"I thought . . . I'm sorry. I truly am. It was a misunderstanding. I was wrong."

Lora smiled, slim and sinister. Even drowning in his brother's robe, she looked surprisingly dangerous.

"Aren't you one of us?" Aubrey asked.

Honor fidgeted in the chair. She looked down at her lap, then back up. "I haven't had the best of luck with our kind. In the least, really. So I do apologize again. I was only seizing the initiative."

"Bollocks," snapped Armand's true love, closing her fist around the knife. "Seizing the initiative would have been running away from the school. It would have been avoiding us entirely. Not threatening a man bound to a wheelchair."

"Well, I didn't *know* there were more than the two of you," Honor retorted, fierce again. "I sensed *you* at Iverson and your friend at the visitors' tea, but I had no idea the Marquess of Sherborne was *drákon*, too. I was startled. I thought all the English dragons were up in Darkfrith."

"Ah," said Aubrey. "Darkfrith. North country, I believe?"

Honor stared. "You don't know about them?"

"As I said." Armand lifted his hand again. "We're a small family here."

"But then—where did you come from?"

"We have no notion," Aubrey said. "Rather hoping you did."

The small-lips expression reappeared. Only this time, instead of *secretive*, Mandy thought it signaled *crafty*.

He asked, assessing, "Are you the black dragon Eleanore saw? With the airship?"

"No, I don't—I can't Turn into a dragon. Or smoke. I don't have that Gift."

"But you can vanish. I saw that for myself."

She looked puzzled. "You did?"

"In Belgium. In the woods. Don't you recall it? Last summer, with the villagers and the Germans bombing everything?"

"That . . ." Honor's eyes closed; her brow puckered. "That was last summer?"

"Yes," cut in Lora, impatient. "Of course it was. With the *war*, remember?"

"I was . . . there by accident. I do recall it. I didn't mean to go there, but sometimes I can't control wh—where I end up."

The knife spun faster. "This vanishing act of yours. You can travel from place to place with it? Travel all the way across countries at once, without going to smoke at all?"

"That's right."

Aubrey asked, "Is that a common Gift?"

"No. It belongs only to me. So, I *was* there in those woods. I did vanish. But I haven't been able to do it much since." She glanced at Mandy. "You said there's another dragon around?"

Lora answered. "Not too terribly around. East of here. Traveling with a zeppelin, as far as I could tell."

"There are only two tribes of *drákon* in all the world that I know of. The English in Darkfrith—that's in York—and the Zaharen in the Carpathians. If you are not members of either tribe, you are outlaws. Outlaws are punished, by the way. Severely so. If another dragon has discovered your family of three, that's very bad news for you."

"And *you*, from Spain," scoffed Lora, still narrow-eyed and dangerous. "Are you an outlaw, as well?"

"Oh, yes. They'll slaughter me if they can. They keep trying." Honor gave a shrug, matter-of-fact. "It's why I thought I'd be safe here, down in the south. I've never heard of dragons in Wessex before. You must be very cunning, to have kept yourselves hidden for so long."

Armand felt the beginnings of a headache creeping over him. Nothing about this girl seemed especially trustworthy, but at the same time—weirdly—everything about her did. "Don't heap us with flattery just yet. We only found out about any of this around six months ago."

Seven fine months ago, he had been at Eton, breaking rules, not giving a damn about his studies, and stewing at his father's hand-scripted, well-publicized list of restrictions for his youngest son, which Mandy had taken perverse pleasure in tacking up outside his bedroom door:

No motorcars.
No smoking.
No drinking.
No girls.
No war.

Naturally, Mandy'd done his best to become intimately acquainted with all of those things, even the war part, although now that he'd actually witnessed the reality of men machine-gunning each other into ground meat, he was better able to appreciate what a stupendous fool he'd been.

Seven months ago, he'd been a different person. Callow. Young. Blind to anything that wasn't strictly about the glory of himself.

Today he was something else, something new and mostly raw and unpolished. He was not only an almost-dragon, but also apparently an illegal one.

He didn't know what to make of that.

Lora smacked the butter knife briskly into her palm. "But who is Rue?"

"Rue is—was the Marchioness of Langford. That's the Alpha line up there, the Langford family."

"I looked up all the marchionesses in the peerage," Mandy said, his headache searing stronger, "from forever ago until now. No Rue."

"That wasn't her given name. I think her given name was Clara, or Clarissa. Like that. But everyone called her Rue."

"You seem very familiar with her," said Lora.

Honor's gaze dropped back to her lap. "It's only folklore."

Aubrey shifted in the wheelchair. The smell of his ointment wafted through the room, acrid and foreign.

"Miss Smith," he said. "Honor, if I may. Will you . . . pour me a cuppa? Sugar, no lemon."

And Mandy watched as she turned to the service, easily

maneuvering the pot, the cup, the sugar spoon, the saucer. Her hands were pale and graceful, her movements precise.

"You're highborn," he said, not making it a question.

"There are no peasants in Darkfrith. There are only patrician savages, and slightly less patrician savages. That's all."

"You said you were from Spain."

"No, *you* said that. I live in Spain now, but I was born in Darkfrith." She walked cautiously to Aubrey with the cup and saucer, watching Eleanore the entire way. "I ran away as a child."

"You're rather still a child, aren't you?" Lora said, the sneer in her voice returned. Mandy could feel her hostility still, a slow-burning heat. She did not forgive easily, he knew.

"I'm old enough to have experienced more of the wiles and rules of the *drákon* than *you*, evidently. And how do you even know about Rue Langford, pray tell, if you've never heard of the Darkfrith line before?"

"Letters," replied Aubrey, not drinking his tea. "From her to us."

"Oh." Honor looked at him, rubbed a finger against her lips. "May I see?"

"Wait." Lora pointed the knife at Honor. "What did you mean before when you said it was the first time you'd felt a 'Weave' come near? What's a 'Weave'?"

"Oh," said Honor Smith again, "that's simply what I call it when I vanish."

And even though the crafty pinch had disappeared from her mouth, and Mandy's headache was spreading red and throbbing behind his eyes, something in the vicinity of his stomach pitched over. The voice that sometimes lived inside him—the dragon-voice—came awake.

It whispered, *She's a liar.*

HONOR SMITH LIVED IN Spain with a kindly pair of adoptive parents and a Great Big Secret that they knew nothing about; she'd Woven to England from Barcelona about three months past. According to her, she'd been in her bed late one night, listening to the clip-clopping of the donkeys traversing the cobblestone *carrer* beneath her window, and the next morning she'd awoken on a pavement in Manchester, tucked under a flowerbox adorning the side of a bank, cold damp stone pressed against her bare back.

"You don't get to keep your clothing when you Weave?" I asked.

She threw me a significant look. "No."

I have to admit, I felt a little smug about that.

She'd awoken very early in the morning, the air murky with a yellow sulphur fog that had probably mostly hidden her from anyone walking by. And it was thanks to that fog that she was able to run without getting caught until she found a street of row houses and an unguarded back gate, and a line of men's laundry—still wet—strung up between two tiny yards.

"So you stole it?" I interjected. "Some poor bloke's work clothes?"

"I had to! I didn't have anything else!"

I pursed my lips at her. Armand only rolled his eyes, no doubt remembering all the things I'd nicked during our time together.

But Honor Smith was not the light-fingered thief I was. Two days later, when she'd tried, starving and reckless, to snatch an unfinished pasty off a café plate, she'd been nabbed.

"There'd been a riot of cotton workers or something, and the jail was full," she said, slowly consuming a scone, a dab of cream on her chin. "So they tried to just send me on my way. But I told them I had naught and no one and they took mercy on me, I suppose. They sent me to a foundling home instead."

"Lovely mercy," I murmured.

She gave me a glance through her lashes. "I had a cot. I had a meal."

"Soup?"

"Better than starving," Armand said, as if he would know. "May I ask, Miss Smith, how old you are?"

"Sixt—seventeen."

I shook my head. "Fifteen, right?"

"Sixteen," she said firmly.

"Small for your age," I noted.

"No more so than you," she shot back.

Armand held up his hands, silencing us both. "Have you tried writing a letter home? Reaching your adoptive parents that way?"

"I write letters all the time," she said darkly. "I never get responses."

"Three months," Aubrey said. "They must be . . . worried."

Armand was staring down at the round moon surface of his tea.

"Mail's a wreck with the war. Spain's far and on the wrong side of everything. Likely nothing's gotten through."

The clock on Aubrey's desk began a light, pretty chiming.

"Crikey, is that the time?" I stood. "I'll miss dinner!"

Mandy laughed and Aubrey smiled, but Honor only nodded.

"It's a *school*," I said with dignity to the Louis brothers. "If I'm unaccounted for, there will be a search. If there is a search, I will be punished. And then good luck visiting me there again, Lord Armand. Or getting permission for me to come visit here, Lord Sherborne."

"Go," said Aubrey, losing his smile.

Armand took me by the arm, leaned close in to my ear. "See you soon anyway."

I walked to the window nearest me and pushed it open. I went to smoke, and as I was flowing away, the last thing I heard was Honor Smith saying, incredulous, "She *can* Turn."

CHAPTER 17

I WAS DIFFERENT AFTER THAT. I wasn't fully certain why. I had known that Honor was one of us before I invited myself to her tea, and I knew the same after. And, truth be told, I still didn't like her. But after that day, I was transfigured, my mind pried open, my deepest thoughts unleashed. Even something about Iverson felt altered, the result of an alchemy of ancient stone and fresh sorcery, maybe.

It warmed the cold walls. It swirled the stagnant air, churning up motes and impossible possibilities. It settled over my body and into my hair and eyes and lungs, unseen magic risen from the netherworld to prickle my every atom.

Change was coming, I could tell.

Change was already here.

I am not the only lost dragon. I had a family once, Langford or Za-haren. I had parents.

I might still. I might.

But change is perilous, you know. Change isn't merely new beginnings. It means endings, too.

CHAPTER 18

ORMALLY AFTER DINNER I would retreat to my tower. But that evening I made my way to the school library, where I found the book I wanted and then the girl I wanted, alone again at a table far from the cozy group of students clustered around the warmth of the hearth.

I slapped the book down on her table with both hands (it was very heavy). Honor looked up at me, unperturbed, as if she'd been expecting me to show up lugging a tome the size of an oil painting.

"Darkfrith," I said, and pointed to the atlas I'd procured. "Show me where."

She said nothing, just bent her head and began to rifle through the pages, finding Europe first, then England, then York. I stood over her and watched her fingers trace the railroad lines that cut across the cities and hamlets, paralleling dotted telegraph lines and the ghosts of Roman-built roads.

"It should be . . ." She smoothed a circle around a particularly blank bit of the map. "Here."

I peered down at the page. A solitary dot had the word DARK-FRITH printed beside it in minute letters. "Not a lot there."

"No. That's rather the point."

I sat down in the chair beside hers. She hadn't removed her hand from the page, only kept making those slow circles with her fingertips, rubbing heat into the paper.

"Do you miss it?" I asked.

Her hand stilled. "No."

"Never?"

She sat back, her eyes half-lidded. The chatter from the girls by the fire washed over us in fragments: *Walter said don't—silk chiffon with pleats—artillery shells, right there on the road—Tillie's party had the jolliest—his letters are censored of course but—flowers, flowers all around—*

"It's very green there," Honor said at last. "Lush. Misty and hilly."

"England is green all over."

"Spain isn't. So I might miss that." She blinked a few times, slowly, like a dreamer coming awake. "Otherwise, no. They're animals there. There's not anything to miss."

"Did they really try to kill you?"

She sighed. "Listen, you shouldn't attempt to find them. I know that's what you're thinking. I heard you're an orphan and perhaps you think they'll help you find your parents, or find yourself, I don't know. But I do know this: the weak are prey there. The abnormal are culled. Criminals—and you *are* a criminal to them, Eleanore, merely by virtue of being apart from them right now—are imprisoned and then executed."

"Oh, come." I couldn't help my laugh. "We are still talking about modern England, are we not? How are they going to *execute* me? Chop off my head? Burn me at the stake? This is the twentieth century, Honor, not the Dark Ages. We have laws. They can't just go around jailing and murdering people."

She gave me an unreadable look. "Perhaps. Perhaps not. Anyway, you can Turn, so there's that."

"What do you mean?"

"It's not a Gift many females have. In fact, hardly any do. So they might use you as a breeder instead."

My laughter died away. "Are you jesting?"

But I knew that she wasn't. Absolutely nothing about her was anything but solemn. She was a statue with endless dark eyes.

"That's . . ." I struggled for words. "That's barbaric."

Now she smiled. "You're learning."

She flipped through the pages of the atlas again, leaning over it intently. Her eyebrows furrowed; her tongue popped out to worry her upper lip. In the half-light she became an ordinary schoolgirl once more, thin and young.

She looked back up. "If you insist upon finding dragons, go here instead." She spun the book around to me.

It was a map of mountains, THE CARPATHIAN RANGE written in a curve along their base.

"Your castle," I remembered. "From Art Instruction."

"It's not mine," she protested, blushing. "It's—it's called Zaharen Yce, and it belongs to the Zaharen. To the ruling family there. I think. I mean, I haven't been in some time, so I suppose it might have passed on to someone else by now, but . . ."

"But you *have* been," I said, when it appeared she'd run out of things to say.

"Yes." The blush grew stronger.

"Weaving."

"Yes."

I twisted my tongue around the unfamiliar syllables. "*Zahaaren Yeece*. You said back in class it was the castle of a prince."

"It was once," she answered. "Once upon a time. Now, however . . . just be careful. If you go."

I studied the map, its dearth of dots and lines, the enormity of those inked-in peaks. Either the mapmaker had gotten lazy or else the modern world had barely brushed these mountains. I counted three train tracks and a handful of villages—no telegraph lines—for the entire page.

"Remote," I said.

"It was never meant for the softness of human lives."

I didn't need the stack of pages between it and the map of England to tell me that wherever this dragon castle stood, it was a damned far distance from where I was now.

"Was he a very handsome prince?" I asked casually, and glanced up to watch her blush deepen into the color of bricks.

Right.

"And these Zaharen, they're not as awful as the *drákon* in Darkfrith? There's no . . ." Stupidly, I felt my own face begin to heat. " . . . breeding?"

"A female who can Turn will cause a sensation wherever she goes. I think you should stay hidden. I would. I'm going to. But no matter what you decide, if you meet them, *any* of them, I suggest you never turn your back to them. And note every escape route. And carry a pistol on your person."

"You mean it," I said, feeling sick.

"Eleanore, they'll keep you any way they can. With honey or with vinegar, it doesn't matter to them. They'd bottle your soul if they could."

She gently closed the atlas, rising to lean over it with both palms spread flat upon its cover.

"In Darkfrith lies a hidden field, formally forbidden to anyone but the Alpha and his council. It's green and fertile, like the rest of the shire. Should you look upon it, all you'd see is sweetgrass and thistles. But feeding the grass and thistles are the bodies of generations of runaways. When you hike through that field, your feet follow their lumps." She straightened. "Don't try to find the *drákon*. But if you do, remember that I warned you."

I watched her walk away from our table and out of the library.

I hadn't said aloud the obvious:

It seemed that the *drákon* had already found *me*.

⊱ ✦✦✦ ⊰

I WAITED IN MY bed for Armand. It sounds salacious, but I waited with all my clothes on, and a candle burning, and the spiders at my ceiling creeping-crawling sleepily, delicately, along their perfect webs.

I was thinking about that castle Honor had painted. About the bones of the dead dragons that held it in place, and the bones that shaped the grasses of that field in Darkfrith. About being forced into someone else's bed—a stranger's bed—merely because I had this Gift I'd never asked for and scarcely controlled and hadn't even suspected existed until my sixteenth year of life.

They're animals there.

I'd thought I understood what that meant. More than once I'd thought of myself as an animal, as a beast, but I would never, *ever* force anyone to—

A horrible new thought struck me. Was that why the black dragon had been grinning?

I pulled another blanket over me, shivering. The sea beyond the tower breathed and released, breathed and released.

Armand glided silently into my chamber, smooth silky vapor transformed into flesh.

He Turned by the bed, bent over and kissed me before I could move. Only my hands betrayed me, my fingers going stiff with surprise. But only for an instant . . . because then I was melting. The candlelight was gone; the sea and spiders and my uneasy thoughts were gone. There was just Mandy above me, his lips caressing mine, and our shared breath and the sensation of him—*male, whiskers and warmth*—consuming me.

I felt made for this, dragon to dragon. I curled my arms around him and kissed him back and shivered once again, this time not from dread or cold.

A word whispered through me, a word with a source I could not pinpoint, a word I knew and loved and feared:

Fated.

Armand's lips shifted, murmured an invitation against the curve of my ear.

"Come with me. I've something to show you."

He returned to smoke, lingering at the edge of my window, waiting.

I got up, walked to the bureau and pinched out my candle. Then I followed.

He took me to the pebbled beach we'd visited before. The tide was lower this time; the Channel seethed and splashed in the dark distance, hissing secrets to itself.

Armand Turned to boy, picking his way carefully over the uneven ground to a crooked sapling that grew, stubborn, from the base of a bluff. I followed as smoke (why stumble my way across the pebbles?) but Turned back to girl when he stopped and picked up a burlap bag that had been resting against the sapling's roots.

He held it out to me. I accepted it, frowning.

It was heavy. And filled with song.

"I told you I'd save the beach," he said.

I opened the bag. Inside were wee fish and clams, tiny crabs and ribbons and knobs of seaweed. All of it transmuted from life into metal. All of it pure gold.

"This is where you've been at night?" I stirred my fingers through the top layer, feeling the flutter of a hundred small melodies spiraling up my arm. "Collecting these?"

"I didn't want you to worry about them."

"I didn't even hear them," I confessed, staring down at the dull gleam of the fortune inside the bag. I picked out another starfish, this one a little larger than the last, its arms thinner and feathered with golden fronds.

"Most of them were buried still, or out in the far waters. I wanted to get them before they washed ashore."

I dropped the starfish back into the bag. Above us and beyond us, the real stars watched and said nothing, throwing sparks against their field of jet.

He must have gone swimming for many of these creatures. He could swim and I could not; he must have been out here in this autumn sea these past few nights, diving through unlit waters, braving sharks and minefields and the unknown monsters of unknown depths. For me.

So I would not worry.

I looked up at him.

"Honor says that because I can Turn I'll be used to—to make babies for the other *drákon*. Because it's a rare Gift. For a female."

He gazed at me, silent, his jaw tight. The wind danced between us, laced through his hair. My skin was cold and the world had gone shadowed and sea-whipped and deep.

"Will you marry me, Armand Louis?" I asked.

He took the bag from me, placed it on the pebbles, and lifted both my hands.

"I would never let them have you," he said. "No matter what happens between us. You know that, don't you?"

"Yes."

"Fireheart. Is this truly what you want?"

"Yes."

And I meant it.

His palm cupped my cheek. "You told me to wait to ask you again. Back in Germany. You told me to ask you under the light of the sun."

"Well," I said, "I think this works, too."

He smiled: a beautiful smile, a glorious smile, one that made me glad I'd said what I did and to hell with whatever would come after. He pulled me to him and I wrapped my arms around him and we clung to each other against the wind, against the salt and the stars and the caroling gold at our feet. Someone somewhere was burning a wood fire and that became part of our moment, too, the sugar-smoke fragrance of pine borne up into the night.

I twined my fingers through his hair; I matched his smile with my own. When our lips touched, it felt like the first time ever.

Because it was, I realized. The Eleanore and Armand of bare

seconds past—two alone, two apart—had transformed. We were joined into something new.

One, not two. Together, not apart.

Don't take me now, I pleaded silently with the stars, my eyes closed, my body alight. *Please let me have this for as long as I can.*

The Channel breathed and released. The earth turned, and the stars sighed.

CHAPTER 19

HERE IS THE DREAM that stole me away much later that night:

I'm floating through clouds, dancing atop their mists, colors such as I've never seen blossoming with my every step. I'm wearing a ball gown composed of diamonds. My skirts capture the colors of my dance in dazzling sweeps of fire.

I'm dancing alone, spinning, dipping, weaving. And then, all at once, I'm dancing with Jesse.

He's the boy I first met, not the star. Tall and fine-looking and very much alive. He captures my gaze as we spin, summer storms in his eyes and rainbows in his hair.

"Do you mind about it?" I ask. "Me and Mandy?"

His smile is rueful. "Yes."

A pang strikes my heart. My next step churns the color of ashes. "I'm sorry."

"As am I."

"You were my all," I try, because it is true, and he has to know it.

"As you yet are mine, dragon-girl."

We slow until we're both standing still, my one hand in his, the other upon his shoulder, his palm a warm spot at the small of my back. The clouds billow around us in scoops of flavored ice, rose and mint and mulberry and orange.

My gown grows weighted. One by one the diamonds begin to fall, tumbling raindrops through the mists.

"He loves me," I say.

"I know."

And because it is a dream, and in dreams your heart speaks for you, I admit, "I think I love him, too."

Jesse smiles again, sadder than before. "I know."

The diamonds are falling. I dig my fingers into the rough cotton shirt covering his shoulder because I feel everything coming apart.

"I'm not ready to die, Jesse."

"Knots are tied. Time has been bent. The hunters approach, and you must be prepared."

"Who? Who are they?"

But he only shakes his head, his gaze going to a place I cannot see. "Do not become their prey. Remember who you are. Obey your heart, not their enchantments."

All the diamonds are gone. Where my body should be are only mists of shifting colors. I know I'm about to wake.

"Wait," I say, urgent. "Is this real?"

"Only you can decide," he answers, and we drop through the clouds together, until we both dissolve into light.

CHAPTER 20

ALTHOUGH THE NIGHT HAD come and gone and left me changed, rendered me new, the next morning dawned a regular school day. Armand and I had agreed to keep our engagement a secret for as long as we could. I was likely still underage (who knew?) and even if I was not, the announcement would send a shock wave throughout the community.

Shock waves, I knew, had repercussions, and some of ours would be momentous. The only person who'd be happy for us would be Sophia, and only because she loved trouble even more than she loved rebellion.

So I sat in Literature class and listened without listening to the poems being recited by my classmates, thinking about Armand and trying *not* to think about Aubrey. I still hadn't quite yet reconciled myself with the guilt of keeping all of this from him.

Aubrey, with his endearing smile.

Who'd given me my own little dragon. Who'd survived an

aeroplane crash and prison camp and all the fresh agonies of his everyday life with nothing but patience and cheer. Whose eyes lit up whenever he saw me.

I needed to tell him.

Oh, God, I *really* didn't want to.

Hullo, Aubrey. Guess what, I'm marrying your brother and oh, by the by, apparently there are some rather beastly drákon *headed our way who mean to enslave me and do heaven knows what to you and Mandy and Honor. Thanks ever so for being the Alpha, because I think that means you're in charge! Cheerio!*

Caroline, my deskmate, kept squirming in her chair and muttering under her breath. She clutched her assigned book of poems with both hands like it would save her from drowning. It had a green cloth cover and gilt lettering that flashed *Pleasant Sonnets from the Field*.

"*Sweet* peas," she kept muttering. "*Sweet* peas with petals so bright."

"Miss Jones," called my professor from the front of the room, and I looked up. Mrs. Huckle was bony and gray-haired and stoop-shouldered, as though she had been listening to too much bad poetry for too many years and it truly weighed upon her soul. She met my look and raised both eyebrows, perhaps because the effort of telling me aloud that it was my turn was simply one more burden than she could abide.

I came to my feet. Caroline squirmed again and someone else's heel tapped a nervous tattoo against the floor, then stopped.

I didn't need to glance down at my own book of poems. I'd

already memorized my piece.

I mustered my courage and began.

Her garden blooms at night.
Her eyes do not see yours.
She dreams of darker lands,
And travels to places you cannot follow.

Her name is Chaos.
Look not at her face.
Look into her soul,
And grow lost there.

You are mired in her winter and spring.
You feed her yearning, nectar on her lips.
In these shadows, she opens to you,
And you take your place there.

She is your fate;
She is your bliss;
Your bright death.
There is no hope.

I'd been speaking to the window behind Mrs. Huckle, one that showed a rectangle of sky and clouds and the blood-red crown of a beech tree, because we were on the third floor and on this side of the castle, the beeches grew tallest. But as I finished I allowed my gaze to drift downward, into the steely eyes of my suddenly invigorated professor.

"That was not from your assigned reading," she said.

"Was it not?" I lowered my lashes. "I beg your pardon."

"Where did you find that—that piece?"

I held up my book. It was smaller than Caroline's book of sonnets, white with black lettering that read simply, *Longing*.

"From the library," I said. Her eyebrows began their upward climb again, so I clarified, "The library at Tranquility, I mean. I assumed, since it came from Tranquility—the duke's personal collection and all—that it would be acceptable."

"Why, dare I ask, would you make such an outrageous assumption?"

"Mrs. Westcliffe has always assured me that His Grace is the epitome of taste and style," I said innocently.

The name inscribed inside the book was not actually that of Reginald Louis, but that of his late wife, a woman with a whisper of my own tempestuous magic in her blood. Even so, I fancied a dead duchess wouldn't carry as much cachet as a living duke.

Mrs. Huckle's shoulders sagged even lower than before. I'd only added to her burdens.

"The tastes and styles of a duke, even one as elevated as His Grace, are not necessarily ones appropriate for immature young ladies. You will receive ten demerit points for this, Miss Jones. And next week you shall recite for us a *proper* poem from your *assigned* reading."

"Yes, ma'am," I said, my eyes downcast, and took my seat.

Caroline leaned as far away from me as she could, and Sophia, seated just behind me, gave my chair a kick. But I ignored them both. Instead I drew my index finger down the spine of the forbidden book, one that had once belonged to Aubrey's mother.

I needed to talk to him, and soon.

YET WHEN YOU THINK about it, school is really a form of prison, and I had no opportunity of escape until nightfall. I attended my classes and ate my dinner, and was attempting to sneak up to my tower without attracting too much notice when I was waylaid by Sophia.

She pushed her arm through mine and hauled me toward the library, where most of the students lingered after meals, embroidering and telling tales and deciding whose reputation next to slice into tatters.

"Sophia, I'm tired. I'm going to bed."

"Are you?" She shot me her canny, *the-fun-has-only-just-begun* look. "But it's so early still. Come sit with me. We'll read poems aloud to each other, the goody-good sort about chaste maidens or lost little bunnies. It'll be fine practice for you."

"No."

"Jacks, then. We'll play for hairpins."

"No."

"Goodness, Eleanore! Will you hide from them forever? Don't let a gaggle of silly geese drive you from the game."

"'Silly geese'," I echoed dryly. "Don't you mean your bosom friends?"

"There is room for us all in my realm."

"How very enlightened of you. Especially considering how many times you've called me *mudlark* and *guttersnipe* since we've met."

"Compliments," she said seriously. "To your triumphant endurance over difficult times."

I brought us both to a stop. "I see. You've heard about the engagement."

Armand must have told her. There could be no other explanation, and my gut twisted. I knew they'd been friends since childhood but still, I thought we'd agreed—

Sophia leaned in close, squeezing my arm. "I had *not*! How thrilling! Have you told the headmistress yet?"

"No," I said, alarmed, "and neither shall you. It's supposed to be a secret for now."

"For what possible reason? It's stunning news! You should share it with the world! Imagine the looks on their faces! Imagine *Chloe*—"

"Sophia—"

"And Westcliffe! Ha! I cannot *wait* to see—"

I gave her a shake. "Sophia, Aubrey doesn't know yet."

Her delighted expression faded. "Oh. And the reason that matters is strictly due to his position as the *de facto* head of the Louis family. Protocol. Isn't that right?"

I looked away. "Right."

The open doors of the library allowed a spill of ambered light into the hall ahead of us. Girlish giggles swelled and subsided, and someone was dealing cards. I heard the *slap-slap-slap* of cardboard meeting wood as clearly as if it were right in front of me.

"Because it's not possible for a girl to love two boys at once," Sophia said, in the hardest tone I'd heard her use yet.

"Of course not."

But I knew that was a lie. It was possible. Not fair, perhaps, but absolutely possible.

Armand existed and I loved him. Jesse existed and I still loved him. Aubrey, though—

I glanced back at her. "Just don't tell anyone, all right?"

She released my arm to take up my hand, gazing down at my unadorned ring finger. "Here I am again, keeping your secrets."

"You're terribly good at it," I coaxed.

"Don't toady up to me, Eleanore. It doesn't suit you."

"Do it for Aubrey, then."

It was the most brilliant thing to say and I knew it, even if resorting to it did make me feel faintly ashamed.

She dropped my hand. "Very well. Perhaps it won't be long to wait, anyway. I wager Mandy means to announce it at—"

But she cut herself off with an even cannier look than before; my alarm flared anew. "At what?"

"I might have overheard a little something after dinner, as everyone was leaving. A conversation between professors."

"Well?"

"Come to the library," she said, dragging me along again, "and you'll find out for yourself."

She steered me to a table that already had Lillian and Malinda and Stella clustered around it, their heads together as they gossiped over a box of stick candies. As usual, they'd claimed the spot nearest the warmth of the hearth—and therefore the most popular place in the chamber.

Needless to say, I'd never sat there.

"Ladies." Sophia greeted her underlings with a grin, pulling out a chair, and then one for me when I hadn't moved to do so on my own. "What news?"

Lillian, holding a letter in her hand, gave me a scowl. Even after all these months of attending school together, she still acted like she couldn't believe that I dared to exist on the same planet as she.

"Um," she said. Her mouth was ringed in a ghastly shade of green. The final inch of her lime-flavored stick was pinched in her other hand.

"Yes?" Sophia prompted, helping herself to a peppermint stick.

"Mamá writes that she purchased a new hat."

"A new hat. Fascinating. Tell me more." But it was clear Sophia wasn't truly listening. She was crunching on her candy and eyeing the doorway, expectant.

"It's saffron taffeta, with a band of fox. To go with her stole."

"Her stole! Smashing. What else?"

"Er . . . I suppose that's it. She did mention that the weather in Dovedale was miserable lately, what with all the rain. Papa can't fish at all, and if it keeps up they're afraid it's going to positively ruin his hunting party."

"What a pity," Sophia murmured, with a glance at me. "Don't you think so, Eleanore?"

"A tragedy of monumental proportion," I agreed. At the top of the candy pile was a pink-and-cream stick scented of strawberries. It glistened by the light of the fire, long and smooth and enticing.

"It *is*," sniffed Lillian. "Of course *you* couldn't understand, Eleanore, but *gentlemen* of a certain stature are expected to host others on their estates. Papa's party is the talk of the season. We have all the very best birds, you know. Everyone says so."

I tore my attention away from the candy. *This* was why I had never wanted to sit at this table. "I just think it's funny, is all, that your father and his *gentlemen* spend their days ambling about shooting defenseless birds and hooking fish, when there are regular men out there in the trenches fighting for their lives. I bet they wish birds were all they had to shoot with *their* guns."

"What are you saying? Are you saying my father doesn't care about the war? I'll have you know we've lost *three* footmen to France! And I'm sure you don't know *this* either, but it is a very hard thing, to do without footmen!"

I nodded in sympathy. "How *does* one go on?"

Her green lip curled. "As if you know anything about anything! The closest you've been to the war was at your pathetic old orphanage. No doubt you hid under your bed every time the sirens sounded!"

"No, I ran out to greet the Huns in their airships bearing champagne and roses. It was the only polite thing to do. You ass."

Lillian sucked in a breath, but before she could reply, Sophia interrupted.

"Wait . . . here we go . . ."

Mrs. Westcliffe had entered the library, speaking in low tones to the pair of teachers at her side. All three paused in the center of the room, taking in its occupants as the conversation in the chamber died down. I thought perhaps Westcliffe's gaze lingered on me a trifle longer than it had on anyone else, but couldn't be certain.

"Good evening," she said, and a soprano chorus of voices chirped back, "Good *EEE-ven-ing*, Mrs. Westcliffe."

"I have some happy news to share. We are all well aware of the circumstances of the brave young men who currently reside at the Tranquility at Idylling Recovery Hospital. The Marquess of Sherborne has suggested throwing a small party in their honor tomorrow night—"

Before she could speak another word, excited chattering (even more sharply soprano) drowned her out. She lifted her hands.

"Young ladies! If you please! Ahem! Thank you. A *small* party, I said. Dinner and perhaps a brief dance. I know it is very short notice, but as only the eldest two years of students are invited to attend—"

She got no further. She faced the teachers and made a smile that was mostly rictus, but as the population of the library was comprised nearly entirely of the eldest students, there was no overcoming the noise.

Lillian looked at me and mouthed, *I told you so.*

Beneath the table, Sophia tapped her fingertip once, hard, against my ring finger. She wasn't smiling.

***

BY THE TIME I got to Aubrey that night, he was already asleep.

I decided not to wake him. Not yet.

Coward, remember?

***

IT USED TO SEEM odd to Armand that although he had been born in this place, this saw-toothed joining of land and sea, upon the small spit of an island that held the castle of his ancestors, he still didn't quite *fit* here. He wasn't quite *right* for land or sea.

He hadn't fit in London, either. Or at Eton.

But he realized now that it was only because he had not yet discovered the natural home of his heart. No, wait—*that* was Eleanore.

The natural home of his spirit, then. *Anima.*

That would be the air.

He rippled through the night, a sheet of smoke so thin the wind could rip him to pieces if it wished. Happily, it didn't seem to. He and the wind were partners tonight, skimming the surface of the world, flowing fast above the limestone cliffs of his birthplace, fast above the rough rocky beaches. Fast above the chopped black sea. He let the wind sweep him far from the safety of land, out so far there were only stars above and reflections of stars below, and their singing in the silence, ringing through him clear as Sunday bells.

swift wings take you, worthy beast, one of ours. your joy rises to us.

When? he thought in response. *When do I get my wings?*

Not tonight, plainly. Not last night, not the night before, nor any of the nights before that when he had been out here trying to Turn from smoke to dragon.

But all he could do was smoke.

Lora had become a dragon within days of her first transformation into vapor. Obviously he hadn't expected it to happen *exactly* the same for him, but still . . .

It galled him to admit it, but he'd thought that if she could do it, so could he. Especially since he felt so confident aloft, so completely at ease to be broken free of gravity. So, yes. He'd expected the next Turn to come to him, certainly before now.

It was as though there were a switch inside him, like an electrical switch, stuck in the Off position. He needed to flip it. He knew that he *could* flip it, if only he tried hard enough. He'd come this far—he was living smoke, by God. He heard the stars and the stones and he could actually *breathe fire*.

But he could not manage this.

When? he thought again, frustrated, pulling himself free from the silken arms of the wind, clouding into thickness. The Channel rocked and churned beneath him. *When?*

when it is willed, the stars sang.

Great.

He made himself into a smoke-dragon shape; spread wings, long tail. He held himself like that against the wind and *willed* himself into flesh—and all that resulted was a human-shaped Armand dropping like a meteorite from the sky to the water, splashing long and deep into the cold.

He broke the surface again, gasping. The Channel heaved him about, a toy tossed to sea; the waves were much more ominously massive up close than they had seemed from above. Between their swells he glimpsed a ship in the distance, a series of dim blue lights illuminating its prow. He must be many miles from shore if there was a ship out here willing to risk its lights.

The saltwater burned inside his nose and mouth. Mandy returned to smoke. The sea pushed him free and he twined up high once more, finding his way back home.

She'd left her window open for him. He glided into her room and became a boy by her bed (dry, clean, abruptly chilled), drawing back the quilts to tuck in beside her. Lora made a soft sleeper's sound and rotated toward him, her arms folded to her chest, the top of her head beneath his chin.

He smoothed back a strand that tickled, then kept smoothing, because her hair smelled nice, and, honestly, it just felt good. He imagined doing this every night for the rest of his life, and felt nothing but wonder at the thought of it.

My wife.

He wanted them to be equals. There were other dragons out there, ones who might try to steal her from him. If they came, he would need every possible defense he could muster. Not only for Lora's sake, but for his brother's as well. Even Honor's.

Mandy had wealth and social standing, and in the human world those things went a very long way. But the *drákon* were not human. What he needed were wings. Talons.

He allowed his hand to rest against the pleasant heat of Lora's nape. She mumbled again, and he touched his lips to her forehead, tasting salt and sweetness.

I'll save you, no matter what comes.

The gods had blessed him this far. Surely they wouldn't mind giving a bit more.

The drumbeat of the Channel filled the room.

Armand closed his eyes and dreamed of ice and blood.

CHAPTER 21

THE PARTY AT TRANQUILITY (or "soirée," as Mrs. Westcliffe was now calling it, as if that would somehow coerce her students into a less manic state) consumed the population of Iverson, even the younger girls who weren't invited. Classroom lessons slipped by unheeded. All that mattered now was which gown to flaunt, and which jewels, and whether egret feathers or sprays of diamonds were more à la mode for evening coiffures.

It was merely a dinner with some dancing to follow, but you'd think with all the fuss that the king himself would be in attendance.

That afternoon found Honor and me together on a bench placed against one of the giant animal hedges that slinked along Iverson's grounds. The creature behind us appeared to be a wolf, ears pricked, tail straight out. Jaws agape. I was glad I couldn't see it.

It was the final few hours between classes and twilight, slightly too early still to retire and dress. We were pretending to watch the game of croquet on the front lawn that had sprung up, fever-like, between our two years.

Honor had the stack of Rue's letters on her lap (Aubrey had apparently lent them to her) and was perusing them page by page. Beyond the clusters of girls in white and purple uniforms strutting about with their mallets, a solitary old man stood in the distance before another hedge, a pair of shears in hand.

It was Mr. Hastings, the Iverson groundskeeper. Jesse's great-uncle.

I watched uneasily as he chopped away at stems and dusky leaves. It seemed to me that his hedge was transforming into a distinctively serpentine shape.

"What shall you wear?" Honor asked, without looking up from her reading.

I glanced back at her, distracted. "What?"

"To the marquess's party. What will you wear?"

"Oh. I don't know. I don't really care."

Now she looked up. "You don't?"

"It's only a dinner dance. All the other girls will dress up and be beautiful, and I shall be happy simply to eat the food."

"And—you'll be beautiful, too."

"Well, I'll be what I am. I'm fine with that."

Her brow wrinkled. "It's not as though you have a choice about it, Eleanore. It's what happens to all of our kind."

I made a face.

"Find a looking glass," she insisted. "It's already happening. You've noticed it, haven't you? How you've grown recently? Er . . . filled out? In a few months, you're going to look just like them, cheekbones and lips and eyelashes. That's the way it always is."

How did this girl keep managing to exhume my most painful, secret wishes? For as long as I could remember, I'd hoped for a family, and by her very existence she offered me the possibility of one. In the orphanage and even here I'd gritted my teeth at the unremarkable features reflected in my mirror, and now she was saying that would change, too. And I could tell that they meant nothing to her, these words. That she thought she was informing me of the most hum-drum facts imaginable.

You had a tribe, you're going to be beautiful, dragons will snatch you away.

I almost hated her for that.

Honor carried on, oblivious. "Still and all, it's an event hosted by your Alpha. I cannot fathom that you don't care."

"Right. About that." I nudged the toe of my boot into a tuft of shaggy grass, pressing down the blades. "What is this 'Alpha' busi-ness? What does that mean?"

"Why, it means what you think. It means . . . he's the male who rules you. Who guides and protects your tribe."

"The male," I repeated. "So it's never a woman?"

She laughed. "Females cannot lead."

"That's ridiculous. Of course we can."

She shrugged and looked back down at her letters. "That's how it is, ridiculous or not."

Sophia's mallet connected with her ball with a sharp *crack*. It careened across the lawn and knocked someone else's ball halfway to the rose gardens.

The elder girls cheered, and all the tenth-years groaned.

Honor rustled the sheets of paper in her hands. "I was told, growing up, that obeying the Alpha and his line, following all the rules of the council, would ensure our tribe's survival. That keeping our heads down and confining ourselves to the shire was more important than anything else, even life or death."

"Grim."

"Yes. That's why it's so shocking, what Rue and Kit did."

I thought back to what I remembered about the letters. "Running away? Hiding Mandy and Aubrey's line from this Darkfrith council?"

"Yes, but not just that. Kit was the Alpha, you know. He was Christoff, the Marquess of Langford. And he took his role very seriously. Abandoning the tribe must have been a heartbreaking choice. Still, I understand why they did it."

I stared at her. "You do?"

"Rue says why right here, on this page. 'They never guessed where Kit and I went, or why. They never thought beyond Europe, certainly not so far as a land of warlords and rice fields and misted mountains. A land where dragons are worshipped instead of butchered. A place where our boy, your great-grandfather, could show his true face to the sun and fly free.'"

"Sorry," I said. "I still don't understand."

"They had another son," she explained slowly, as if I were exceptionally witless.

"Well," I said, defensive, "I didn't know they had any at all. Except for that one she mentioned, I suppose."

"She does write about her *children*."

It had been a while since I'd read the letters, actually.

Honor took in my expression and sighed. "Rue Langford bore five children in Darkfrith, two of them males, all of them healthy. And all of them were grown by the time I—by the time their parents left the shire. But this is apparently another son, born much later than the others. And there must have been something wrong with him, because otherwise his *true face* wouldn't matter. Do you remember what I told you about the abnormal? What they do to them in Darkfrith?"

Culled, she'd said, and all at once the happy chatter surrounding us, the willowy gangs of prancing debutantes and the gently fading sunlight all seemed very far away.

"So they fled to Asia," she said. "Rice fields, yes? Warlords? And dragons *are* worshipped there."

I couldn't believe it. "Do you have any idea how much we've agonized over those damned pages, trying to figure out what she meant?"

"It's all right here," she said calmly.

Someone hit their ball hard again, and a round of cheers followed. A couple of girls began to argue loudly over the score. Across the green, against the tall dappled woods, the serpentine hedge was gaining a slender head. A single raised foreleg with a hint of terrible claws.

"Parents *should* protect their children," Honor muttered, suddenly ferocious. "*I* would. I would do anything for my child."

I watched in silence as Mr. Hastings clipped the outline of the final claw, then moved on to the next leg.

꧁ ✦ ꧂

TRANQUILITY HAD TRANSFORMED ITSELF for the night from a hospital into . . . well, into a place that wasn't as depressing as a hospital. I'd attended exactly one party at the mansion in all the months I'd lived in Wessex, a birthday celebration last spring for Aubrey (who hadn't even been in attendance, since at the time he was busy dying in the prison camp). But just as it had on that evening, Tranquility now blazed with light, and the elaborate tiered gardens in back were festooned with merry torches and colorful paper lanterns.

The evening was warm enough to dine al fresco, which was lucky, since all the rooms inside the manor house were filled with either wounded men or their caretakers. Small, round tables dotted the patio above the gardens, already set with plates and silver and neatly folded slips of pasteboard that had our names inscribed upon them.

The table farthest from the doors had *Miss E. Jones* seated between *M. of Sherborne* and *Lord Armand. Miss H. Smith* was there as well, along with a colonel, Mrs. Westcliffe, and one of the doctors.

Not Becker, I noted. Nor Chloe, either.

I stood in line behind Honor and waited my turn to make my greeting to our host, who sat in his wheelchair next to Armand and a man in a scarlet uniform—the colonel, I presumed. I allowed my fingers to be clasped by the scarlet man, then Mandy (who kissed my glove), and finally Aubrey, who didn't go as far as a kiss, but who placed both of his ruined hands around mine and smiled.

Mrs. Westcliffe, right behind me, released a sigh. Perhaps she was remembering that festive evening last spring as well, when the duke had still lived here, and had closed his fingers firmly around hers.

She visited him in his asylum. She never spoke of it, but I knew she did.

The patio was choked with girls in magnificent dresses and soldiers in uniforms: men with casts, men with slings, doctors in khaki and nurses, too (although the nurses seemed to be mostly off by themselves near the steps that led down to the gardens, chortling over flutes of champagne). There was music coming from somewhere, real music played by real people, but I couldn't see its source. It seemed to float up from the paths below us, unwinding from the dark between the torches.

Mandy and Aubrey would be busy for a while yet with the receiving line. I wandered away and secured my own glass of champagne, figuring I had to be nearly old enough now to drink it in public. I'd find out, I guessed.

I leaned against the patio railing and gazed upward. The stars barely twinkled tonight, elusive behind a high, misty haze that draped over us like a veil. I didn't see Jesse, just mostly the moon, frost-white above the woods, casting a phantom halo against the mist.

My empty hand brushed the folds of my gown. It had a skirt of ivory satin, thick and heavy, that blossomed from a tight black velvet bodice with a whisper of lace. I'd worn the nicest frock I owned, likely due to how Honor had gone on about beauty and Alphas and obedience. But as my palm met that satin, an unexpected thought took me.

Leave the dress. Leave it all. Go to smoke, right now. Breathe deep. Fly free.

Instead I lifted my hand to cup my elbow, my arm pressed against the unyielding shape of my corset. I took a sip of champagne and let the bubbles pop in my mouth, dry and prickly all the way down my throat.

The smell of sickly sweet jasmine and sugar rolled over me. Chloe Pemington's signature scent.

"You think they actually want you here," she said softly, leaning against the railing as I did.

I angled a glance at her. Her hair was swept up into sleek chocolate curls; her skin was radiant; her face was flawless. I wanted to believe she wouldn't always be this perfect, but deep down, I was fairly certain she would.

"Their welcome's been rather clear," I said, and took another sip. "Or can't you read place cards?"

"Sitting at their table doesn't make you one of them, Eleanore. You'll never be one of them."

"I am already one of them. I'm just not one of *you*. Nor would I wish to be."

"Noble?" she goaded, still soft. "Prosperous? Celebrated?"

"Pitiful." I looked at her fully. "I would never wish to be as pitiful as you are, Chloe. Because you've lost, you see, but you're not smart enough to realize it yet. You need to let Armand go. He's not yours. He never was."

Her lips flattened. "You truly *are* unhinged. I wonder that they ever discharged you from that place. Doctor Becker says—"

"Chloe," I interrupted. "Listen. You're a fine nurse, I'll give you that. I think you make a difference here for these men at the hospital. All you have to do is smile at them, really, and I imagine their pain lifts away on the wings of angels. But I swear that if you mention Becker to me at all—if you ever try to wrangle us together again—I will hit you so hard you'll lose teeth, and I don't care who sees."

"You wouldn't dream—"

I took a step closer to her. "I'm crazy, though, aren't I? Of course I'll do it. I'd be happy to."

We glared at each other, and the night stretched over us, and the music drifted by, and for a wild teetering instant I thought I really might be daft enough to strike her here at Aubrey's elegantly structured soirée. My fingers itched to try.

"What an awful stench," chimed in Honor, from behind me. "Is that someone's perfume? It smells like rotting flowers. It's—oh. I suppose it must be yours, then."

She came to stand at my side, smiling her mild, enigmatic smile at Chloe.

"You might want to check the bottle," Honor said to her. "I think you'll find it's gone off."

"No," I said. "That's the way she always smells."

"Does she? Dear me."

"And what would *you* know of it," Chloe jeered, but her voice betrayed a wobble. "What would either of you know of quality? Of anything rare or refined? You're that other charity girl, obviously. Birds of a feather muck together—*that's* true enough."

"Eleanore was right," Honor said, sounding surprised. "You *are* pitiful. Go away now."

To my shock, Chloe did. I watched in disbelief as she lifted her nose and turned and melted back into the crowd, surrounded almost immediately by attentive men begging to bring her drinks and food and heaping helpings of blind devotion.

"Did you do that trick with your voice to make her leave?" I asked. It was another Gift, one I sometimes had and sometimes not: the ability to command certain people (people with smaller minds, I suspected) by manipulating the tone and tenor of spoken words.

"No, I only looked into her eyes. I saw her fear, and she saw me see it. No one wants their true heart bared to a stranger. Especially not someone like her, with all her buried dreads."

Honor swept both hands briskly down the front of her dress, as if wiping away dust. She was wearing my second-best, cornflower blue velvet and a wrap of gauzy silk. It looked quite nice with her hair.

"You think she has buried dreads?" I asked, doubtful.

"Oh, yes. I recognized it right away. It takes fear to see fear."

I didn't really know what to say to that, so finally I offered, "Well, thank you. For coming to my rescue."

"I thought it best if you didn't knock out her teeth. Not tonight. I can understand why you'd want to, though."

"I'm starving," I said. "Do you think they'll serve us soon?"

"Let's go sit down and find out."

And that was how Honor Smith and I became something close to friends.

WITH MRS. WESTCLIFFE ENSCONCED at our table, there was no chance of any sort of flagrant impropriety, such as conversation about anything more meaningful than what we were eating (Westcliffe: "This *consommé fermier* is exquisite!"), or what we might expect to eat soon (the colonel: "Beefsteak, extra rare! Puts field rations to shame, by gad!").

Oh, and we also discussed the weather. Naturally.

Armand kept his foot against mine and Aubrey, I noticed, didn't eat or drink anything; I knew it was difficult for him to dine neatly with his hands. But he was beaming and chatting, taking extra care to lure smiles from Honor, once even eliciting from her a small laugh (which she quickly smothered with her napkin).

I sampled everything presented and tried to savor it; I was hardly going to pass up a feast. But mostly I was aware of all the things that were happening beyond me.

The pressure of Mandy's foot.

A bandage around Aubrey's neck that was coming loose.

The headmistress's watchful eyes, moving from me to Armand.

Chloe conversing at a table nearby, using her breathy voice again, the one men always seemed to believe revealed the real her.

Sophia speaking under her, much more normal.

The moon glowing. The stars twinkling.

The music from the gardens. The slow, aching notes of a violin as it crescendoed into a solo.

The paper lanterns strung in the trees, bobbing with the breeze; bright jewels of light against the dense dark night.

"Miss Jones, may I have the pleasure of this dance?"

I blinked and came back to myself. Aubrey had wheeled away from his place at the table to approach my side. He had a hand lifted to me.

I glanced down at my dessert plate, bemused. I'd finished my pear compote and hadn't even noticed.

Aubrey misread my hesitation. "I can't go all the way down the steps," he said, jerking his chin toward the gardens, "but I can manage things well enough up here."

I realized there *were* dancers around us now, most of them down on the paths. They swept in and out of the light, skirts flaring, faces gleaming. It was a waltz, and everyone below us spun and turned like miniature dolls inside a music box.

Armand had taken his foot from mine. I threw him a look but he was already rising, moving to bow before Honor. He hardly limped at all.

"I don't know this dance," she said.

He helped her to her feet. "It's easy. I'll show you the way."

I stood as well. And I and Mrs. Westcliffe and the colonel and the doctor (whose name escaped me completely, even though he'd told me twice) all watched as the Marquess of Sherborne placed his feet upon the patio stones and braced his forearms against the arms of his wheelchair and slowly pushed himself upright.

I'd been right before. Aubrey was very tall indeed.

I took his arm, not his hand. His steps were short but even as he led us to the center of the patio where the tables had been cleared away and a handful of other couples twirled.

Not Mandy and Honor, I noted. They'd gone down to the paths, and I thought that was probably for Honor's sake, so she could feel less conspicuous in the dark.

Aubrey and I faced each other. I settled my hand lightly atop his shoulder and moved near enough that he could find my waist.

His eyes were silvery clear. A thick lock of blond hair flopped down over his bandages to rest against his forehead; his brother had the same unruly curl.

"I'm not very good," I warned him. "Mrs. Westcliffe says I fight to lead."

He inclined his head. "Luckily, I am the veriest expert. My skills are so . . . famous, I've had offers from the . . . moving pictures companies. You're in safe hands."

And we stood there together, swaying in place to the music, while everyone else waltzed looping circles around and around us.

Aubrey drew me closer. "I'm seriously considering . . . making this my new career. 'The Marvelous Mincing Marquess.' Something like that. What d'you think? Will I . . . razzle-dazzle them?"

"I'm going to marry Armand," I said.

We stopped swaying.

I wished, with my whole heart, that I could steal the words back.

He brought both of his hands to my cheeks. I felt linen and the warm, careful stroke of his uncovered fingertips. I gazed up at him without moving as he lowered his head to mine and pressed his lips to my cheek.

"Of course you are," he whispered. "Of course, my angel."

And everything shifted. Like someone had suddenly held a prism to my eyes that split clear light into rainbows, I felt Aubrey's lips and realized how different things were supposed to have been. How, had I not made that one reckless promise that one reckless night last summer, Armand would be gone now, lost to the stars, and the only other male dragon left to me in my world would have been his brother.

Mandy was supposed to have died that night. It ought to have been just Aubrey and me flying back home from the prison.

Just Aubrey and me. Meeting up for tea, laughing and dining and coming to know each other. Bound by the wonderful, dreadful secret of our blood.

And it wouldn't have mattered that he was burned from the war or stuck in a wheelchair. That he couldn't Turn. All that would have mattered was that he was *like me*. Beyond everything else—his title and money and those easy, tender smiles—I might have fallen in love with that.

Yes. I would have.

But I'd changed that outcome. With one vow to the stars, I'd erased Lora-Aubrey and created Lora-Armand-Aubrey instead.

I breathed in the scent of his ointment and the mellower, more pleasing fragrance of him, the man, and thought miserably, *This is even worse than I'd imagined.*

He pulled away. "Think I'll sit down now."

I nodded, everything I wanted to say stuck in my throat.

I'm sorry, I'm sorry, I'm sorry.

I started to walk back to the table with him but he patted me on the arm and sent me a too-shiny look that stopped me in my tracks. So I stood there and watched him trundle away, and find his seat, and roll himself haltingly back into the warren of his mansion.

None of the other dancers ever stopped dancing.

A shadow crossed my eyes. I turned away from the doorway that Aubrey had vanished beyond and discovered someone else standing before me. He was also tall, ebony-haired, in formal evening dress but not a uniform. He proffered his open hand to me along with a hard, slight smile. He was immensely handsome.

My throat closed. All my skin crawled into bumps.

The black dragon had found me.

CHAPTER 22

I FELT MY BREATH HITCH. I felt my soul contract.

"Don't," said the man at once, taking me into his arms even though I had not accepted his hand. "Don't Turn here. Everyone will see."

He began to twirl us around, his movements as smooth and graceful as mine were not.

"You are an extraordinarily difficult young woman to find," the man said. He seemed about Aubrey's age, perhaps a few years older.

English, I thought dizzily. *His accent is English, not Romanian or Transylvanian or whatever Zaharen is. Shit.*

"May I have your name?" he asked.

I found my voice, reedy thin. "No."

His smile returned. "Very well. I'll call you . . . Promise. How about that?"

"I'm not a runaway," I blurted. "I've never been to Darkfrith, or wherever you're from."

He maneuvered us into an extra fast twirl. "I know."

I was getting sick to my stomach. I had to keep my focus straight between his eyes or it got worse, and I wondered if, like Honor, he could see all the fears behind my gaze.

His eyes were black, as it happened. They matched his hair.

His scales, my mind added.

"My name is Everett," he said. "Joseph Everett Michael Langford. But please call me Everett."

"No," I said again.

He went on as if I hadn't spoken. "And since apparently you're not in a sharing mood, Promise, allow me to hazard a few educated guesses about you. You're around seventeen years of age. You're a pupil at that school nearby, the one in the castle on the isle."

I swallowed.

"Your parents, whoever they are, are not close at hand. Otherwise they'd do better than to allow you to become a dragon in public, even if it *was* at night."

"*You* were a dragon," I said, suddenly braver.

"I was hunting," he replied. "And I needed you to see me."

The waltz ended. The patio echoed with polite applause.

"So, despite the fact that you can Turn, you are alone," Everett continued. We stood facing each other; I realized belatedly that he hadn't released me, and jerked away from him. He shook his head. "It's a damned shame."

"I'm engaged. To another *drákon.* I'm not in the least alone."

His smile grew wider. "*Another drákon!* Really! How many of you are there down here?"

"Plenty," I bluffed. "And *none* of us are runaways, all right? We're just . . . here. Minding our own business. So it would be really grand if you'd leave us be."

"I'm afraid your business, Promise, is my own. All this"—Everett swept the air with his hand, his fingers scooping up the veiled night and the stars—"is my business. And if you've heard of Darkfrith, then I don't doubt you know that."

"Are you the Alpha?"

The smile he sent me now seemed somewhat more genuine than the last. "No. I'm merely the *very* interested messenger."

Beyond his shoulder I saw Mandy cresting the steps from the garden, Honor a blue-gauze fairy at his side. Mandy was saying something to her, but Honor's attention had landed on Everett and me.

Time slowed, peculiar and moon-frosted and thick.

Her eyes widened. She yanked free of Mandy's arm and disappeared back down the steps.

Armand paused to watch her go.

Everett turned his head and noticed Armand.

I grabbed my skirts and picked up my feet—which had gone heavy as lead, as bloody boulders—and forced myself forward toward Mandy. His gaze locked on mine, and his expression transformed from bewilderment into fixed intensity.

I heard Everett murmur, "We're not nearly done, child," but by then I had reached Armand, or he had reached me, and time was normal again and the lanterns above us swayed green and red and turquoise and Mandy was grasping me firmly over the slippery satin of my gloves.

"Lora! What is it?"

I twisted around. I meant to point out Everett, but he wasn't there. I scanned the crowd milling about the patio and realized he wasn't *anywhere*.

But he *was*. He had to be. And now he knew where I lived.

I was shaking. Armand scowled and pulled me to him, and he felt so good, so real and warm and *safe* beneath his layers of silk and wool and starch, that I knew what I needed to burn away my fears.

I wrapped my hand behind his neck and drew his head down for a kiss.

Our lips met. He made a sound that wasn't a word, but that I could tell meant *yes*, and *now*. The universe became a rushing river in my ears. My heart hammered in harmony with his.

"It's all right, everyone," I heard Sophia calling out from beyond the river of noise whooshing through me. "They're quite, quite betrothed."

❧

So, ONCE AGAIN, I was the talk of the school. Only this time, instead of receiving looks of carefully filtered malice, I was receiving ones of openly vivid envy.

I was too done in to pay them much attention. I'd not slept the entire night, most of which I'd spent at Tranquility, in Armand's bed, with him beside me.

I hadn't felt comfortable sleeping in my tower; no one knew better than I how the castle was full of chinks. It was full of people, too, but most of them were juvenile girls who'd sooner offer me up on a platter to the devil himself than lift a finger in my defense. At least Tranquility teemed with soldiers and guns. (Although I wasn't certain what protection any of them could indeed offer against a full-grown dragon.)

"Don't worry about Langford," Armand had whispered last night, his head next to mine on our pillow. "You have me. You'll always have me."

I'd drawn my hand up his arm, exploring the shape of his muscles there, the finely winged arc of his collarbone, the dip in the joint of his shoulder. His room was very dark at night, much darker than mine ever was. The brocade curtains on his windows ate up any little bits of light. We were secret and alone, sealed away from all the outside troubles of humans and dragons and stars.

It had to be true. I desperately wanted that to be true.

Mandy's hand reached up to capture mine. His fingers stroked my skin, found the spot where his diamond ring would go and fell still, covering mine. My palm pressed against his neck. I felt his pulse there, a strong good rhythm against me.

"Always," he said again.

"Thank you."

"I love you," he said.

I scooted closer, our faces sharing heat even though I still couldn't see him at all.

"I love you, too," I'd said. Because admitting it in the darkness somehow felt less like the loss of Jesse and Aubrey, and more like an inevitable truth.

We'd kissed then.

And then we did more than kiss.

And my body became something lithe and happy, and the true meaning of *inevitable* was this *drákon* who would wed me and the breathless night that cradled us and my own hungry rapture that expanded outward to become his.

And I did not sleep.

I WORE HIS RING the next day. It was the final proof of my nonconformity, I assumed, for the students who skirted past me in the halls with their pop-eyed gawps, and the professors who stared at my hand as I scratched down my notes, and for the headmistress who sat upon her dais at breakfast and had no *consommé* to praise and no visible weather inside the castle to comment upon, so she only ate kippers in silence.

She'd witnessed the kiss on the patio last night. I should probably be grateful that she hadn't perished of shame on the spot. I was proving to be a rather shoddy Iverson Girl, and I was actually a little sorry for it.

But I won, I thought silently to her, as she laid down her fork and her gaze skidded across mine. *I did what you said. I've won.*

Her eyes lowered. Her mouth had a slant to it that I could not interpret.

"I've won," I said out loud, but under my breath.

Deep down, though, I knew there were fresh battles to come.

If only I'd realized how quickly they would arrive.

CHAPTER 23

FOUR DAYS. THAT'S HOW long it took for Everett Langford to show up at my school to put the next part of his plan into action.

I was sitting in French class, paying no attention the conjugation of verbs that our professor was chalking in large, loopy letters upon the room's slate.

J'espère. J'espèrerai.

Armand's diamond was singing to me. It sounded like a cradle-song, restful and low. Every time I moved, the stone showered me with sparks.

"Ahem."

We all looked at the doorway, where Mrs. Westcliffe stood in a sheath of black bombazine. Our professor dropped her chalk, picked it up, and pasted on a smile.

"Oui, madame?"

"I require Miss Jones," Westcliffe said to the room at large. I was seated right in front of her, but she acted as if I wasn't there at all.

"Bien sûr," responded my professor, who knew exactly where I was, and made a poking motion at me with the chalk. *"Dépêchez-vous, mademoiselle."*

I gathered my books.

Westcliffe didn't wait, just turned around and clipped off.

I followed, making certain I remained a few steps behind. If she wasn't inclined to even look at me, I wasn't particularly excited about whatever would come next.

We reached the door to her office. She opened it and stood back, allowing me to enter first.

I'd been in this chamber enough times to have it memorized down to the minutiae; being summoned here repeatedly for scoldings had seared the details into my memory with unspeakable clarity. I could close my eyes and picture precisely the arrangement of the cherry furniture, the china figurines (mostly cherubs and lambs), and the cloisonné vases stuffed with expensive crisp lilies. I even knew how many candles would be burning in the chandelier above her desk. (Ten until six o'clock; the full twenty after that.)

But I did not close my eyes as I walked in, so I saw at once the couple that rose from the pair of chairs before Westcliffe's desk. One was Langford. The other, a woman with auburn hair and the same shining black gaze.

"Miss Jones," said Mrs. Westcliffe. Her voice sounded tight. "May I introduce the Earl of Chasen and his sister, Lady Fay Langford. My lord and lady, Miss Eleanore Jones."

I made myself smile, although it stretched small and strained against my teeth. I dipped a curtsy as I'd been taught, murmuring "How do you do?" as I straightened.

Back not turned to them: Check.

Escape routes: The windows, the chimney (was the flue closed?), the door.

Pistol on person: Negative. Damn it.

Lady Fay had a smile much more believable than my own. She came toward me with both hands outstretched.

"My darling girl! My darling! How splendid to find you at last!"

I couldn't stop myself; I retreated a half-step to avoid her, and she laughed, a sound as soothing and lovely as water rippling over stones. Her hands dropped back to her sides.

"But I forgot! You don't know, do you?" She threw a sparkling glance to Langford, then to the headmistress. "She doesn't yet know."

Westcliffe walked to my side. I felt her hand pass along the small of my back, the briefest of touches, before she moved to stand behind her desk.

"I did not feel it was my place to inform her," she said.

"Of course," said the black dragon. "Allow me. Miss Jones—Eleanore, if I might be so bold—I know this will come as a shock to you."

I shook my head. I knew what was happening and still couldn't believe it; Everett Langford kept talking.

"We are your family. Your cousins, to be specific. You are the daughter of our dearest aunt and uncle, Kiki and Valentine Langford." He shook his head exactly as I had, his words going rough with feigned emotion. "And *you* are little Jane. We thought you lost, child. All these years, and we thought you lost."

What a performance.

"How utterly fantastic," I said, flat. "And you have evidence of this familial connection, I expect?"

"Miss Jones," warned Westcliffe.

"No, no!" protested Lady Fay. "She's perfectly sensible to ask. Anyone would. Yes, my dear, we do. We have papers, of course. The church ledger recording your parents' marriage and your christening. The constable's report that sent you to the foundling home—oh, if only we'd known! But I think you'll find *this* the most convincing proof."

She dug into her reticule and pulled out an envelope. I accepted it from her warily, making certain our fingers made no contact.

Inside the envelope was a daguerreotype. I held it up to the light. A young couple stared back at me, sepia-toned, pale-eyed. The woman held a baby in her arms. All I could see of it was a mop of fair curls beneath a cap, a round face poking up from yards and yards of frothy lace.

That baby could have been anyone. I couldn't even tell if it was a girl.

The mother, though. I had to admit . . . the mother looked like me.

"Where are my parents now?" I asked.

"Passed on, I'm afraid." Lady Fay dabbed at her eyes. "Influenza, both of them. You barely survived it yourself."

"We've come to take you home," the black dragon said kindly.

"To take your rightful place among us."

I gripped the daguerreotype more tightly and stole another half-step back.

"That's very generous of you, but I'm afraid you're too late. I'm engaged to be wed soon. I could not possibly leave my fiancé."

"Fiancé," Lady Fay echoed sadly. For some reason Everett was letting her do most of the talking; perhaps it was because her voice was so unnaturally soothing. "Precious girl, I'm afraid you're only barely sixteen years of age. We'll have to discuss this. An engagement at this point—you are so very young!—seems precipitous."

I was older than that. I knew it, even if I could not prove it. But I had no doubt that these two had all the papers they claimed and then some, declaring to the world that I was the underage, long-lost daughter of this poor dead couple, and that now I belonged to them.

They'd bottle your soul if they could.

I looked at Mrs. Westcliffe. "Ma'am, would you mind if I spoke with the earl and his sister alone?"

She squared her shoulders. "I would be remiss in my duty if I left at this point, Miss Jones. As credible as the earl and his sister may be, you remain my responsibility. I shall stay for the duration of this interview."

I had the feeling she was speaking more to Everett and Fay than to me. A warm, unfamiliar heat began to spread behind my breastbone: gratitude.

The black dragon turned the full force of his gaze to her. "You will go."

I heard the whispering sly silkiness hidden beneath his tone, the dark pitch of the Gift that would overcome her scruples and compel her to do as he said.

Yet Westcliffe remained unmoved. "I beg your pardon. I shall stay."

"Please," I pleaded. "Five minutes, that's all."

I hadn't tried to compel her. I'd only put all my frustration and hope into my entreaty.

She clasped her hands in front of her, considering me. I thought of how austere she appeared on the outside, how rigid and long-skirted and finely combed. But she wore that perfume that belonged to the woods. To untidy nature. Spring and tangled blooms.

"Five minutes," she agreed, reluctant. "I shall be right outside, Eleanore."

"Thank you."

We all watched her leave. Fay placed her manicured hand against the door and eased it closed as I circled around her, keeping both her and her brother in front of me.

"I can't believe you picked *Jane*," I said. "Jane Jones? Are you serious?"

"Jane Langford," Everett reminded me. And then, to Fay: "I told you."

She shrugged. "Change it to whatever you like, then. We can fix the papers to match."

"I'm confident you can, but I'm keeping Eleanore, thanks very much. Eleanore Louis. *Lady*," I added, to make myself extra clear. I held up the daguerreotype. "Who are these people?"

"Photographer's sample," said Everett. "I found it at a shop in Chelsea. Remarkable resemblance, isn't it?"

All those years I'd endured the bleak, bare-brick misery of the orphanage, and then the asylum, not knowing who I was. Imagining what my parents must have been like, what they'd looked like, who they'd been. Waiting for them to miraculously show up and claim me and explain that every bitter hour of my life spent outside their care had been a terrible mistake.

That I was wanted. I was loved.

Instead, I got this. I got these two strangers distorting my dream into their own personal sideshow, for their own personal benefit.

The unfamiliar warmth in my chest heated into a much more familiar burning: anger.

I tossed the daguerreotype back to Everett. "So everything you've said is a load of rubbish."

"Not everything. My dear, orphaned little dragon—oh, yes, gossip spreads so quickly in these quaint country villages, doesn't it? After the dance, it wasn't difficult to get tongues wagging about *you*. We may not know who your parents actually were, but there's no question you're one of us. And it *is* time for you to come home."

"I'm not bloody going."

"Eleanore—"

"Miss Jones," I corrected him frostily, and he smiled.

"Do you know how we first came to know of you?"

Not from Jesse. Not from the stars. They wouldn't betray me like that.

He reached into his jacket pocket and pulled out a folded sheet of newsprint. He snapped it open with one hand and showed me its front. It was one of the German broadsheets that featured a pen-and-ink illustration of me. The monstrous, mechanical dragon version of me.

"You made the headlines, and we've been hunting you ever since. As you only went after the Germans, we figured you to be an especially wily English runner. We also figured you to be male. You surprised us all."

I managed a sneer. "Huzzah for me."

"You are a riddle. An inexplicable, yet joyous discovery. You're also quite famous, which honestly doesn't do the rest of us any good."

Fay had moved to stand against a window; the daylight behind her darkened her figure and face. "Attacking zeppelins and soldiers in full view! What were you thinking?"

"I was *thinking* of saving lives." A new notion took me. "And why the devil aren't *you* out there doing that, anyway? Why aren't *you* going after the airships? I saw you that night. You could easily rend them to pieces."

Everett concentrated on refolding the newsprint. "We do not involve ourselves in the affairs of men."

"My gracious. I can't decide if that makes you more of a selfish bastard, or a lazy one."

"There are many more humans than there are dragons, Miss Jones. There always have been. A few less Homo sapiens on the planet is no loss to us."

I clutched my books to my chest, speechless.

"So you must understand," said Fay, "why we cannot allow you to continue on like this. Why we cannot allow you to run loose."

"Are you attempting to threaten me?"

"Not at all," she said, but her chin lowered, and her hands disappeared into the folds of her dress.

"You know that I can Turn. You won't want to risk losing that. I don't see how you're going to hurt me."

"Hurting you is the last thing we want," she said.

Everett leaned a hip against Westcliffe's desk. He placed a finger upon the letter opener near him and spun it around and around in a circle, like time speeding through the flat hands of a clock. "But there *is* Lord Armand. And his woefully heroic brother."

I smiled again, though my insides clenched. "Oh, are you threatening them, then? That's going to be rather more difficult for you. The sons of a duke and all. Lords and *drákon* in their own right."

"Barely *drákon*," Everett said. "Far removed from the rest of us, with blood as thin as whey. I sense only one full dragon among you."

"You're wrong," I lied. "We are three."

"We are hundreds," he said gently.

"Then we are public," I countered, leaning in. "As public as we need to be. And if you didn't like me in the papers all the way over there in Germany, I wager you'll be even less thrilled about it happening right here."

I bit my tongue before I said anything more. The air had gone cold and dangerous and both of them looked at me now as if I were a puppy that had inexplicably bared a grown wolf's fangs. A menace that needed to be contained.

I became excruciatingly aware that I was trapped by myself in a room with two beings absolutely unknown to me. Two black-eyed, animal-hearted unknowns.

Everett rubbed his cheek, studying me. The letter opener spun itself out.

"There is a grotto in the foundation of the island beneath this castle, is there not?"

I said nothing.

"The stones sing of it," he explained. "A human weakness, to build a fortress atop such a flaw. You'll not find Zaharen Yce so imperfect."

"Zaharen Yce?"

"Our ancestral home. A stronghold like this one, but of course far superior."

My mind whirled. I'd thought that they were the English dragons—Langford was the name of the Alpha line from Darkfrith, wasn't it?

Everett pushed off the desk, looming closer. I retreated until my back bumped a wall. "Eliminating that grotto beneath us would likely obliterate this entire school. One or two adult *drákon* could easily handle it. Any bodies found would seem bloodied from the rubble. I think most, however, would remain entombed in stone. Lost to the sea. All those young, promising lives, simply . . . wiped from existence."

My jaw dropped. He smiled, apologetic.

"Won't you come?" implored Fay.

A rap sounded on the door; it swung open. The headmistress

surveyed the three of us.

"Five minutes," she announced. "And I believe Miss Jones has had enough excitement for one day. If you will call upon us again, Lord Chasen, Lady Fay? We have a Visitors' Tea on Sundays. We would welcome you then."

"Certainly," said Everett, slipping back into his gentlemanly façade. "We understand it is a great deal to take in at once. We wouldn't want to overwhelm the girl."

"Wait," I said, as they both moved toward the door. "I thought—I thought that Zaharen Yce was the home of the—of another family. I thought that you were from Darkfrith."

"Oh," said Fay, with a lift of her fashionably plucked brows. "That was true once, I believe. But you'll be happy to learn that you have quite an extended family, sweet Jane. Darkfrith is our English seat, to be sure. But we Langfords have been at Zaharen Yce for generations."

What?

Everett pinned me with his gaze. "And like it or not, you *are* a Langford, Lady Jane." He offered a nod to Mrs. Westcliffe. "Until Sunday, then."

"You must run away." Aubrey said.

I sat hunched on the floor with my head in my hands, my hair falling in long, straight curtains that blocked my view of anything but hair and my borrowed robe and a plush section of Aubrey's rug. It was very late, and even though I knew the rug I stared at was actually sage-colored, in the shadow of my body it looked more like the color of death.

"Both of you. Tonight," Aubrey added, and it was Armand, cross-legged at my side, who answered.

"No."

I heard the squeak of Aubrey's wheelchair as he shifted upon the seat. The crackling of the fire in his hearth.

"Be clever," he said. "Think it through. They'll . . . take her otherwise."

"We can't run," Armand said.

I lifted my head. Aubrey's bedroom was cloaked in darkness. Beyond Tranquility, far out over the Channel, a storm brewed. Lightning flashed. But we'd closed the drapes, and the only illumination we'd dared was from the fire the maids lit hours past.

Shadows licked over us. Anything might be hiding in them.

Anyone.

Stop.

"I'll set up an account at the bank," Aubrey was saying. "Draw . . . funds as you wish. Whatever country. Just go."

"Aubrey," sighed his brother, ragged.

I pushed back my hair. "Don't you see? It's not only the school, it's you as well. They know about you."

"Me?" The marquess let out a thin puff of air that might have been intended as a laugh. "So?"

I wasn't going to be the one to speak the truth aloud: that if we fled, we'd have to take him with us. And we couldn't, not tonight or even any night soon.

He'd barely survived the summer. He needed rest and constant, professional medical care. He did *not* need to be stuck on the back of a dragon darting through storm clouds to parts unknown.

Yet Aubrey held me in that awful, shining look. "Do you imagine, Miss Jones . . . I am so helpless?"

"That's not fair," I protested. "It's not about being helpless or not. It's about them outnumbering us. *All* of us."

"All three of us," Mandy clarified softly. Because we *were* three now, not four.

I'd gone to Honor before smoking here. I'd barged into her room, where I'd found her seated alone on her bed and staring at nothing in the lackluster light from the lamp atop her desk, her hands knotted in her lap.

I'd told her everything, Everett and the dance and Westcliffe's office and his threat about the grotto.

"Leave me out of this," was all she'd said when I was done. "I want nothing to do with any of it."

"But you're one of us. You *have* to care."

"I don't. Just let me be."

"Honor—"

"I am in earnest, Eleanore. This is your quandary, not mine. I told you not to find them. I told you to stay away."

"*They* found *me*!"

Her hands wrung but her face was stony smooth. "No matter. You've been discovered. If you have a shred of decency, you'll keep my name to yourself."

"'A shred of decency'! That's rich, coming from you. Everyone in this school is in mortal peril, and you won't help at all?"

"I cannot."

"You can. You won't."

She stood. "I want you to leave now."

"I'm going! Only tell me this first. Why did you say that the Langfords weren't at Zaharen Yce, when they are?"

She blew a breath through her teeth, a long, hissing sound.

"Why?" I demanded.

"I told you it had been some time since I'd been there," she'd answered eventually.

"Well, how ruddy much time could it have *been*?"

"Enough. You've not traveled as I have. You don't know. So leave me alone. I've done everything that I can for you. Now get out."

And that was how Honor Smith and I severed any prospect of becoming friends.

"I'll be all right," Aubrey said now. Firelight turned his bandages gray and smoky orange. "Don't need you . . . here."

"Bugger you," said Armand rudely. "We're not running away, and that's that."

Aubrey clenched his jaw. "You have to protect her."

"And I shall." Armand took my hand. "We'll go with them willingly. Together."

I wish I could tell you that I was a fine enough person to have replied, *No, of course you can't come, Mandy, I could not possibly risk your life for mine.* Or, *No, your brother and father need you more! You must not abandon them.*

But the words inside me were these: *Oh, thank heavens. Thank you, yes. Yes, yes.*

I was the worst sort of person, one suffused with both shame and relief that I wouldn't have to confront alone whatever was to come; that I would have his strength and surety at my side.

All I was able to say was, "Okay."

Armand gave my hand a squeeze. Perhaps I hadn't needed to say more, after all.

CHAPTER 24

AS WE WERE A properly (or at least publically) betrothed couple, Lord Armand was granted the special privilege of paying calls on me at Iverson—after classes, for one half hour each day. We'd hoped for a stroll through the rose gardens, as it was open enough that we could spot anyone else nearby. But the squall that had whipped the Channel the night before had rolled inland, and the day was slaty dark and soaked in a fast, cold rain.

Thus, Lord Armand was escorted into the conservatory, where his fiancée awaited him (very properly) next to the koi pond. A half dozen settees tempted from beneath the potted palms and fruit trees, but the pond had the advantage of a small fountain bubbling up from its middle. I'd figured any bit of extra noise to conceal our conversation would be helpful.

We sat side-by-side on its stone edge, not touching, and pretended we were speaking of flower arrangements and tulle and the color of icing on cakes.

Miss Swanston was our nearby chaperone. *She* was pretending to sketch one of the pomegranate trees, which had realized it was autumn despite its location inside the castle and was shedding leaves at an impressive rate.

"Is there a way to get married before Sunday?" I asked, my voice low.

Armand considered it, then shook his head. "Not without proof of your age. *Real* proof."

"Why not do what they did? Fake the papers. How hard could it be?"

"Yes, Lora. I'll just tap into my many underground criminal connections and have some falsified documents inked right up." I knocked my knee into his, and he added, hopeful, "Unless you actually *do* have some criminal connections?"

"No."

He scowled down at his feet. "No. Anyhow, Sunday's only four days off. I'm no master forger, but I'd bet that's not enough time."

"It's all the time they had."

"They," he said, "are far more evil than we. Likely criminal connections galore."

I subsided moodily, twisting my engagement ring around and around my finger. I told myself that marriage probably wouldn't make a difference to the Langfords, anyway. A group of creatures who threatened to murder an entire school simply to get their way wouldn't give a fig about church ceremonies.

The diamond in my ring was singing to match the rainfall, a

wistful, glimmering melody rising up to encompass us. Armand was watching the koi, their zipping paths, orange and red fire beneath the lotus leaves. He touched a finger to the surface of the water, spreading ripples that sent all the fish scurrying to the other side.

"Jesse said you were born on a steamship, didn't he?"

He had, ages ago. It was the only information the stars had been willing to give about my birth.

"So?"

"So, we know approximately how old you are. And we know you ended up in London. What if there was a record of it somewhere? What if the ship's log recorded your birth? Or the newspapers? Perhaps it was news?"

"One baby being born," I said doubtfully.

"Perhaps you were more than a baby, even then. A lord's daughter. A wealthy merchant's. A princess."

I almost laughed, and then smacked my palm to my forehead.

"A *dragon*," I realized. "And we might recognize their names now. If they used Langford or Zaharen or anything like it, we might . . . might . . ."

"Anything at all," Armand agreed, meeting my eyes. In the rainlight his had darkened into midnight, soft and deep. His lashes were tipped in silver. "It's worth a try."

"But likely not before Sunday."

"I'm afraid not. We'll have to go on as we are for now." He leaned closer. "In sinful bliss."

The rain peppered the glass dome arching over us. The fountain burbled. The air was heavy with the fragrance of storm and soil and sea. And of Mandy: spice and clouds, magic and desire.

His hand covered mine, a lovely warmth against my skin. We leaned nearer still. I closed my eyes.

"Ahem."

It was Miss Swanston, sounding remarkably like the headmistress. Mandy and I both jerked back; I'd forgotten all about her. He sent her a smile while I ducked my head, embarrassed. Neither of us spoke for a while. I returned to twisting my ring.

"Why does it sing so softly?" I wondered aloud.

Most diamonds were much noisier, even the smaller ones. Last summer, when all the rich mums had shown up for that year's graduation, the din of their jewelry had been nearly deafening.

Armand said, "Because I asked it to."

I looked back up at him. "You did?"

He nodded, the corners of his lips still smiling.

"I didn't know we could do that." I turned the stone upright and lifted my hand level to my chest, like I was admiring it. The diamond continued on with its serenade.

I stole a quick glance at Miss Swanston. She was frowning at her sketch, her pencil flying. Another leaf feathered down from the tree.

"Louder," I commanded my stone.

Nothing changed. Armand's smile grew wider.

"Please sing louder," I tried.

Nothing. I gave my hand a shake.

"Wait." Mandy touched the tips of his fingers to mine, holding me still. "Louder," he murmured to the diamond.

And it obeyed. Our serenade boomed into an earsplitting aria. I winced and Mandy gasped out, "Softer!" and it calmed again, a pretty sparkle on my hand.

"Gads," I said, disgruntled, eyeing it.

Mandy dropped his fingers from mine. But his smile was wider than ever.

"How did you know you could do that?" I asked.

He shrugged. "I've been able to do it since summer. After my first Turn. I thought you could, too."

"Well, I can't. Can you—does it work on any stone?"

"I don't know. I imagine so." He looked around the conservatory, speculative, but I was already shaking my head at him. We were encased in limestone. If he commanded the walls or the floor to yodel, I could only imagine what would happen to my ears.

Still, I couldn't help but feel a twinge of jealousy. "You have all these Gifts I don't."

All right, only two, but even so . . .

Armand's smile faded. "I have you, Eleanore," he said, serious. "And that's really all that counts."

❧ ⟞⟝ ❧

THE RAIN DRONED ON through Sunday, so that when Lord Chasen and Lady Fay made their way into the front parlor, she was laughing and patting at her hair, and he was dusting the water from his cuffs. They swept into the room trailing the scent of the storm, both of them elegant and groomed to the nines despite the silvery drops beading them.

They appeared so very—normal.

Mrs. Westcliffe stood ready to greet them, lifting her hand to show them the way to the table where Armand and I already sat.

Mandy came to his feet. I remained as I was, striving to look inscrutable.

Everyone else in the room—mostly students today; the parents hadn't braved the squishy roads—went quiet. I hadn't spoken of the Langfords' visit to anyone at the school except Honor, but in the manner of all juicy secrets, the tale had gotten out anyway. It was rumored now that I was an heiress, or a contessa, or the missing daughter of a tragically banished king. The girls from my year literally turned up their noses at the gossip (Mittie: "A princess! Really! I'd sooner believe she kissed a frog and made him a prince!") but even they stared at the fact of glamorous Everett and his sister unmistakably making their way to me.

A noble fiancé *and* a noble family, all within days. Nearly everyone in the parlor looked as if they couldn't quite believe that ratty, tatty Eleanore had turned her fortunes around so entirely.

I had to concur.

I waited until they were near enough that I didn't need to speak above a murmur.

"Lord Chasen, Lady Fay, my husband-to-be, Lord Armand Louis

of Idylling. Armand, the Langfords."

As introductions went, it was barely civil. Yet everyone smiled. Lady Fay settled with a puff of skirts into her chair, and Armand and Everett reached across the tea table to shake hands. I couldn't see who let go first, but the chill between them practically slithered across my skin.

I began to pour, making certain my diamond showed. I was proud that my hands didn't quiver at all, even though there was a fat knot of nerves writhing in my stomach.

"What a darling little parlor," Fay was saying, ignoring my ring. "In such a darling little school."

She dripped with false sincerity. In all honesty, nothing about the parlor was especially darling or little. It was jam-packed with mirrors and chintz and eavesdropping girls, but suddenly it was *my* parlor. In *my* school. And there were those curried chicken sandwiches being served *plus* ham and cheddar, so I raised my chin and said, "Indeed," in my best Iverson Girl accent.

Fay's gaze slid back to mine. "I'm sure you'll be sorry to leave."

"I would be, yes," I replied.

Beneath the table, Armand's foot tapped my shin, a warning.

"Sweetheart," he said.

Everett looked away, trying his tea, but Fay's smile grew even more syrupy. She had a role to perform, and she wasn't going to let me spoil it.

"*Wait* until you see the Music Room at Zaharen Yce! You're going to absolutely *adore* it! All the ladies of the castle have taken their tea there, for centuries and centuries. It's simply fabulous! I can't wait to show you the whole thing. You'll die, I swear."

"I'd rather not," I said.

Her façade faltered.

"Die, I mean," I added, and offered my own saccharine smile.

"Such a delightful wit," Everett said. "Have you always been so literal?"

"I wouldn't know. Perhaps *you* could tell *me*, since apparently you've known me since birth."

"Sweetheart," grated Armand again, with another kick.

I took up the sugar tongs and lowered my voice.

"Here is our only offer. We're getting married, no matter what you say or what you think or what you do, and therefore we shall *both* accompany you to Zaharen Yce. To *visit*, not to stay. Or else you slink home empty-handed, and I swear to God we will do whatever we must to ensure you leave us alone for the rest of our lives, even if that means our lives end tomorrow."

"Or tonight," Armand added, scary soft.

I glanced up at Everett through my lashes. "Or this goddamned instant," I whispered, and dropped the sugar tongs back into their bowl. My teacup brimmed with melting white cubes.

I let them melt.

I'd had plenty of time to think about this moment, about how it was going to unspool here in this chilled gray parlor of mirrors and stone. Lord Chasen and Lady Fay fully believed they held the upper hand, and perhaps they did.

Or perhaps . . .

Perhaps, deep down, I was more ambivalent than I cared to admit over the potential, tragic demise of all my horrid classmates. Perhaps, deep down, I wouldn't mind so very much should Iverson Castle tumble into the sea, or should my true face be revealed. Perhaps I was ready to be done with protecting a gaggle of rich, uppity schoolgirls who enjoyed nothing more than making me squirm.

Perhaps the dragon in me was aching for a fight.

And perhaps, deep down, these Langford dragons could sense it.

Fay eased back, silent. The earl crossed his legs and contemplated his tea. After a moment, he picked up the tongs, captured one of the last sugars, and plopped it into his cup.

"We journey swiftly," he said, without looking up. "And we don't exactly travel by rail."

I folded my hands across my lap. The nerves in my stomach were crawling up my throat, but I was able to reply, "That won't be a problem for us," with perfect aplomb.

⊱──❖──⊰

"So this is it," Sophia said two days later, sitting on my bed. She surveyed the case and trunk that were rapidly filling with my new wardrobe. "Truly *it*. You're leaving Iverson."

I shrugged, struggling to fold a chemise on the bit of unoccupied bed she'd left me. I'd turned down Almeda's offer to have Gladys pack my things. I wasn't the neatest hand at folding, but I had no desire to open my trunk again in a month or so to the stench of a dead rat or rotting coffee grounds or whatever else my maid might think up to bid me *adieu*.

"Leaving this absolute *utopia* of a rock pile," Sophia went on, kicking her feet back and forth. "No more tedious lessons all the day long. No more boring professors. No more drafty classrooms and curtsies and wretched seafood for every single meal."

"Apparently so," I said, tossing the chemise, more or less folded, into the trunk. It was already nearly full, and I had several dresses to go.

I tried pressing everything down with both hands. As soon as I released it, the mass of clothing sprang back up.

"You lucky bitch," Sophia said.

"Best not let Westcliffe hear you talk like that, my girl. You'll find yourself out of Iverson, as well."

She flopped back on the bed. "Let them give me the boot. I'd welcome it."

"To be sure. Right up until the moment you'd have to live under same roof as Chloe again."

Evidently, Lady Chloe had abandoned Tranquility the day after the soirée, and was currently licking her wounds back at her family estate. What a shocking coincidence that her selfless desire to serve as a nurse had withered to dust as soon as she'd discovered that Armand was engaged to me.

Sophia directed a snort at the ceiling. "I shall never live under the same roof as my cherished stepsister again. I'll strangle her in her sleep first. Infect her with the Spanish flu. Ship her off to the front with one of her moony Tommy boys. How soon before you invite me to this marvelous castle of yours?"

"It's not my castle," I replied. "And I'm not going over there, I'm going up north, remember?"

That was the lie we'd decided upon over Sunday tea. That Armand and I were to visit all the delightful Langfords up in York, and not the ones residing in the castle made of tears and ice in the Carpathian Range, because no one in their right mind would attempt to cross Europe these days. Not for a mere family visit. No trustworthy train service, no reliable restaurants or hotels, no truly safe roads or shelter—but plenty of bombs and bullets and poisonous gas to go around. Only an idiot would want to wade through all that.

Not that we would be wading *through*. We would be soaring *above*.

Obviously, I couldn't explain *that*.

"Why *are* we going to Zaharen Yce instead of Darkfrith?" I'd muttered through clenched teeth at the tea. "Why risk it?"

Everett had flashed me his attractive smile. "Because that is where the Alpha awaits you, of course."

Of course.

At least I knew that I could fly higher than a bullet shot from the ground.

Usually. Probably.

Sophia whisked her hand through the air, chasing away my logic as she would a gnat that had ventured too close to her person. "Castle, villa, your ancestral mansion in the Yorkish hills. I don't care which. Invite me."

"Darkfrith's still far away, Sophia, and apparently quite rustic. You'd be bored to tears."

"Oh, *Lord*, Eleanore, *try* me. I'm dying to break free of this place."

I knew the feeling. So why, now that the moment was actually at hand, did I feel so doleful about it?

Because you're leaving against your will, my mind answered. *With the enemy. So they won't eat everyone here alive.*

Oh. Right.

"Lucky," Sophia groused again, still kicking.

WE WERE TO DEPART first thing the next day. So that night, with Mandy asleep in my bed, I smoked alone back to Tranquility.

Aubrey was also asleep. Or if he wasn't, he was doing a very good job of pretending to be so.

I stood over him and watched him breathe. Then I leaned down and kissed him on the lips.

His eyes opened. I paused, met his look. Then I cupped my hands to his face and kissed him again. I wasn't trying to be cruel, but when I pulled away, his lashes were damp with tears.

"I'm sorry," I whispered. "I had to know. What it would be like, I mean. Before I'm gone."

He nodded.

"I promise to send Armand back home to you and your father. I'll return with him if I can."

He nodded again.

I stroked my fingers down his cheek. "Goodbye, dearest Aubrey."
And I left.

THE MORNING WAS BRACING and bright, and Mrs. Westcliffe stood beside me at the castle's main doors. We watched together as Armand (just arrived from Tranquility as if he hadn't spent the night in my bed) and his chauffeur strapped my trunk and case to the back of the motorcar.

As far as the headmistress and everyone else at the school were concerned, the car would transport us to the train station at Bournemouth, where we'd join up with my devoted new family, and together we'd all begin our happy jaunt to York.

The car *was* taking us to the Bournemouth station. Everett and Fay *would* be there. But none of us were climbing aboard a train.

A few dozen girls were on hand as well to wave their handkerchiefs at me—or, more likely, at my fiancé. They were mostly the younger students, some still in ringlets. I don't think any of the elder girls had quite yet forgiven Lord Armand for removing himself from the marriage market.

"Well," said Mrs. Westcliffe, as the last strap was secured. She glanced at me, then began to adjust the folds of the scarf tucked around my neck. A frown creased her brow. "This would appear to be goodbye. At least for now."

My fists were clenched with apprehension or cold, or both. The sea winds snatched at my coat and dress, whipping hems about my ankles. A line of leaves the color of dried blood somersaulted end-over-end down the drive.

"I wanted to graduate," I said. "It was important to me."

I'd surprised us both; her eyes lifted to mine, and the frown faded.

"And so you shall. When you come back to us, Lady Jane."

I pulled away, uncomfortable. "Please don't call me that. It's not my name."

"It seems that it is, though." She gave my scarf a final tug. "You'll grow used to it, I am certain. One becomes accustomed to a good many situations in life that might feel at first . . . ill-suited to whom we thought we were."

I laughed miserably, and the wind snatched at that too.

Armand approached. He bowed to Mrs. Westcliffe and held out his arm to me.

I rested my hand atop his sleeve. Felt his steadiness.

Took a long breath.

"Your family awaits," Mrs. Westcliffe said. "When you return from your trip, you may take up your studies here once more."

I looked askance at her. She looked directly at me. We both knew I wasn't coming back.

Iverson's headmistress held out her hand. "Farewell, Lady Jane."

"Farewell," I said, and we shook on it.

As I mentioned, there was no one from my year to squeal at us and flutter white handkerchiefs goodbye as the motorcar purred away from the castle, not even Sophia.

But there was Mr. Hastings, standing motionless beside one of his animal-hedge sculptures, neither waving nor smiling.

And Honor Smith, watching from one of the library windows, a rippled suggestion of a dragon-girl, trapped behind glass.

CHAPTER 25

And so it begins: all my careful knots and plans, unraveled. In my desperation for her, I have struck a fresh bargain.

At least she will be with me soon.

CHAPTER 26

RUE HAD WRITTEN THAT she'd discovered a place where dragons could be themselves. Where we could fly as we wished, and frolic as we wished, and apparently people were delighted to have us around and would not run and scream in a wild panic for their lives.

It sounded lovely, if implausible. In my mind's eye, I saw the rice fields and green terraced mountains. Black-haired ladies in elaborate headdresses whispering behind lacquered fans. Gruff men with swords, and homes with sliding paper walls and roofs that curled up like shepherds' crooks at the tips. The air would be scented of tea and spices so exotic I had no name for them. Birds would flock in poetic lines, flowers would forever bloom . . . and dragons gleamed against cerulean skies, alight beneath the blazing sun.

It would be a land that was, in short, precisely the opposite of staid, stately Bournemouth.

I watched the town take shape with my head against the motorcar window, my breath fogging the glass. I was attempting to hold on to Rue's dreamland, to *not* think about the reality of my own world, but Bournemouth would not let me dream.

In spite of the brisk weather, the sidewalks and cafes swarmed with humanity. Couples walked arm-in-arm; small children and barking dogs darted across the busy streets and back again. Flower girls and newspaper boys hawked their wares as loudly as they could, and men with mugs of gin or ale spilled out of tavern doors, laughing or arguing with equal fervor. The air surrounding me smelled not of tea or spice, but of ocean and coal and sewage.

I was beginning to feel acutely sorry for myself. Not only was I being forced into a journey I did not wish to take—into a potential fate I did not wish to accept—but in the upcoming days, I was the one who was going to have to do the lion's share of the work. Armand would ride on my back, but I'd do all of the flying, and breakfast was ages ago and lunch barely a memory and I hated these vile Langfords with all my soul. And who knew if they'd even bother to pause for supper before insisting we depart for their stupid castle? They were grown, and I was not; perhaps they could fly for days on end without touching ground.

And what was I going to do at Zaharen Yce once we got there? How would Mandy and I ever get away again? Although I'd insisted this was to be only a visit, I'd be a fool to trust the Langfords as far as I could spit. Were we to be their prisoners? Guests? Something in between? I'd promised Aubrey I'd send Armand back to him, but what if the Alpha *never* let us leave?

What if the stars took my life while I was there? What would happen to Mandy then? Or to Aubrey, back at Tranquility? Or even to ungrateful Honor?

But this was my darkest, ugliest fear, one I hadn't shared even with Armand: What if the Langford Alpha desired to marry me— or just breed with me—himself? What would I do then? Would I let that happen, if it meant saving Mandy's life? Saving Mandy's life *again*, actually?

I would.

I would hate myself, but I would.

Normally I enjoyed the fact that Armand and I were able to be together in silence, neither of us needing to obscure the space between us with noise or natter. But when the motorcar passed a pastry shop with piles of iced biscuits and cakes displayed in the windows, I heaved a sigh so heavy it was probably heard all the way back at Iverson.

Armand leaned forward and murmured to the chauffeur. The car pulled to a curb (instantly surrounded by a pack of admiring chimney sweeps), and Mandy hopped out. When he returned, he was carrying three waxed paper bags stuffed with pastries.

"I find few situations can't be improved with chocolate macaroons," he said, handing me a bag.

I'd finished them all by the time we reached the station.

He was right. I felt improved.

THE SEA HERE WAS a much tamer brute than that surrounding Iverson's isle. Bournemouth was known for its happy, golden beaches; for waves that never rolled in so belligerently as the ones that gouged the cliffs back on the island. But because these happy, golden beaches were so chockablock with happy, golden beachgoers, we had to wait hours and hours before all the people had cleared out.

The beach we stood on now was flat and open and overall an excellent launching point for a giant winged creature. Yet even in the hazy nights that drenched these shores, dragon scales would glimmer. We had to be quick.

It was around midnight, and the sands were at last deserted. There was a dance (*A Seaside Serenade!* announced the placards along the streets, *Benefiting our Boys at the Front!*) drawing to a close at a private club far down the curve of the strand; I could see their firefly lights jouncing in the distance. Snippets of music still traveled the breeze, but it reached me patchy and thin, like a poor telephone connection.

Armand and I huddled together beneath the dark sky (no moon; no stars; I hoped no zeppelins), going over our provisions. Everett and Fay did the same nearby. Since Mandy and I had traveled like this before, I knew already that we had all that we needed: his knapsack with our extra clothing and my shoes, the cuff that Jesse had made me, some food, maps, money, a compass—but it still reassured me to check.

(I'd wanted to bring some sort of weapon, too. Last summer we'd traveled with a pistol and a knife, but Mandy had pointed out that the Langfords would hear the metal singing, so we couldn't really conceal them. And it might not strike the most politic note with the *drákon* at Zaharen Yce to show up armed.)

I kept my hands tucked under my arms and occasionally bounced up and down to ward off the chill. Since we were so close to leaving, all I had on was my day dress and chemise, and the autumn wind could bite.

Mandy, however, was well bundled in thick, heavy clothing and gloves, boots and a long leather duster, aviation goggles around his neck. We'd learned the hard way that the heavens were always frosty, no matter how temperate the globe below.

His cane had been abandoned to Tranquility. He was sure he could go without it now, and anyway, there was no easy place for it in our rig.

Everything else—all my belongings from Iverson, everything I'd packed away, make-believing it would travel with me to northern England—resided in a locker now at the train station, and I supposed likely would for some while. Unless the Germans blew it up.

Or I never returned.

Also around Armand's neck was a platinum chain with a sturdy clasp. I removed my engagement ring carefully from my finger, handed it over, and watched him string it down the chain so that it tapped against his heart.

Everett lifted his voice above the *hush, hush* sound of the sea. "Pity you can't Turn, after all, boy." He was addressing Armand, but his eyes were on me.

I knew you were lying about him, his expression said.

I shrugged without comment, met Mandy's gaze. With his back to the others, he gave me a ghost-thin smile. It had been his idea, to hide the fact that he could go to smoke.

"They think I'm less than they," he'd reasoned over our macaroons, back inside the auto. "Let's help them to think it. A little hidden edge for our team."

"Are you certain?" I'd asked. I'd thought he'd at least want them to know he was *drákon* enough to manage smoke.

"Why not? Having them believe I'm earthbound might come in handy in a pinch. Surprise on our side, and all that. We're heading into their territory. About to smack right into their rules. Let's face it, we could use any advantage."

Which was damned true.

"Indeed," piped up Fay now. She plastered on her insincere smile. "If the Turn hasn't come to you by now, Lord Armand, it likely never will."

"Like it never did for you?" I inquired sweetly. Fay resembled Mandy tonight, dressed in men's pants, woolens, and a long winter coat. Neither of the Langfords had mentioned whether or not she could Turn, but it wasn't nearly cold enough on this beach for so many layers.

We looked daggers at each other, both of us now smiling. Then Everett touched her arm, and she dropped her gaze.

Armand set the knapsack at our feet; all it lacked now were the clothes on my back.

"Ready, Promise?" called Everett.

"Eleanore," I countered, then caught myself. "I mean, Miss Jones."

With his hands in his trouser pockets he sauntered closer, his hair windblown, his mouth a straight line. He perused me up and down and up again. It was a thorough examination, much more so than any gentleman should ever offer a respectable lady. I dug my bare toes into the mush of the sand. Despite the wind (and despite the fact that I was nothing near a respectable lady), my skin began to warm.

"Have your boy signal if you can't keep up, *Miss Jones.*"

"We'll keep up," Armand replied before I could snap, *He's not my* boy. Which was just as well, since it's likely what Everett was goading me to say.

Another long look from Lord Chasen, this one encompassing us both. Then he turned his back to us and rejoined his sister.

He peeled off his jacket. I wasn't certain if he meant to disrobe entirely or not, but even as I was averting my eyes the earl went to smoke, and Fay was scooping up his garments to stuff into her valise. Then he was a dragon, a black metal demon towering over us, head lifted and neck arched, yellow eyes aglow. He was a fearsome sight, quite as much as I remembered from that moment on the zeppelin.

I hated to notice how very small we stood before him.

To his credit, Armand ignored the demon and his burning yellow gaze. My fiancé, my lordling, my second and last true love, placed his hands upon my shoulders and pulled me in for a very ardent, very *lingering* kiss.

"We'll keep up," he whispered against the corner of my lips.

So, yes, unquestionably I was smaller than Everett, both as a girl and as a beast. But that night on the beach, with Armand secure on my back and my own body a golden arrow waiting for release, I took us up into the air with just as much magic powering my wings.

WE HUGGED THE COAST. making our way to the dimmed, sparse spiderweb of lights that was Dover, and then a hard right over that slithery stretch of sea that separated my homeland from Everyone Else.

The wind was a song in my ears. Armand was a lithe weight upon my spine. I said a silent goodbye to England with just a glance over my shoulder.

Farewell. I hope to God to find you again.

Armand stroked his hand down my back, then bent low and kissed my neck.

I faced forward, followed the blended pitch shadows of Everett and Fay as they glided over the waves.

As the night was so misty, I wasn't terribly worried about aeroplanes or dirigibles, but I remained alert. There were four of us now with *drákon* senses. Surely we'd notice anyone approaching before they spotted us.

We'd dined before we'd left; Armand and I had insisted upon that. Yet by the time the sun threatened to rise, starvation gnawed at my seams, and I was close to coming undone. I was actually considering alerting Mandy that I needed to stop when at last Everett began to descend.

We found a clearing in a forest next to a village (Bavarian, as it

turned out). We touched earth, put on our human faces, and presented ourselves to the local inn as a foursome travelling from Munich,
eager for a hearty breakfast and rooms to let.

I was glad that Mandy was fluent in German, since Lord Chasen
and his sister apparently were as well. My own command of the German language was limited to *ja*, *nein*, and a few choice swearwords,
so all I had to do was sit in silence as I devoured everything that was
placed before me.

I SLEPT AWAY THE day. It was a dense, heavy sleep, as smothering soft as
a blanket of cotton wool, and I let myself be smothered by it. I don't
believe I dreamed, but occasionally I did rise up close to conscious-
ness, called by the tolling of bells. Church bells, I supposed, marking
the hours as the sun slipped by.

And, of course, I awoke hungry.

I rolled over and opened my eyes and Armand sat at the edge of
our simple iron-frame bed, already dressed and shaved and holding
me in his warm blue look.

"Dinnertime," he said, and I stretched my sore muscles with a sigh.

Everett and Fay awaited us in the public room, a place crammed
to the gills with villagers and their families. The air tasted heavily of
vinegar and grease and the tears of children denied yet another bite
of dessert. Our table was already piled with an impressive amount of
food; perhaps this far from the front, the war had not yet inspired
rationing. The Langfords had started the meal without us.

Fine by me. Less of a wait.

I helped myself to sliced goose and pickled whitefish and a salad of red cabbage. Everett pushed over a tankard of lager. Beneath the noise of the chamber, Fay whispered something to Armand, who nodded and whispered something back, and both of them glanced at me and I had that prickly, uncomfortable feeling you get when you know others are talking about you, and you have no notion of what they're saying, good or bad. Not that Mandy would say anything bad about me, I knew. But it rankled being the only person around who could not safely speak.

Was it going to be like this at Zaharen Yce? I had supposed all the *drákon* there to speak English, but perhaps only the Langford family—the Darkfrith version of our kind—did so. I wasn't clever with languages; my brief lessons in French at Iverson had more than proved that. Attempting to learn even the basics of German or Romanian or . . . or whatever it would be, was going to be an exercise in frustration.

I twisted the ring on my left hand, vexed. I wanted to ask exactly where we were. I wanted to ask how much longer we'd be flying. How soon we'd reach the castle. Yet there were potential enemies surrounding our table entirely; likely this was the only tavern for miles around. Many of the customers were muttering over their brews and staring openly at us, no doubt because we were new.

I hoped that was the reason. I hoped it wasn't anything more, like how we looked especially foreign. Or even, perhaps, another species from them.

A waitress, harried and perspiring, came over to refill our tankards. She glanced at my scraped-bare plate, then bent close with a hand on her hip and said something into my ear, her tone rising slightly to end on a question.

I turned to Armand, but he was back to conversing with Fay.

The waitress lifted her eyebrows at me.

"*Ja,*" I said.

She pivoted off behind the bar.

Twenty minutes later she returned with an entire platter of beef dumplings, topped with diced onions and garlic and dabs of sweet mustard.

"*Für das Baby,*" she announced, and patted me kindly on the shoulder.

Armand and Everett regarded me with identical expressions of slack-jawed astonishment. Lady Fay only laughed.

WE SOARED ON INTO another night, and then another. Each new village we encountered in the mornings proved more and more remote. More and more mysterious. And lofty—during the second night the plains melted away, and all around us mountains began to claw their way up into the clouds.

Gone were the ordinary shapes of the houses and steeples I knew, ones that I'd encountered anywhere from England all the way to Prussia. The villages we visited now appeared almost medieval, deliberately pinned and fixed in another time: stout stone structures with thatch roofs; onion-domed churches that glowed pale and gold through the ebony nights. No automobiles, no railroads, only cobblestone streets and horses and people huddling around hearths behind closed doors. Rock walls ringed everything, spreading out in ripples to surround gardens and homes and eventually entire villages.

We were well beyond Germany now.

"Transylvania," Everett informed me over our breakfast that third morning. "A land of dark blood and even darker legends, of dream thieves and winged beasts that slice the very ether into ribbons of stars."

I fought a shiver. Perhaps he was only attempting to intimidate me, but it was easy enough, in this archaic place, to believe in dark blood and dreams.

He had spoken quietly but in English; we were the only guests this morning in the taproom of the alpine hostel we'd found. The day beyond the room was emerging a seething sick green; snow clouds shrouded the sky, obscuring the harsh peaks of the mountains. A fog crawled down the slopes, curling invisible tendrils into my marrow. It felt charged, as if with an electrical current. The air itself felt charged and crackling. Dangerous to breathe.

I watched that greenish sky thicken. The first of the flakes began to fall, lacy patchwork against the glass panes.

I wanted to rest. I wanted to eat and rest and rest and rest. I did not want to keep flying; if we never arrived at Zaharen Yce, that would be just fine by me. But I knew by that tension in the air that we were close. We had to be close. And I'd only have this one last day for sleep.

Our server shuffled up and placed a second platter of charred sausages upon our table, along with a pot of warm cornmeal porridge topped with salted cheese. She was around sixty, thin-shouldered and wide-waisted, and no matter how frankly I stared, she would not meet my gaze. Instead she curtsied and backed away from us, uttering something musical and strained as she touched her curved fingers to her forehead.

Her words sounded familiar to me, and at the same time, wholly unknown. They scratched at the back of my memory—

In my mind's eye, I glimpsed a face. A man's face, blurred and sharp at once, as though from a dream. He was dark-haired and smiling and a bar of sun lit his eyes and the air smelled of heather and a woman laughed and said *sandu*—

But then it all vanished. Just as swiftly as it had come, the memory (the dream?) was gone.

I sat there, blinking, as Everett pierced one of the sausages with a wicked-looking fork, releasing streamers of grease.

"What was it she said?" Armand asked.

"Hmm?" Everett began to slice the sausage.

"Our hostess, just now. She says the same thing every time she comes over. Doesn't sound too happy."

"She's thanking us," Fay answered, "in the local language of the mountains. It's Hungarian and Latin and Romanian blended, with a dash of French tossed in for good measure. Fairly difficult to master unless you've been steeped in it. Anyway, she's gratified that we're staying at her simple little refuge." She sampled a spoonful of the porridge; I'd never seen Fay eat in any manner other than ladylike, and there was no grease on *her* plate. "Literally, the translation is, *I am grateful that you adorn my home, Noble Ones.*"

"She doesn't look especially grateful," I commented, because it was true. Whenever the woman was at a safe enough distance from our table, all she did was glower at us from the kitchen door. The cook, the source of much banging of pots and pans and all of our burned sausages, hadn't ventured out at all.

"Nothing personal, I expect," said Lord Chasen. "Probably she just doesn't like dragons. Not all of us are as agreeable as my sister and I."

Armand and I went still. Everett feigned surprise.

"I told you, children, we're in the land of legends now. The *drákon* have been entrenched here for centuries. More than centuries. Aeons. These mountains are our birthplace. We sparked to life in the seam between the welkin and these diamond-dusted alps. Did you imagine the humans here would not recognize us for what we are?"

I propped an elbow on the table. "If they *recognize* us, then why did you make such a fuss back in England about people seeing me? When apparently you all live out here in the bloody open?"

He smiled, unruffled. "The humans populating these little hamlets remain here at our pleasure, and they know it. We adorn their homes, their places of trade, their tea houses and markets and butchers' shops. We are their pride and their terror. No one speaks the truth beyond the local walls." He speared another sausage, plunked it with a *splat!* upon my plate. "No one dares."

Past the kitchen door our hostess watched us, one chapped hand clamped along the wood. As soon as she noticed me looking, she dropped her eyes and scooted back into the shadows.

"What does the word *sandu* mean," I asked, "in this local language?"

Fay thought about it, then lifted a shoulder. "Nothing, as far as I know."

I frowned down at the food on my plate, the aroma of cornmeal and heather filling my head.

"Storm's coming," Everett noted, as the fat green clouds bubbled behind him. "Good thing we'll all be home soon."

CHAPTER 27

I'D NEVER FLOWN THROUGH a blizzard before. The promised storm had arrived with howling force, and the night had gone surly and speckled, the heavens erased, the ground a smear. The wind was no longer a song in my ears, but a scream. I *had* flown blind once before—*once*, in daylight, through heavy clouds—but this was entirely new and honestly terrifying.

Ahead of me, I knew, was the serpentine figure of Everett, cutting our path through the sky, but he was as invisible as everything else. All I could see was the storm, and all I could feel was the ice expanding between my scales. Armand hunched low against me, both arms around my neck, but I was so cold I could no longer tell he was there at all. I only knew he held on by twisting my head around to check.

The citrusy perfume Fay had splashed on hours past, a day ago, a world ago, was all that kept me on course.

Snow crusted my lashes, thick and solid. It caked my face and wings. The wind was a constant push sideways, and I was a ship with no rudder, constantly struggling to right us again. My body grew heavier and heavier. A mere three hours into our flight, it felt like someone had poured wet cement over my entire being.

I have to land, I have to land, I cannot land, there is no land and no way to land . . .

It was too much. My wings no longer wanted to beat. Lifting them became a Herculean task; holding them stiff for a glide became impossible. We were bobbing now despite my best efforts, dipping violently up and down and Armand made a noise that I couldn't understand, and we were sinking because I could no longer keep us aloft, we were going down—

Armand made the noise again, and this time the wind released it to become a shouted word in my ear:

"Look!"

He was jabbing a finger to our left. I squinted to see what he had.

A shadow took shape through the storm. One, two—three of them, long and winged, their silhouettes unmistakable. They were dragons, other dragons, flanking us, and when I looked to my right I saw three more. The nearest one flapped close enough to look me in the eyes, then jerked his head downward.

All six began to descend. I followed.

I don't know what might have happened had they not arrived when they did to guide us in. To this day I don't know, and so I suppose I must be grateful to them for ensuring that Armand and I did not end the night as messy stains upon some Carpathian mountainside.

Regardless of everything that came after, I am grateful for that.

The ground rose up quickly. I assumed it was the ground; I saw the shadow dragons jolt in place and fold up their wings, and they didn't seem to be falling. Within seconds it was my turn, and my feet scuttled for purchase through the drifts of slippery snow—there was indeed rock or dirt beneath it—and then Mandy was sliding off my back, and I went to smoke. I had to; it was either Turn or collapse under the weight of the ice encrusting me, and I wasn't going to collapse in front of these strangers.

We were in a courtyard of sorts. Well, what I could see of it looked like a courtyard: there were walls all around (they did cut the wind some) and a large alabaster fountain with a pond at its base, all of it completely captured in ice. The dragon shadows had become human-shaped, and Lady Fay was plunging toward us with her head down and a hand against her face to protect her eyes from the gusting snow.

Mandy got free of his duster, held it open for me. I Turned to girl inside it, shivering (it was bloody, *bloody* cold up here; good God, I'd never been so cold). Fay reached out, grabbed my elbow, and began to drag me back along the way she had come. I grabbed Mandy and dragged him after me.

We passed through a massive entranceway, engulfed at once in light and heat. I had a brief impression of iron doors, of silk wallpaper painted with red birds on branches, of candle flames flickering behind clear glass sconces, their prisms chiming an alarm with the sudden wind. The ceiling yawned so high and shadowy I couldn't see the end of it. Beneath my feet was a rug of tangerine and rum, ancient and thin as a whisper. And from somewhere, everywhere, bloomed the soft music of diamonds—what had to be *thousands* of them. It seemed to emanate from the very walls around us.

Fay released me without a word, walking calmly now toward an older, stylishly dressed couple waiting at the base of an imposing sweep of stairs. Everett must have Turned and gone ahead of us all, for he already stood beside them, wearing a robe of quilted damask.

I brushed a hand across my face, swiping away hair and melting snow. I was a city rat, right and proper, not some country milkmaid who'd never known splendor, so I knew how it would appear if I gave in to my desire to stop and gawk. Instead I angled a glance up at Mandy; he was as damp and disheveled as I knew I must look.

He yanked off his aviation goggles and wrapped them around his fist, and it struck me then how much older than I he had somehow become. He couldn't have been born more than a year or so before me, but he looked so much . . . *more* now. So stern. Wary. Angles and edges and sharp corners I didn't recognize.

Armand looked full grown, while I still felt like a schoolgirl inside, guessing at rules, outmaneuvering my elders, trying to blend in and stand out all at once.

Mandy returned my glance. He reached up to tuck a lock of hair behind my ear.

With an unexpected ferocity, my heart swelled with him. I loved him, I feared for him. We were neither of us *really* adults yet, but here we were, outnumbered and surrounded by the very creatures I'd been warned to avoid. So I suppose I feared for us both.

What had we done?

More people filtered in, lining the atrium walls. People of all ages and shapes, men and women and a sprinkling of children, even though it had to be well after two in the morning. Some of the newcomers were dressed as servants, but most were not. A few were wearing the same sort of damask robes as Everett (our dragon escort, I presumed). Candlelight glazed them all in dusky gold, glittered slick across the surface of their eyes. No one spoke, but unlike me, these *drákon* were not afraid to stare.

We are hundreds, Everett had said to me back at Iverson, and I was beginning to understand what that meant.

Don't look at them, I told myself grimly. *Don't hunt for any hint of yourself in their faces. Don't look.*

The doors shut behind us. The winter wind pushing against my back eddied and died.

But for the diamond-music, but for the drumming of my heart, the silence surrounding us now was absolute.

Armand offered me his arm. We finished the length of the atrium in a decorous stroll, chins up, dribbling water with every step.

The Marquess of Langford—who else would it be?—and his wife watched our approach. He was silver-haired and slim, with a narrow hooked nose and unsettling green eyes. The woman at his side hardly reached his shoulder, but there was something about her—an aura of elegance, an innate poise—that made her appear anything but slight. Her auburn hair was swept up into a knot and woven with pearls; they matched the choker at her throat.

"Well," announced Lord Chasen to the hall, "here they are at last, our little lost dragon and her paramour."

"Everett," chided the woman in a tranquil tone. "It would be pleasant if your manners reflected the occasion."

"I beg your pardon." Everett dipped his head in mock apology. "Mother, Father, may I introduce Miss Eleanore Jones and her *friend*, Lord Armand Louis. Miss Jones, Lord Armand, I present the Most Honourable Marquess and Marchioness of Langford."

So, the woman *was* his wife. The Alpha was wed still. Relief made me almost giddy—followed instantly by the realization that I'd better establish my own position right away.

I offered my most polished curtsy, duster and all. "How I hate to remind you yet again, Lord Chasen, but Lord Armand is not only my paramour, but also my fiancé."

A stir rustled through the watchers, a sibilant hiss that didn't quite resolve into sentences.

Fay rolled her eyes at her father. "This is how they've been the entire way. Such a pair."

"Indeed," agreed the marchioness. She closed the distance between us, grasping both of my hands. Armand rocked forward a small, stiff step, which she ignored. "I fear I cannot blame you, Miss Jones, for taking offense. My son has a knack for ruffling feathers."

"It's a gift, rather," drawled Everett.

The marchioness's eyes were the same impenetrable black as her children's. Her grip was firm. The pearls wreathing her hair and throat hummed and gleamed.

She didn't *seem* the kind of person who'd be content with her husband taking a mistress, but then again, who knew with these dragons?

"Everyone is so eager to meet you," she continued. "But first, won't you come into the parlor and get warm? The storm stole over us with such fury. We have a fire in the hearth and sandwiches prepared."

"Yes," I said, and Armand shifted again, even stiffer than before. "That is, I should like to dress first. If you don't mind."

"Certainly. Baird?" She glanced to our right, and a brawny man who looked more like a pugilist than a butler stepped forward. "Baird will show you to your rooms."

"Miss Jones and I will share a room," said Mandy at once.

"Is that so?" murmured the marchioness, and for the first time she looked directly at him. "Such modern notions young people have these days. Yet I am an old-fashioned hostess, Lord Armand, and I run an old-fashioned household. Unwed couples do not share a bed in this castle."

Mandy smiled, and my skin prickled. I returned my hand to his arm.

"So sorry," I said, before he could give voice to whatever lurked behind that smile. "Perhaps I wasn't entirely clear before. Lord Armand is my lover. I won't sleep here without him. If that is against your *rules*, my lady, my lord, then this visit is over before it begins. We will not be dictated to. We have come all this way at Lord Chasen's insistence, but I have no qualms—none at all—about heading back out into that storm this minute if I must."

Another hiss slid its way through the gold-shadowed hall. Fay pressed her fingers against her mouth; the Alpha regarded me with hooded eyes and a stoic mien. His wife never moved.

I'd never spoken so boldly to an elder before, and definitely not about something so intimate. I was knackered and nervous all together; my body buzzed with exhaustion, but my mind was ticking hot like the engine of a locomotive. I'd meant everything I'd said, though, except for the last part. *That* had been a bald-faced lie.

We *would* leave if we had to, but I had plenty of qualms about it.

In case you didn't know, the key to a successful lie is to maintain all its subtle constructs: your facial expression, eye contact, firmness of speech. You don't want to oversell it, but one tiny misstep, one ounce of indecision, and a cunning observer will tear you to pieces.

No one had to tell me that this Alpha and his wife were cunning. If they were anything like Everett and Fay, they'd already taken my full measure and made plans to lock me up tight in the dungeon, forever and ever. Wouldn't *that* be a fine ending to my life?

I cocked my head, attempting an air of disinterest. I did not drop my gaze.

"Do you truly not know who my parents were?" I demanded. (If your lie starts to unravel, your next best hope is a strong diversion.)

"Truly we don't," said the marchioness, after a moment. "But I confess that you do remind me of someone, Miss Jones."

"Oh?" It was hard to keep the excitement from my voice.

She lifted a hand to the butler. I was burning for her answer but knew from her smile that it wasn't going to come.

"Escort them both to the Winter Suite, Baird."

"Yes, my lady."

❦❧

THE WINTER SUITE. *A suite composed of winter,* Armand thought, and it was difficult to see how he was wrong. The walls, the floors, the ceiling: all of it icy, all of it frosty pale and shimmering. But no real winter crept through this chamber. Thanks to a pair of fireplaces at either end, it was warmer than the castle hallways, and brighter, too. They'd been given a room composed not of ice but of heavy white stones—some type of quartz, he would guess. But *between* those stones, between . . .

Diamonds.

Studded throughout the mortar were diamonds of all cuts and shapes, both raw and polished, large and little, smoky and clear. Some were bigger than peas, others no more than grains of dust. And their *singing* . . .

"Softer," he commanded the walls, the ceiling, the floor, and the deliriously potent music that had been coursing through his soul began to gentle.

Lora, warming herself by one of the hearths, threw him a look from over her shoulder.

"This place," she said, and that was all.

"I know."

It was like a dream and a nightmare entangled. He could envision, all too easily, how Zaharen Yce and its songs and its dragons could swallow them whole.

He walked to the dressing chest by the sleigh bed (draped in white shantung; everything layers of white, inside this room and out) and placed the knapsack upon it. The goggles. Removed the chain from around his neck.

How small their belongings seemed here. How meager.

Just like our defenses.

"What did you think of the Alpha?" Lora asked, coming over.

Mandy gathered his thoughts. "He's a quiet bloke, isn't he? I don't believe he spoke a word the entire time."

"You're right." She sounded surprised.

He worked at the straps on the sack. "You know what they say about still waters, though."

"That they'll drown you just as thoroughly as the other kind?"

He smiled, although it didn't strike him as particularly humorous. "Exactly."

They unpacked the knapsack together, pulling out their crumpled clothing and spreading it upon the bed. Before he'd finished, she'd slipped free of the duster and let it drop to her feet. At the edge of his vision she stood nude and pale and glorious.

His breath caught.

No; he needed to focus now. To concentrate on where they were and why. But his mouth had gone parched and his body taut, and when she shifted to pick up something from the bed, he was fully overwhelmed; her scent and that brief, searing instant of Lora, her hair to her waist and the smoothest skin, edged in diamonds and firelight.

The world around them melted away. The whole of everything was simply, immutably *her*.

Mandy closed his eyes.

He felt her fingers trace a pattern on his cheek. Trail slowly down the pulse of his throat.

"They're waiting for us," he managed, still not looking at her.

"I know."

This is what you want, the dragon-voice within him whispered. *This is always what you want.*

Her lips grazed his chin. Her hands tugged at his shoulders.

He surrendered to what they both wanted with a relief so piercing it felt like pain.

SO. WE WERE LATE. The tepid tea was whisked away and replaced with a fresh, hot pot; the beefsteak-and-horseradish sandwiches were more room temperature than not, but at least the servants didn't attempt to remove those as well. I might have bitten off someone's hand had they tried.

Our hosts were not so boorish as to inquire why Armand and I had kept them waiting. Nevertheless, I'm sure they knew. I'm sure they all knew.

The parlor, as the marchioness had called it, was predictably huge and tall and chilled with the storm still blustering beyond the windows. Even so, it might have been easy to think we were in a conventional (if extremely posh) manor house back in England. All the furniture was rich and rare, all the paintings were oils, all the vases and figurines and books lining the shelves were tasteful and spotless.

But the black marble mantelpiece framing the fireplace held nothing atop it except a scattering of loose opals, rainbow glints that danced with the light.

And the fashionable chairs and settees were draped in animal hides, shaggy and thick, from their tops all the way to the floor. The ripe stink of slaughtered creatures flowed around me, primitive enough to raise the hairs on my arms.

My eyes watered. I lowered my head and sucked in a silent breath as my body tingled with a bizarre combination of pleasure and alarm.

No one else appeared to notice, not even Armand. We sat with the Alpha and his family and a handful of others in front of the fire, and everyone sipped their drinks and ate their food as if this were the most ordinary evening in the most ordinary home ever.

What an astonishing pack of actors we *drákon* had turned out to be.

I regarded the china plate balanced atop my lap. I thought the pelt beneath me might be bison. It smelled wild like that, wild and wheaten and sour.

I took a bite of my sandwich. It was insanely good.

"How was your journey?" inquired the marchioness, pouring me a second glass of wine. No one but Armand, I'd noticed, had touched the tea.

"Tolerable," Everett offered, just as I said, "Compulsory."

Everett's smile bent thin as a blade; his father aimed at me a vague, dissatisfied frown.

"Oh, forgive me," I said to the marquess. "Are we not supposed to speak of that?"

I was attempting to provoke him, I admit. Perhaps it was the wine, or the opals crooning, so eerie and low. It was disquieting enough, dealing with that dead-animal stink. The Alpha's constant, silent stare did nothing to soothe my nerves.

"You're an outspoken chit," he commented at last, in a tone that might have meant anything from *and I am going to crush you for it* to *outspoken chits are so awfully delicious.*

I lifted my chin. "I find it useful when dealing with extortionists to speak in truths."

The frown intensified. His wife shook her head and tsk-tsked, and Mandy had stopped breathing.

Everett yawned, stretching his arms above his head. "All these histrionics. You make it sound like I'm a pirate or something, and I kidnapped you at gunpoint."

"Threatening to murder my entire school should count as gunpoint."

"*Did* you?" inquired the marchioness, facing her son.

Everett held up his finger and thumb in a small, pinching motion.

Just a tad, it meant.

And she *smiled.* "I've taught you well, haven't I?"

The pelt beneath me slid an inch or so down the cushion of my chair; I pulled myself upright again. The world was spinning, spinning, right off its axis.

I said, "It's you, isn't it?"

The marchioness's ebony eyes returned to mine. Her lips mirrored her son's knife-edged smile.

"You're the Alpha," I said.

"Of course," she replied. "Who else?"

CHAPTER 28

I COULD NOT SLEEP. OR perhaps I did in fits and starts; if so, I couldn't tell. By all rights I should have been halfway to a coma by now—all the flying, all the anxiety, all the surprises of the past few days should have drained me dry.

But I was awake in the pillowy white bed the marchioness (*the Alpha,* my mind corrected) had assigned us. Awake for each of the scant hours left winding through this early morning, my eyes dry and gritty, my respiration subdued. I stared up at the ceiling. At the walls. At Mandy, who at least slumbered beside me but still with that faint, stern severity, as though even his dreams gave him troubles.

My world had never really stopped spinning after that moment in the parlor, I realized. I could not make it stop spinning. So many big things, *significant* things that Honor Smith had told me about our kind had been dead wrong.

The Langfords *were* ensconced here, not just in England.

A female *could* lead.

And, as I'd learned over my meal of sandwiches and wine, there had been no princes of the Zaharen for well over a hundred years. No dragon nobility of any sort left, save the English.

But Honor had gotten that painting of Zaharen Yce right. Its location and name and that of the native *drákon* who'd thrived here once—once upon a time, as she'd said. Plus Rue and Darkfrith. All of that had been right.

I didn't know yet if she'd been right or wrong about the *drákon* bottling my soul. Maybe it was just another story she'd concocted for reasons of her own.

I exhaled hard, irritated. The diamonds all around me echoed it, turning my sigh into a pretty lullaby, but that only irritated me more.

When I flipped back the covers and sat up, Mandy didn't rouse. I told myself that at least one of us was going to be rested for whatever the day would bring, and that would have to be good enough.

The window nearest the bed was shrouded in white organza. I shoved through the panels to find that the blizzard and its cap of clouds had tumbled off. The Carpathian sky now arced blue-green above me—not the rotten green of yesterday's storm, but a green as sharp as glass and glistening with the last of the stars. Mountains cradled my view, shadowed still but brightening with the dawn into turquoise and seafoam and canyons of purple velvet.

My nose touched the frigid pane; my breath clouded into steam. It was beautiful here, there was no denying it. Beautiful in a way that felt like a wound inside, like a piece of my soul that had been sheared off, but I'd never realized it until I'd found it again.

Ever so slightly, that thought stung. Liking any aspect of Zaharen Yce seemed like a betrayal, although I could not say exactly of what or whom. I didn't want to fall under the thrall of this place, not to its dragons or its mountains or its savage clear sky. I didn't want to ache for any part of it after I left. Because I *would* be leaving.

We would, I corrected myself, with a glance back to Armand in the bed.

We.

My hands tested the window's latches; they opened easily. The pads of my fingers came away smeared with oil.

I stuck out my head, examined the stars once more.

There, in the heart of heaven—there, nearly gone but not quite—flared a golden-green light.

Jesse! I hadn't seen him in so long!

I went to smoke before I could think twice about it. The winds caught me up and swept me higher, higher, until I tore free of them as a dragon and took charge of my own path.

Celestial music swirled around me. *fireheart, home at last!*

Jesse, is that you?

Yet I was too late. I thought I might have heard the beginning of his reply, a song so distant it was more a ricochet, a memory—*lora, don't tell them*—but in that second the sun seared a line of fire into the aquamarine horizon, and all the stars blinked out.

I circled, searching for any sign of him, but the day had come and there was no erasing the light.

Don't tell them what, Jesse? I wondered. *Don't tell what?*

Zaharen Yce was a crystalline toy castle glued to a crystalline toy mountain. I'd tilted back toward it, beginning to descend, when the sky above me was severed by a single serpentine strand. Another dragon twisted through the green to join my side.

Everett, as shiny dark as the ground was bright.

His eyes glowed with the dawn, nearly as brilliant as my scales. He grinned at me (I thought it was a grin, not a snarl), and with a scarce tipping of his wings, flipped under me, around, above and then back to my side. I'd not changed course, and he'd done it all so quickly, I'd hardly had time to register what had happened. But then he did it again, fleet as the wind, graceful as a swan, and I knew that he was showing off.

Very well.

I opened my wings wider, rising up. I went as high as the highest peak I could find, then plunged down toward the virgin snow until I was inches above a wide, smooth slope. I skimmed its surface faster than I'd ever flown before, never faltering or dropping too low, my talons scoring fresh lines down the white.

The snow hissed beneath me. The mountains shone, and the black dragon swooped beside me, mimicking me, the pair of us dodging trees and boulders that rushed by so swiftly they were little more than precarious blurs . . . and I could not hide my own smile.

I don't think I'd ever flown for pleasure before, not purely for pleasure. Flying had always been a means to an end for me, a way to get from here to there, or from down to up. How astonishing that I'd never realized how madly, exhilaratingly *fun* it could be.

At the base of the mountain, in what had to be a field covered in powder, Everett flipped to his back again, landing with a puff against the snow. I pulled up and watched, baffled, as he spread his wings and writhed on his back—rather like a dog enjoying a good scratch against the ground—until I realized what he was doing.

When it was done, he floated up beside me, still grinning. He had made a snow-angel, just as we'd used to do in the orphanage courtyard after a heavy storm. (Or a snow-dragon, actually. I doubted that any true angels, those beings so pure of heart and noble of spirit, had our dagger-tipped wings.)

I dipped lower, ready to try my own. But before I could land, the black dragon beat me to it, pouncing upon his own shadow, dancing and whirling his tail around until all that was left was a cyclone of crystals, spiraling upward to rub out the sun and sky in a frenzy of white-and-gold glitter.

CHAPTER 29

*D*ON'T TELL THEM WHO *you are*, I was singing to her.

But as her life grows shorter, I grow weaker. That was the deal struck; I cannot reach her as I used to do.

If I could, I would shout it down from the azure, to her or to that damned Armand, whichever of them might hear: *whatever else comes, don't tell them who you are.*

CHAPTER 30

ANDY AWOKE ON HIS stomach, one arm stretched out and one tucked under, saturated in a sense of loss. And of cold—the arm that was out from the covers felt chilled as death.

His dead-chill fingers curled into the linens. He narrowed his eyes at Eleanore's empty side of the bed, then at the empty rest of the room.

She was up already. That was fine; she tended to rise early, no matter how little she'd slept the night before. He had no reason to feel this abnormal, tugging sensation unpleasantly deep in his center. No reason for this disturbing sense that he'd lost something—her—when she was likely only having breakfast somewhere in this ridiculous riddle of white stone.

He was not her owner, not her master, and he had no reason to be wishing she'd waited for him. Lora was entirely trustworthy.

The rest of the rotters here, however, were not.

He found them all in the dining chamber. He assumed it was the dining chamber, as it was lengthy and crammed with potted ferns and footmen and a table even longer than the one at Tranquility anchoring its middle. The windows were dressed in more of those useless gauzy curtains that did nothing to block out the light, which is why he was blinded momentarily when he first walked in.

The shadow-people gathered about the dining table shifted, probably facing him. Years of tart professors and bitter rivals at Eaton had trained him well; Armand had the sense to pause, not to squint, and to wipe all expression from his face.

Shadow-Chasen released Shadow-Lora's hand. She sat back in her chair.

Mandy still hadn't moved. An odd combination of aromas washed over him, as if a draft he couldn't feel had pushed straight at him: it was lust and hope and coffee and eggs and confusion. An apple-spice tinge of something else—embarrassment?—beneath.

Then his vision settled, and Lora was looking at him with the corners of her lips gone tight, which meant that she was displeased, and the marchioness was smiling serenely. He realized the apple-scent belonged to her, to the Alpha, and it was amusement, not embarrassment.

Lora wiped her hand against her thigh.

Chasen said, "A clear diamond, though. So very human."

"It is perfect," Lora retorted, and the displeasure was in her voice as well.

Mandy felt some of his unease lift away. If she was peeved at

Chasen, things were still fine. He walked to the side table laden with chafing dishes, took a plate, and began to serve himself.

The marchioness explained, "The tradition among our sort is to match the color of the stone in the ring to the color of the fiancée's eyes."

Our sort. Evidently Mandy wasn't quite sorted into the correct pile.

"How adorable," he said. He moved on to the bacon and tomatoes; it was a real English breakfast set out, not a pot of cornmeal mush in sight. "Yet I must defer to the lady in this matter. Lora, my love, would you prefer a lavender diamond?"

"I want only what I already have," she said.

"And there we are." He glanced up from the bacon, shot a bared-teeth smile at the Alpha. "My fiancée is pleased enough with her human-colored stone. All is well."

Her smug amusement didn't fade. "I'm curious about your background, Lord Armand. You unquestionably have some element of *drákon* in you, as does, I am told, your brother. We have no records of English runners from Darkfrith in recent history, but there have been plenty of thin-blooded bastards produced by the Zaharen. Is there Romanian in your family line?"

"As far as I know, we are fully English." He took the chair across from Lora, softening his smile for her, even as she straightened and sent the marchioness a withering glare. "The dragon in me is courtesy of Rue Langford and her husband."

Lord Chasen emitted a short, scornful laugh just as his father said, "That is not possible."

"It is entirely possible. My mother was descended from Rue and Christoff Langford. We have the letters to prove it."

The marquess clenched a fist upon the arm of his chair. "Every single offspring of Christoff and Clarissa Rue, every *single* descendant, myself included, has been identified and tracked."

"Every single offspring but the last," Lora corrected him. She looked at Mandy, ignoring the monumental silence of the others. "Is there more bacon?"

He shoved his plate at her. "Have mine. It's soggy, anyway."

"Pardon me," said the Alpha in her low, cool voice. "Are you suggesting that Clarissa Rue and Christoff—two of the most formidable, influential dragons in the whole of our history—had a secret child, one they somehow managed to keep hidden from the tribe for the sum of its life?"

"It was a boy," Lora offered, clearly enjoying herself. She reached for Mandy's plate, chose a slice of bacon with her fingers, and tore off a bite. "They had him after they fled Darkfrith. Apparently he needed protection from the barbarism of you thick-blooded lot."

"And it must have worked." Mandy took back his plate before Lora could move on to his eggs. "As here I am, quite as much a descendant of your two most formidable dragons as *you*, Lord Langford."

"That is not—" the marquess began, but his wife held up her hand, only that, and with a thin whistle of air through his nose, he subsided. Two bright red spots of rage burned high across his cheeks.

"It *could* be," she mused, thoughtful. "They did disappear all those years ago, and there is something about your eyes, I think, reminiscent of Christoff."

Armand paused. "You know what he looked like?"

"We have a portrait of them both in the gallery. A Reynolds, I believe? Do you recall the artist, my dear? In any case, yes. Upon rumination, perhaps there *is* a slight resemblance. Or perhaps you're merely a very skilled manipulator, Lord Armand."

He shrugged. "No doubt you see what you want."

Lora tossed her napkin upon the table. "Well, *I* want to see the portrait."

The marchioness, after a studied moment, lifted her own napkin, folded it, and placed it beside her juice glass.

"Then so you shall."

THE INTERIOR OF THE castle was a disconcerting combination of brilliance and gloom, of song and silence. Of things human—and very much non-human. I hadn't noticed it as much last night, maybe because it had been dark and I so tired and anxious. But in daylight, Zaharen Yce was a strange and marvelous creature, with a haunting beauty resonating through its arches and coiled staircases, in the finely carved dragons that danced along its balustrades and cornices, in the unspoken mysteries behind its many closed doors.

I could still smell the animal stink of the skins covering the chairs and settees, and I could still hear the diamond-music rising through the halls. But there was more than scent and sound and sight here. As I accompanied the marchioness to the portrait gallery, I realized there was a kind of *awareness* pressing down upon me. A heavy sentience of immense proportions, held in place by these thick stone walls, pinned beneath the thick stone floors. It felt living to me, watchful.

I remembered what Honor had said about the castle, about how it was affixed to the side of the mountain by the bones of the beasts who had built it. In that moment, her story seemed absolutely plausible.

The dragon ghosts of Zaharen Yce sifted through the weighted air, brushing ice against my skin, combing frost through my hair.

Steady on, Jones, I chastised myself, but I couldn't help rubbing my hands up and down my arms. *Keep your wits about you.*

"He's quite your shadow, isn't he?" murmured the Alpha, at my side. I glanced at her, and she tipped her head toward Armand, walking a few paces ahead of us with Fay clinging to his arm.

"He loves me," I said, because it countered everything she was implying, plus it was true.

"Loyalty is a commendable quality, Miss Jones. I require it amongst all our kind. But love and loyalty needn't be fused. One may exist without the other."

I shook my head at her, perplexed, and her silky tone became even silkier.

"He will never fly with you, will he? He will never Turn and rip into the ether beside you. You will never witness his dragon self, because his human blood has drowned it. It's not his fault, of course.

But perhaps, in this case, Lord Armand's ambitions have exceeded his actuality. Perhaps your love for each other exists merely because there was no better option available to you at the time."

I'm certain she saw the storms on my face, but before I could speak, she asked, "Do you know how many female *drákon* can complete the Turn?"

I'd been wondering, obviously. I'd been guessing not many. Not if all those stares from last night had meant anything.

"Including you, Miss Jones, there are now precisely two. Two females out of all our tribe left with this Gift."

"You're the other," I said, not making it a question.

She gave a nod. A girl in a maid's uniform opened a door to our left, popped out, saw us, and recoiled back inside just as rapidly. The marchioness never turned her head.

"Everett wouldn't have attacked your school, you know."

"I do *not* know," I snapped.

"My heir is far too shrewd, and far too well disciplined to draw that sort of attention to us. I approved of his stratagem because it brought you here, but I assure you, it was only a ruse. I disclose this to you now because it seems to have colored your view of us."

"It was a damned realistic ruse."

She smiled. "It was meant to be. However, I promise you that in all my years as our leader, I have resorted to lethal measures only once, and only to eradicate an extraordinary threat from one of our own. Everett wasn't even there."

Ah. That made everything *so* much better.

We had reached the portrait gallery, a long corridor punctuated with radiant windows of chamfered glass. As Armand pivoted to locate me, the marchioness placed a hand on my forearm to keep me where I was. She leaned in close, her mouth to my ear. She smelled of freesias and face powder and meat.

"You could be a leader here, Eleanore. You could be a queen, the bride of an Alpha instead of a Giftless boy. You could be the moon to Everett's sun, a power unto yourself, and together the two of you could champion a new era for us all."

I looked into her eyes and saw that the *awareness* pushing down on me, that watchful and ghostly presence, lived inside her, too. I wanted to shiver, and made myself not.

"Consider it," she whispered.

"Lora?"

I joined Mandy's side. Fay and her father had moved ahead, dim in the shadows, then bright in the sun. Every wall was covered in artwork, nearly all paintings of bewitching, unsmiling creatures with piercing flat eyes. Everett was already standing before a particularly large canvas framed in flaking gold.

"Far be it from me to speak against my esteemed mother," he declared to no one in particular, "but I can't see the family resemblance."

Oh, but *I* could. *I* saw at once in the face of this long-ago marquess Armand's slanting eyebrows, Armand's beautiful long eyes, Armand's beautiful long lashes. True, their coloring was different— Christoff's hair was blond and his irises green, his complexion a warm tan—but there was so much of the boy I loved reflected in the features of this other *drákon*, I almost forgot to look at Rue.

She gazed back at me gravely, a porcelain doll with lustrous dark eyes and rich, flowing brown hair that rippled and curled all the way past her waist. They were both garbed in the elaborate fashion of their era, in shiny satins and starched lace; Rue's hooped skirts took up half the painting. But there was no powder covering their hair or their flawless skin, only jewels. Lots and lots of jewels. Just as a secret dragon might wear.

Look and admire us, Rue's eyes said. *We're only pretending to be what you see.*

She was real to me now. Not just faded words scrawled on paper, but a being with a face. With a soul.

"So," I said quietly, pressing my cheek to Mandy's shoulder. "Now we know who they are."

"Yes. Now we do."

The light bathed us in its snow-pale glow and the painted gemstones bedecking Rue and her husband seemed to catch it, to wink back at us. I rubbed a hand across my face, then straightened. Since Rue was real and Christoff was real, *all* of the *drákon* portrayed here, I realized, were likely related to Armand and Aubrey.

And maybe to me. Surely somehow to me.

I was eager suddenly to see them all. If I didn't dare scrutinize the living dragons in this castle to discover hints of my own origins, I could let myself inspect these paintings as much as I wished. They would never tell.

I moved down the hall, passing portraits of stately men and gorgeous women, of *drákon* children arranged in bunches like posies of sweet, dangerous flowers, everyone standing or seated and looking so serious. I scanned a few of the names inscribed upon the plaques at the bottoms of the frames, but mostly, I just looked at the faces.

I looked for me.

One oil had been hung off from the rest, with nothing else around it. It was even larger than the one of Rue and Christoff, dominating a particularly darkish section of the hall. I noticed it primarily because it appeared so deliberately shunned.

I walked over, curious.

The painting depicted yet another *drákon* husband and wife, their hands tenderly clasped, their wedding bands brightly prominent. They, too, were done up in the fashion of more than a century past, dripping with gemstones and lace. The artist's brushstrokes were graceful and detailed, and in nearly all respects the portrait resembled the others in the gallery, but for two very startling facts:

The husband in it was the man from my memory-dream in the taproom, dark-haired and smiling.

And the wife beside him was Honor Smith, my schoolmate, looking very much full grown.

CHAPTER 31

I SEE YOU FOUND THEM."

I had been standing there, open-mouthed, when the Alpha showed up beside me. I threw her an astonished glance.

"What?"

She nodded to the painting. "The last Zaharen prince and his bride. You were asking about *drákon* royalty last night, I believe? And I told you there were no more. These two ended the line. I made certain of that."

"What?" I gasped again, fainter now. I felt as though I could not quite catch my breath.

Certainly this isn't Honor. Certainly I do not know this dragon prince, I have never, ever seen him before—

"Prince Alexandru of the Zaharen, and his wife, Réz. They were contemporaries of Clarissa Rue and Christoff, as a matter of fact. Or of their children, actually. It was Kimber, the eldest son and heir of the Langfords, who took over the Zaharen after the prince and princess fled the castle."

Sandu, laughed the woman's voice in my head, and by God, in my memory now, didn't she sound more than a little like Miss Honor Smith?

Sandu.

I pressed a hand to my forehead. What on earth was happening?

I felt Armand approach; his strong, sturdy heartbeat. I felt the connection between us, that invisible thread that tied us, turn brittle with shock as he saw what I did.

"Fled?" he echoed. How could he sound so composed?

"Vanished, more like," replied Everett. "Because of her."

"What did she do?"

"She was a time weaver. The most treacherous one of us ever known. You wouldn't guess it, would you, just by looking at her. But she betrayed us, all of us, by joining with our human enemies. Did her best to hunt us down and wipe us out, down to the last infant. Makes one ill to consider it. Especially since she was born English, not even Zaharen."

"Oh, my God," I said out loud.

Everything, *everything*, was coming into horrifying focus.

She'd known about the castle and the prince and the Zaharen, but not that the Langfords lived here now.

She'd known that we'd seen her in the forest in Belgium, but not that it'd been last summer.

She'd even admitted the *drákon* were trying to kill her.

And Honor hadn't known how to waltz, I realized. For some

reason, that struck me as the most obvious clue of all. Why hadn't I considered it before? At the party at Tranquility, she'd told Mandy she didn't know the bloody *waltz*, the very *first* dance taught to any modern young woman.

Even just this morning: *We have no records of English runners from Darkfrith in recent history . . . .*

"She weaves through time, not just places," I said shakily. "She weaves through *time*."

The marchioness sent me a queer look. "Not any longer. Princess Réz is very much deceased. I saw to that myself."

Mandy said quietly, "Her name isn't Réz. It's Honor."

"Yes, her name was once Honor. How did you know? She was born Honor Carlisle, back in Darkfrith. She changed it after she came here."

I was backing up, preparing to fly, because my body already knew what would happen next, even as my mind was still struggling to understand it all.

"She *is* Honor Smith *right now*, and she is back in England *right now* with Aubrey." I faced Mandy, trying to contain to my panic. "We left her alone with Aubrey."

⁅ ❦ ⁆

HE WAS NOT A paperwork type of chap, and never had been. When Aubrey had first signed up for the RFC, he'd known that he'd be offered some sort of safe assignment, one designed to keep him as far from the front as possible. Most sons of the nobility were. But being a Brigadier-General's aide-de-camp sounded to him like nothing more than a long, dreary death by boredom. And it sure as hell wasn't why he'd joined.

Aubrey didn't know if it had something to do with his dragon nature or rather more his human side, but the tedium of ordinary life, the endless lists of forms and regulations and copies of things that needed to be copied and certified and copied again just to keep the Great Military Mechanism clicking along . . .

Good gad. How did anyone endure it?

He had been born to fly.

And he'd done it, too. For a few precious years, he'd had wings, albeit ones designed by man. And it had been magnificent. He'd been made for the sky; it had been his lover and his enemy and his best friend. He'd never been so free as when he'd sent his Sopwith up and up into the yonder, and never so at ease. Not even in the dogfights, with bullets whizzing past his ears and engine grease blown back thick across his face and German machine guns stuttering and the clouds hiding secrets and the sun a high, relentless eye that never shut.

Not even then.

Those days were done. He knew it in his blood, in his bones. He knew it by the skin covering his hands, pink and raw and paper-thin. He knew it by the fire that still smoldered in his lungs, by the toilsome breaths that kept his heart (mostly) pumping. His flying days were behind him, charred to cinders—along with his Sopwith

Pup—back in France.

And so.

Here he sat.

The paperwork he labored over now was heavy. His hands couldn't manage it, so he'd had the footmen stack the archived newspapers all along the surface of his desk. They teetered there in depressingly tall piles, book upon book of old, bound broadsheets, all on loan at his behest from libraries across London.

Slowly, Aubrey was making his way through them. At least he could flip the pages easily enough. When he was done with one volume, he'd summon a man to come and remove it, and then replace it with the next in the pile.

He kept a dish of water at his side, since wetting his fingers with his tongue to turn the pages had left the unpleasant taste of newsprint dry in his mouth. He kept a pot of coffee nearby, too. Studying page after page of steamship passenger lists and society columns nearly two decades old was about as invigorating as counting sheep.

He did it anyway. He did it to help Lora. He did it because although she loved his brother, and would marry his brother, Aubrey could not intentionally stop his own love for her, any more than he could intentionally stop his wrecked heart from beating.

Eleanore had been born on a steamship. Armand had thought that discovering her true name and family might somehow save her from the rest of the *drákon*. And thus, in this small way, *Aubrey* might save her.

It was all he could do.

He was well into the eleventh volume, his eyes glazing, when a discreet tapping sounded upon his door.

"Yes?"

"Pardon the intrusion, my lord." It was Matthews, his butler, staring fixedly at a point somewhere above Aubrey's head. "You have a visitor. A Miss Smith, from the school."

Aubrey uncurled a bit in his wheelchair, his spine creaking. "Oh?"

Now Matthews deigned to look him in the eyes. "She has neither an appointment nor a card, my lord. Shall I tell her you're not at home?"

Not at home. Like he would be anywhere else these days. Aubrey almost sighed.

"No. No, send her . . . in at once, if you please."

Honor Smith inched inside his quarters with an anxious, wary look, her blue eyes large and her frock so threadbare it was difficult not to feel sorry for her, even though she'd abandoned him and his brother and the glorious Lora to the mercies of the dragons of Darkfrith.

"Miss Smith," he said. "How delightful."

"I'm sorry. I would have—I mean, I *wouldn't* have . . ."

What she would or wouldn't have done was destined to remain a mystery, as her sentence only tapered away into an ungainly silence. She lingered near the doorway, rocking from one foot to the other, clearly ready to bolt. As he watched, her cheeks blushed into roses, then into cherries.

Whatever else had passed between them, she was young

and awkward and *drákon* like him, and it was surprisingly excruciating to watch.

Aubrey attempted a smile. "Please, do come in. Have a seat."

"Thank you."

"Tea?"

"Er, no. No, thank you. I've only come for this."

She nearly leapt in front of him, thrusting out her reticule with both hands. He looked from it up to her face, and watched the blush deepen into a shade not so far removed from actual blood.

"Sorry," she mumbled, and drew away again to fumble at the clasp. The reticule opened, revealing a thin stack of papers inside.

"I wanted to give them back," she said, pulling the stack free. "The letters from Rue. I didn't trust any other way to get them to you."

"Ah," he said, and accepted them from her. He twisted in his seat to place the bundle upon his desk. His gaze drifted across the open pages of the old broadsheets before him, and this time he did not repress his sigh.

"What are you doing with all those?" Honor Smith asked in a funny voice.

"Perusing." He grimaced but was able to marshal himself, facing her again without any particular expression. By her own wish, she wasn't one of them. It would be a mistake to treat her otherwise. "Thank you for your . . . visit, Miss Smith, and the letters. I trust you can . . . see yourself out?"

But she wasn't listening; she wasn't even meeting his gaze. Her attention had gone to the newsprint pages flat open on his desk—and the blush on her cheeks drained away to pallor.

She looked like a ghost. She looked petrified.

Aubrey glanced back down at the pages.

He didn't see it at first. It was a smaller photograph near the bottom of the sheet; a larger one of a steamer (*R.M.S.* Nikita Regina, read the caption, THE MOST LUXURIOUS LINER NOW TRAVERSING THE *ATLANTIC!*) had been placed above it. But he then saw it, the frozen-flash image of a man, a woman and a baby—the man frowning at the photographer, but the woman gazing down at her child with a dreamy smile—and the child itself, a bundled wisp of pale hair and eyes and that solemn rosebud mouth—

Aubrey felt light and dazed; that peculiar floating sensation that used to overtake him with the spinning of his Sopwith through the blue, eluding bullets and oblivion.

LIVERPOOL WELCOMES A SEA-BABY! DAUGHTER OF FIRST-CLASS PASSENGERS MR. & MRS. SANDU ZAREN, BORN AT SEA, COMES ASHORE FOR THE FIRST TIME.

The paper was dated May 24, 1898.

"I say." His fingers grazed the printed face of the young mother. "This woman looks exactly like you."

*   *   *

"STOP," COMMANDED THE ALPHA, moving to stand in front of me.

Through the buzzing in my ears, I barely heard her. The gallery was a realm of gray shadow, of spearing bright light. I needed to Turn, to Turn—

"Stop," she ordered again, flinty, and clamped her hands around my forearms. "Tell me what you know."

"I just *did*!" I shook her off. "Honor is there with Aubrey! With Lord Sherborne. She's been there at Iverson all this while, and we had no idea she was dangerous—"

"She's a student at your school?" cut in Lord Chasen.

"Yes! She's been there since classes started. You nearly caught her at the soirée. You nearly saw her, but she hid." I found Mandy's eyes, anguished. "And I *let* her."

The Alpha crossed to her husband, muttering something that I couldn't hear. Fay watched her parents with her arms hugged to her chest, and Lord Chasen scowled down at the floor.

"I am sorry," said the marchioness, facing me again. "I'll gather my guard and head out tonight, of course. But you need to understand that Lord Sherborne is likely already dead."

"No!" The word ripped from my throat, harsh and deep. "That can't be true! She had all this while to kill us if she wished. She never laid a finger . . ."

But I had to stop, because what I was going to say—*never laid a finger on us*—wasn't quite correct, was it? She'd held that knife to Aubrey's neck. She'd threatened to kill him right then and there. Perhaps the only reason she hadn't at that moment was because she'd been outnumbered.

She wasn't any longer.

"We must go *now*," I said.

The Alpha shook her head. "Miss Jones! *You're* not going any-where. You and your consort"—Armand received a derisive look—"will remain here, where it is safe. I will handle this situation."

"We're going too," Mandy said.

"You will slow us down, Lord Armand. We'll have no time to coddle you. And Miss Jones is far too precious to us—to all of us—to risk. If Honor Carlisle truly is back in England right now with your brother, as I said, her work is likely already done. We shall leave tonight."

"We're leaving now," insisted Mandy, through gritted teeth.

"If you are determined to be difficult, *boy*, I swear you will not enjoy the consequences. Do not imagine for an instant that I am unready to secure you both. One way or another, you shall remain at Zaharen Yce." The marchioness turned away, dismissing us, and moved to her son. "Send word to Marlowe. He'll contact the others. Tell him we—"

"Lora and I are leaving right now," Armand said, lifting up both arms. His eyes warned mine; I barely had time to cover my ears before he roared:

"Scream!"

THE DEAD MONSTERS WHO had constructed their castle of tears and ice had embedded a great many diamonds in its frame. There was also the white quartzite that made up the bulk of the fortress, of course; all along, the quartzite had been burbling its own minor refrain.

But in my experience, diamonds always sang loudest.

At Mandy's command, every single one of them, all the many thousands of them, rose into a sound that I could have never imagined, a horrific screeching dissonance that pierced my eardrums and buckled my knees.

I caught myself with a palm against the floor. I was smoke before my other palm could hit the stone, with Armand seconds behind me.

THE SCREAMING STILL HURT as we sped away. *That* was a surprise. Usually becoming smoke dulled all sorts of pain. Even so, within moments we'd found a way out of Zaharen Yce (up a chimney vent with a fire chuckling at its bottom, real woodsmoke all twisted up in us). I burst up into the sky like a missile, soaring north. Mandy was a sliver of gray beside me, scarily thin.

We had the advantage of minutes, at most. The last I'd seen of the Langfords, they'd been doubled over in pain, much as I had been. They might not understand what Armand had done, not at first, but it wouldn't take them long to realize the result.

So we couldn't stay as smoke. Dragons were at least twice as fast.

It was daylight, it was bright, and I decided to throw the *drákon*'s vaunted secrecy to the winds. I Turned to dragon, slowing just enough for Mandy to find my back. He Turned human, grabbed my neck, and we plunged on.

I WOULD DESCRIBE TO you the days and nights that followed. I would, but they were dreadful and exhausting and involved very little sleep, plus a gradual spread of frostbite on Armand's hands and knees until we managed to steal some clothing.

I didn't dare fly too low, because we'd be visible to anyone on the ground with a gun—which was very nearly everyone.

I didn't dare fly too high, because in the clean open light of the sun or the stars, we would be visible to any of the dragons who hunted us.

So I kept us inside the clouds every chance I could, enough so that we both ended up soaked and shivering and still pressing on.

In the sable dark, the stars would lilt, *threads unravel, time comes undone. hurry or be devoured. hurry for your farewells.*

Which was *not* helpful.

And Jesse, damn him, was nowhere to be seen.

A few towns beyond the terrible entrenched line of poisonous gas and flames and uncivilized death that was the front of the Great War, we stopped long enough to pick a pocket's worth of change from a drunken lieutenant, and used it to send a telegram.

AUBREY ALL NOT AS IT SEEMS STOP DO NOT
TRUST OUR FOURTH STOP SHE IS DANGEROUS
IN EXTREME STOP DO NOT TRUST LANGFORDS
EITHER STOP WE ARE ALL EN ROUTE STOP
DISAPPEAR IF YOU CAN STOP

It was a long shot. Getting messages across the Channel was more a matter of luck these days than of money, but it made us both feel better to try. Even if the wire did make it through, we'd likely show up only hours after—but those hours might mean the difference between a living Aubrey and a dead one.

As the sun rose and sank, as the moon smiled, I couldn't figure out why the Alpha and her guard weren't catching up with us. We did have a head start, but we were younger and greener and certainly less rested than any of them.

Then I realized she didn't need to catch up. After all, she knew exactly where we were going.

CHAPTER 32

ITWAS LATE AFTERNOON on a cold, sea-spangled day with dollops of high glossy clouds, and Armand and I were both smoke as we approached Tranquility. Everything looked normal from above; I didn't see any other suspicious bits of vapor lingering around, and all the soldiers and nurses appeared to be carrying on as usual. I actually began to let myself hope that we'd beaten the odds, that we had made it here first, when we corkscrewed down the chimney that led to Aubrey's quarters and Turned human, and Lord Chasen materialized in front of us and punched Mandy in the stomach.

It happened so fast. The room was unlit and the shadows were opaque and then just *there he was,* and Mandy bent in two with a rough gasping cough and I launched myself at Everett.

He was smoke before I could hit him. Smoke, man, smoke, man, and I could not keep up with him, and he struck Mandy again, this time across the jaw, but I was able to catch him in my arms before he fell.

We reeled back and smacked against Aubrey's desk, knocking apart towers of books that toppled noisily to the floor.

Everett stood before us without Turning, naked, sneering, not even breathing hard, his eyes an awful yellow glow.

"I would kill you, Louis, but we need you alive to quiet all those ruddy diamonds back home."

"Go to hell," Mandy snarled, holding his jaw.

The bedroom door opened. We all Turned; the maid who peered inside looked nervously left, then right (but not up, where three distinct clouds of smoke lingered against the ceiling). Her hand fumbled for the light switch.

"M'lord?"

"He's not in there," said a man's voice behind her. "What are you about, then, Millie?"

"I heard people arguing, I thought."

A footman shouldered in past the maid, glanced around (apparently not noticing all the toppled books), and shook his head.

"No one's here. Lord Sherborne called for a motorcar hours ago. Got some telegram this morning and took off."

The maid backed away. "It was ghosts, I reckon. Ghosts of this mad place."

"Ghosts! I never! Get back to work, girl. And don't go spreading stories, neither, or Matthews'll have your hide."

She fled. The footman snapped off the electric lights, closed the door. We all waited for the audible *snick* of the latch catching before Turning back.

"Ambush him again," I whispered furiously to Everett, "and I'll make you wish you were a gelding."

"I owed him that much, at least," Everett growled back. "For being such a goddamned liar. Was it your telegram?"

"Go to hell," Armand said again, not bothering to lower his voice.

"Where is your mother?" I asked.

Everett sent me that vivid yellow look, his gaze raking up and down my body.

"For God's sake." I stomped over to the bed, wrapped myself in one of the canopy curtains. "You can't blame us for lying to you. You lied to us as well. You fully planned to imprison us!"

"Only *you*. Your pet here would have been merely shooed away."

Armand leapt. Everett didn't bother to avoid him. I went to smoke again; that maid wouldn't be too far off, I'd wager. And anyway, I'd seen enough fistfights back at the orphanage to know that interfering now would likely only get me a stray blow to the face. At this point, Armand was giving as good as he got.

They skidded across some of the fallen books (actually old newspapers, I saw now, that had been bound into books), knocking them even more asunder. A ribbon poked out from the pages of the one nearest me.

A jade-green ribbon. Just like the one Aubrey had once wrapped around the gift box of a delicate metal dragon.

There was something written upon it.

I flowed downward to become a girl, crouching to pull it free.

Cottage + H, read the cramped, careful handwriting.

"Oh, no," I said.

I looked up at Mandy precisely as he looked down at me, and Everett clouted him across the head.

Armand crumpled.

I pushed to my feet, horrified. Everett turned to face me, wiping crimson from his mouth. His eyes still glowed.

"Marry me, and I swear I'll let him live free once I'm Alpha."

I dropped to my knees beside Armand and ran my fingers along his skull. An ugly welt was swelling along his temple—but he was breathing. He was breathing.

"Eleanore, kindly pay attention. As irksome as your whelp might be, I won't kill him unless I must. He has Gifts, and thus, he has worth. But be rational. You need to give him up. You know that."

"No," I was saying, still focused on Mandy. "No, no."

Everett sighed. "Off the top of my head, I can think of at least a dozen unattached girls in the tribe who would suit him better than you. He could have his pick. I'll even handle the introductions."

I looked up at last, caught between a laugh and a sob. "What are you *talking* about?"

His voice softened. "I'm talking about the natural order of things. I'm talking about who we are. You are unique, Eleanore. You are special, stronger than any other female of our generation, more Gifted. By the laws of our species, that already makes you mine."

Beneath my hands, Armand took a deeper breath.

"Sweet Promise," Everett said, squatting low beside me; he took my chin between his fingers. "Beautiful one. This is how we survive, by strongest mating to strongest. I knew it the instant I saw you that night, tackling the dirigible all by yourself. You're meant to be with me."

"I *love* him."

He smiled, almost wistful. "I believe you. But I suspect that, in the end, you'll come to realize that love is a human indulgence. We're beyond that. We're better. Love may follow for us, but solidarity must come first. And from solidarity . . ." He leaned nearer, still holding my chin. His lips grazed mine, firm and warm. " . . . comes power."

He pulled back, watching my reaction. His face was a study in grace, in shadow whiskers and comely, blood-smeared edges.

He was so very good-looking. And he left me so very cold.

"I'm going to make you happy," Everett murmured.

"No," I said again, fiercer, and Turned to smoke. I fled up the chimney once more.

← —❧— →

THERE WAS ONLY ONE cottage that I knew. Perhaps Aubrey had meant a different one; perhaps Aubrey, the treasured eldest son of a duke, had never ventured into the rugged, secretive woods of Iverson's island, where Jesse's old home still stood.

Walking there from Iverson would take at least a half hour.

Flying from Iverson—where the Alpha and her guard surely must now be, hunting for Honor—well, flying would get you there in the blink of an eye.

I hoped that Everett had abandoned Tranquility, and Mandy, to chase after me.

I hoped that Aubrey was where I thought he was, and that I could get there before Honor killed him, and that Everett never fully overtook me before I managed to lose him in the dark-bristled crown of the forest.

I hoped that, if I was wrong about any of this, Armand would awaken soon and discover the ribbon I'd pressed into his palm, and end up in the actual right place.

THE CHANNEL WINDS WHISKED me along, tugging me into loops and whorls. Everett *was* smoke behind me (I kept checking), but the winds had him too, and we were both struggling. Still, as soon as I crossed the waters that frothed between the mainland and the isle, I made a beeline for Iverson, pretending that was my goal. I remained aloft just long enough for Everett to register my direction, then dropped into the shadows.

I knew these woods. I knew the beeches and birches, the pines and oaks. How their trunks stretched, how their branches twisted, how their leaves and needles shuddered. I knew the bracken and the brambles and the woolly moss. I knew where the squirrels and the toads and the bugs all slept. Where the streams spilled black and smooth, and where the mists never fully lifted away.

So I became the mist, settled in with it in a bog surrounded by reeds, and forced myself into stillness.

A rook sprang free from a stalk above me, flapping up and up and gone.

Dusk began to fall, a slow purple darkening.

Everett did not appear.

I could wait no longer. I slipped free of the bog and made my way to Jesse's cottage.

CHAPTER 33

HAD ARMAND DIEGO LORIMER Louis, second offspring of a mad duke and a spellbound, forgotten *drákon*, been purely human of blood and spirit, the blow he had suffered to his head would have killed him.

Everett Langford, in his rage, had struck his rival square across the *fossa temporalis*, that tender and spare spread of bone more commonly known as the temple.

Armand's skull had fractured. His brain had been perforated; nerves were damaged. Blood had amassed in places it should not.

A human boy would have slid into a coma, and never awakened again. But Armand Louis was not human.

Not in the least.

With the last dregs of my magic, I willed him *back*.

CHAPTER 34

FROM THE OUTSIDE, THE cottage appeared vacant. I was extra-stealthy anyway, just in case there happened to be a member of the Langford clan slinking about. But all the windows shone dark and the shadows were unmoving, and I had no sense of anyone else nearby.

Blast.

I found the cracked windowpane and made my way inside. I did a swift, desperate tour of the main room, shooting from corner to corner.

It was empty. The kitchen was empty. The pantry and broom closet and coal bin—all empty. However . . .

It was dusky in here; it was always dusky, since the cottage had been built in the heart of the woods. But even in the twilight gloom I could trace the tracks that scuffed through the dust coating the floor. Several sets of tracks. I swept lower, studying them.

A long while ago, someone had walked barefoot through this

room—that would have been me. My footprints were already blurred with newer dust. But cutting through those was a more recent set of prints: one of girlish heeled boots (exactly like the ones supplied to us by the school), the other a series of lines forming long, snake-like marks.

Aubrey's wheelchair.

Not very long ago at all, Honor Smith had wheeled Aubrey into Jesse's bedroom; whether he had gone willingly or not, I could not say. The bedroom door was shut, and I discerned nothing from the other side. No voices, no rustling.

I went back to the kitchen, Turned to girl, and with the tips of my fingers tugged free the largest knife I saw from Jesse's mismatched set. It was a bread knife, long and serrated. Getting stabbed by it would definitely hurt.

As quietly as I could, I crept toward the bedroom door, wary of any little squeak from the floor. I pressed my ear to the wood, but there was still only silence.

No, wait. Did I hear . . . a heartbeat?

I licked my lips, counted to three in my head, then slammed open the door.

Aubrey sprawled dead on the bed, his wheelchair shoved to the shadows. His head lolled and his arms hung limp off the sides of the mattress, and the sight of him like that actually paralyzed me. I stood rooted in horror, just past the doorway.

It was all that Honor needed to slam into me from my left, trying to snatch the knife. I twisted in her grasp, Turned to smoke and escaped her and then Turned back and punched her, as hard as I could, in the face. Yet she was fast, *drákon*-fast; she ducked to the side, and my blow only glanced off her shoulder.

The knife had skidded across the floor. I dove for it, grabbed it, and had bounded to my feet with my arm an upward arc and the tip aimed straight for her belly, when my hand was smacked away, the blade deflected. Someone was yanking me backward, croaking *Lora! No, no, Lora, don't!* in a voice I barely registered at all.

It was Aubrey, standing with his arms wrapped around me. *Aubrey*, tottery and fighting to contain me and *not dead*, and I was hurting him though I didn't mean to, so my hand opened and the knife clanged back to the floor.

"She—" I panted, frantic, staring from him to her. "You—"

"If you kill her," Aubrey said to me, deep and very clear, "you will never be born."

"Oh, my God," I cried, clutching his shoulders. "I thought you were dead!"

"No." He pulled me closer, pressing his face to my hair. "No, my angel. No."

I was weeping, which was asinine, and Honor stood back and watched us both with a tense, unhappy expression and it was only then that everything that Aubrey had said settled over me.

I leaned back, taking in his bandaged face.

"What did you say?" I demanded.

Honor interjected, "He was asleep, by the way, not dead. I wouldn't harm him. I don't *do* that. I don't know why everyone keeps saying that I do."

"Never be born *what*?" I said, insistent, to Aubrey.

Whatever inner fire had been supporting him and restraining me, it deserted him then. Aubrey swayed and Honor and I both caught him and led him back to the bed. As soon as he was seated, I pushed her away from him with both hands.

She didn't fight me, only staggered back a few steps with her arms out for balance. The window behind her offered wild ivy and an amethyst sky, black pines reaching.

"I wouldn't harm you, either," she said. "I just didn't know who had come through the door."

"Righto," I scoffed, wiping at my cheeks.

Aubrey was still struggling to breathe. "Didn't you . . . see the photograph? With the ribbon? Marked . . . the page."

"No, I just—I only saw the ribbon. What photograph? What are you talking about?"

His gaze went to Honor. She slanted me a strange smile, then stepped forward and stuck out her hand.

"Hullo. It seems that I'm your mum."

"Bugger *you*," I retorted, and she actually laughed.

Aubrey twitched on the bed, dark against the paler covers. "Eleanore. Fireheart. Swear it's . . . true."

In the silence of the twilight, Honor's hand gradually lowered to her skirt.

"It's true," Aubrey said again, calm and powerful and in that deep, carrying voice that must have been his all along.

"*No,*" I burst out, anguished. "It can't be her. Not *her*. She's the enemy! She tried—is trying to kill all the *drákon*. All of our kind. They told me so!"

"No," said Honor.

"Then why do they hunt you?" I flung my hand to the window. "They're out there right now, a whole host of them right outside, combing this island for you so they can execute you!"

"I don't know. I don't know what I've ever done to them. They've always hunted me."

I searched for the lie on her face. "There's got to be a reason."

"I fled the shire so that they would not kill me. I stay hidden in Barcelona so that they will not kill me. I never seek them out. I never go near them. That's the truth. Until now, the only dragon I *ever* Weave to is the prince. Sandu. Your . . . your father. And I would sooner end my own life than harm him in any way. Or you," she added.

And I could not see the lie.

"Lora," rasped Aubrey from the bed.

True, he mouthed.

I pressed both palms over my heart.

"What happened to you?" I whispered. "What happened to us all? Why did you—why did you abandon me?"

I didn't realize what I had asked until the words were already beyond me. I didn't realize I had voiced the deepest agony of my being until the words were already spoken, given form and life, and I could not take them back.

But Honor Carlisle only lowered her gaze, shook her head. Her heels tapped the floor as she came closer. Inches apart, we became exactly the same height, even though she was in boots and I stood in my bare feet. The purple night gleamed along the copper of her hair.

"I Weave back and forth, but I can't control it. I never know where or when I'll wind up, or why." One hand reached out, took hold of mine. Her fingers felt slim and cold. "I haven't been to our future yet, so I don't know what's to become of us. I'm sorry. I genuinely didn't know who you were—who you *are*—until I saw that photograph of us in the broadsheet back at Tranquility. But as soon as I saw that baby in my arms, I knew she was you."

She brought my hand to her mouth, pressed a kiss to the back of it.

My body began to tremble. I was aware of it, unable to stop it, and I hated it, hated that I was weak now when I needed to be strong and figure things out. And then Honor had gathered me to her and wrapped her arms around me and, damn it, I was really crying now, silently and furiously, with my mother's slim, cold fingers tangled in my hair.

Her shirtwaist was scented of Iverson, and of me and my tears, and of her. Time and mystery.

"I cannot imagine how this happens," she murmured, her head tucked against mine. "I cannot imagine how Sandu and I lose you. The future is always a revelation to me."

I pulled away suddenly. "You can't stay here."

"No," she agreed, as if she'd only been waiting for me to realize it.

"They'll find the cottage eventually. They'll figure out you're not at Iverson and maybe overhear someone talking about how Aubrey came for you—"

"Told Westcliffe . . . we were going to Bath. See . . . my father. Scholarship interview. Had the chauffeur . . . drop us off out of view. Drive on."

"Westcliffe believed you?"

He shrugged. Honor tipped her head toward the window; she released me to walk over to it.

Aubrey's lie might work, I supposed. The duke *was* in Bath, and he *did* control the scholarships, and the headmistress knew he had summoned me there before.

"All right," I said. "We wait until full dark. I'll smoke out of here and make sure there's no one about, then we'll sneak off the island together and head for—for London. London's a labyrinth, and I know corners the Langfords will never think to search. We can send word to Mandy from there." I glanced at Honor, still staring out at the woods. "St. Giles isn't very pleasant, but it's a lot safer than here."

"No," she said quietly.

"Honor! Don't be an idiot. We've got to—"

"No, Eleanore. I'm sorry, but it's too late." She turned about to face us, slender and small and stained in purple. "They're already here."

CHAPTER 35

AND THEY WERE.

I saw now what Honor had sensed moments ago: the new, ominous shadows amid the shadows, people-shaped and . . . not.

Eyes glowed from the dark, eldritch and huge. The forest trembled. I couldn't tell how many of them were out there, but it was certainly more than we three.

We were trapped inside a house that might as well have been made of matchsticks. Any one of the dragons outside could likely destroy it (us) with the swipe of a foot.

I swallowed, looked at Aubrey. "I'm sorry. I have to."

He did not move from the bed. "I know."

I opened the front door and remained there, making certain Honor stayed behind me. The Alpha stood a few paces away, her long, dark hair cloaking her body, her eyes burning red coals. Everett, human again, stood just beyond her.

A night breeze nuzzled me; my skin went to gooseflesh.

Just the cold, I told myself. *I can do this. I am not afraid.*

Liar, mocked my heart.

"You cannot kill her," I said aloud. "I won't let you."

The marchioness locked those unholy red eyes on mine. "I had credited you with slightly more intelligence than this, Miss Jones. I don't know what she's told you, what nonsense she's stuffed in your head, but you have no hope of changing this ending. I allow that you are important to us, and I do not wish to damage you. Do the clever thing now, child, and step away."

"I won't let you," I said again.

The dragons around us shifted, razorblade talons piercing the earth, massive bodies crowded against the trees. Miles above us, the sea winds moaned, but the stars blazed in silence.

The marchioness's voice slipped into that chilly, silken tone, even as it seemed her eyes scorched hotter.

"Eleanore, you must listen to me now, because I am about to act purely in the best interests of us all. Believe me when I tell you that you do not know who this creature truly is, or the atrocities of which she is capable."

"I know exactly who she is. She's my—"

"I am an innocent," Honor interrupted loudly, pushing around me. I caught her by the wrist before she could leave the front step. "Entirely innocent of your slander. I've never harmed anyone, nor do I plan to. All my life, I've wished only to be left alone."

Everett smiled. "That will never happen."

"That's what I thought," I said, and with my next heartbeat I Turned to dragon, snatched up my mother in my right front claws, and ascended into the night.

It wasn't as easy as that, of course. I had to Turn just beyond the doorway because I was big and it was not, and the Alpha and Everett fell back and went to smoke, and (although I had tried not to) the barbs on my tail ripped furrows along the face of Jesse's cottage, smashed a window, and tore off a sizable chunk of the roof. I was registering all of that while vaulting straight up from a complete standstill *and* clutching a tender soft person in my talons. My wings ached and my lungs burned and my heart throbbed.

But I did it.

We cleared the trees and headed for the stars. Honor held fast, both arms clenched around my leg.

The other *drákon* followed at once, but all as smoke. If they stayed that way I had a real chance of out-distancing them, and perhaps London would work, after all. Or Bournemouth, or Edinburgh, or the North Pole. *Anywhere* else, as long as I could lose them behind me.

I banked toward the towers of Iverson, betting they would not risk becoming dragons so close to the school.

I was wrong.

As I swung near a turret (perhaps I could loop about to confuse them? hide amid the buttresses?) the air went *shooosh* above my head; the slick, shiny shadow of a beast blotted out the purple heavens, larger than I, black as pitch; only the Alpha's eyes revealed her. She darted ahead of me and then writhed downward, attempting to force me to the ground. As I cut left, another dragon rose up from nowhere to almost crash into me: black and red and green, grinning his terrible grin.

I flapped right instead, wobbling, and Honor let out a stifled scream. I grasped her more tightly, then hastily relaxed my grip again—I could barely feel her in my claws. If I accidentally stabbed her, I wouldn't know until it was too late.

Over and over I dodged them, attempting without success to break free to open sky. So far they were the only two to take their dragon forms, but there was smoke everywhere, and no question that I was besieged.

Help me, I pleaded to the stars. *Jesse, help!*

But he wasn't there, and not one of the others answered.

I dipped low toward the sea, low enough to taste salt on my tongue and feel the sting of it along my lashes, then zoomed swiftly upward—yet nothing I tried shook them from my tail. I simply wasn't as *good* at this as bloody Everett and his mother. They had years of flying experience while I had less than even one, and I was already flustered and panting. Every time I managed to shoot toward the mainland, they beat me back. It had been well over a week since I'd fully rested and, by God, I felt it. Likely that was their plan, to wear me out until my wings cramped up and I had no choice but to descend.

We had exactly zero chance of escaping them on land.

I risked a glance at Honor; she gazed back up at me with a miserable face. No doubt she'd worked that out, as well.

My only hope was the fortress, then. All those lamp-lit windows, all those students and professors tucked inside, ready witnesses to every raw bit of reality I hoped the Alpha was not prepared for them to see . . .

Let them hound me *there*, in open view, if they dared.

I targeted Iverson once more, heading straight for its limestone walls and pretty lights. If I could force the Alpha and Everett to Turn back to smoke, if I could gather enough speed—

Something struck me on the head. Struck me *hard*, hard enough to blank my vision and numb my body. Someone was screaming, though, and I heard *that*: a shrill, tinny sound that bounced through me and burst into balloons, green and puce and white, behind my eyes.

I opened my wings and lifted us up, right as we were about to smack into the ground. We swooped above something my muddled brain identified as familiar (*thorns, paths, cold mulch, withered petals tossed behind me in a storm*), and then higher.

The Alpha dove toward me again, whipping her tail at my head.

That's what had struck me, the end of her tail. Lethal enough, but at least not barbed as mine was. I ducked the next blow, only just, but she swung about without pause and came at me again. Honor released another scream—full-throated, nothing stifled about it at all—and the third blow got me across the neck, sending us sideways.

Everett lunged beneath me, snapping at Honor. I jerked away awkwardly, fixing desperately on Iverson. I had to—

time, came an unexpected chorus from the stars. *we come to your time, fireheart.*

Something new sliced toward me. A third dragon. I had the Alpha above and Everett below and nowhere much else to go, because Iverson was now too far away to be useful. I glared at the third dragon, my heart sinking; if more of them were willing to Turn now, we were done for. Honor and I were about to die together.

we come to your time.

Number Three was not so subtly colored as the others, conspicuous in blue and gold, sapphire scales rimmed in perfect gilt. His head angled to find me, dagger wings glimmering, luminous blue eyes and—and—

And it was Armand.

Armand.

If I could have screamed myself, I would have. I would have screamed and wept and called out his name to the wild violet sky.

He shot up like a bullet and slammed into the Alpha. I heard the strained cough of her exhalation, the hard hiss of his. Everett lunged after Honor again, and this time I barely managed to pull her away as his teeth cracked closed.

I went into a spin, at first by accident, then I had the hang of it and kept going. I slipped past Everett and under the marchioness and Armand, and now I *was* near Iverson.

time come . . .

I flew so close and reckless to a window, I almost broke the panes. As it was, I saw my own reflection in it, swift and bright, and beyond my reflection were the shadowy smears of people, real regular human people, students or professors or maids and I just needed them to *look up, look out, look at me—*

time undone . . .

The two dragons battling above me crashed into the castle. A heavy shape whistled down and down past my right, a stone missile haloed with dust: one of the merlons that decorated the very top edges of the roof. It struck the boulders at the base of the cliffs with an explosion that likely shattered glass for miles around.

That would bring them outside—that would *surely* bring them outside—

Everett, at least, thought the same. He snapped his jaws at me again but Turned to smoke as the main doors swung open and people began to spill out along the drive. Voices rose in a babble through the dark.

I climbed to find Armand. He and the Alpha were locked in a deadly embrace, wings batting, claws flashing, scales winking silver-dark-silver in the starlight.

I had to help him. The Alpha was yanking them higher, I could see that. If they got high enough, more of them would Turn and Armand would be killed, but I still had Honor in my grip and no safe place to leave her.

I—

Without warning, I was somewhere else. Without warning, the universe shifted into breathless black, into a cold tugging sensation near my belly.

No, not my belly; it was by my leg—

I was no longer flying but floating, suspended. I looked down at

Honor and she looked up at me. Against the inky void, every inch of her shone bright as a flame.

What—? I would have said, but I was still a dragon, and as a dragon I had no voice.

"Oh," is what my mother said for both of us. She smoothed her hands along the scales of my leg, curved her fingers along my talons. Her hair swayed loose and wavy around her face, as though she drifted underwater.

"Oh," she said again, wide-eyed. "Goodbye! Goodbye! I love—"

My talons closed shut.

She was gone.

A roar spilled through me, deafening. The universe shifted back into purple and stars and smoke and dragons. I had weight again. I realized that I was not breathing, that I had forgotten to breathe— and then the universe tasted of sea mist and stars.

I swiveled about, searching for Honor, but I knew I wouldn't find her.

I had not dropped her. She had not Turned. The Weave she had wanted so badly had finally come for her, that cold black thing, and it had, for the smallest moment, swept us both in. It had let me go, but pulled her all the way to Somewhere Else. Some*time* Else. Now she was just . . . vanished.

Like she'd never been.

A blast of wind shoved me left, strong as a train; I shook my head and fought to regain my bearings. But my wings weren't working as they should. They weren't working at all, in fact.

And I'd stopped breathing again.

time, came the chorus once more, both joyous and sad, barbarous and soft. It echoed across the heavens, carved the wind into hurricane swirls. *fireheart, who belongs to us: the deal was struck. your time is now.*

Oh, I thought.

A whip-wicked beast of sapphire and gold raced toward me through the night. I saw my hands reach out for him. Human hands, belonging to a human body, with no wings attached.

The stars were above, below, above again. The Channel glittered and spun, and still I reached for dragon-Armand, who plunged after me as I fell, his wings tucked and a snarl on his lips.

Goodbye, I would have called to him. I don't know; perhaps I did. *Goodbye. I love you.*

That savage, beautiful face became the last sight granted me from my mortal life.

Honestly, I could not have asked for more.

CHAPTER 36

HERE IS THE SCENE that no one on Earth remembers, but that I have seen recorded and played out over and over in stardust and forfeited memories:

Samuele felt so peculiar. Her body felt light and hot, but her head felt thick and fat, stuffed with yarn. From her perch on the side of the bed, Mama had kissed her forehead and announced that it wasn't a fever . . . but the worried look she'd given Papa as she'd said it made Sam wonder.

What was worse than a fever?

Sam was ten and not dumb. Fevers could kill, even their kind. *Especially* their kind. Papa had told her once it was one of the few human illnesses that could.

She sighed, fretful. She didn't like being stuck in this strange little bed in this strange little room. The hotel was noisy and stank of unwashed people and fetid cigars, and the London street outside her window never seemed to fall into silence. The sheets itched. Papa had had business in the city and Mama had wanted to come this time and Samuele went wherever they went, always, and anyway, wasn't London exciting? Weren't there libraries and street fairs and confectionery shops that sold candies so delicious, they might have been conjured by sugar fairies?

But now she hated that they'd come. She missed her own, actual bedroom back home. She missed the moors and the granite tors and the smoky-soft heather that stretched forever and a day around their house. She missed it all with a sudden piercing anguish, so much so that her face went tight and tingly, and it seemed like her heart might burst.

There were mice in the walls here. Mice scrambling around under her skin, gnawing at her bones.

She was panting. She kicked off the prickly sheets; she was so hot.

Mama and Papa had retreated to the sitting room. Through her own wheezy gasps Sam could hear them talking, though not quite all that they said.

Mama: . . . *heard of it come to anyone so blessed young?*

Papa: . . . *my sister. I should have thought . . . such a lifetime ago.*

Mama: . . . *suffer it. We have to help her.*

Papa: *You know we can't.*

A cold, intense pain sliced through her, so keen it diced her into pieces. It hurt so badly that she couldn't even scream; there was only a tiny gurgling squeal trapped in her throat.

Another mouse inside her, mad to get out.

The muscles of her neck and back went to wood, thrusting her head against her pillow. Her body arched into an impossible bow. She heard the sound of the sheets ripping as her fingers tore into the bed.

Oh, God, it hurt, *it hurt, IT HURT!*

She managed a scream, after all. It came out shrill and cut short, because all at once she no longer had a mouth. She no longer had anything—a head or body or throat—but the pain.

From a tall floaty distance, Sam saw her parents hurry into the room. She saw their faces turn upwards. Mama raised both hands up high as though to pull down—Samuele? the sky?—her eyes brilliant with tears.

Oh, how she wanted to reach back. She tried but she was nothing now, nothing to reach or pull, not any longer. Her entire self was smoke and agony.

"Turn back," Mama implored, still reaching. "Dear one, you must fight it. Turn back."

"Samuele," said Papa softly, his face grim and blanched. *"Draga mea. Nu este ziua ta de a muri."*

(my darling. it is not your day to die.)

From her tall floaty distance, smoke-Sam saw the door leading to the hotel hallway ease open. A woman crept inside, slinky, sinister, swathed in shadows and silence. Her eyes were glowing red poppies; there was something forged of metal in her hand. A gun.

Look out! Sam would have shrieked, but she, too, was locked in silence.

"Found you," the woman said.

Papa spun about, his jacket flaring. Even as he spun, the woman fired. Mama screamed, and Papa collapsed to the ground.

The woman aimed the gun at Mama. "You really ought to have switched solicitors, you know. And Prince Alexandru ought to have been far more careful about being followed."

"What have you done?" Mama cried.

"Corrected a problem that should have been corrected ages past. Will you Weave away now, outlaw, while he yet breathes?"

Mama stood frozen.

"No," said the woman calmly, "I thought not. Your last sighting, nine years ago, was with a baby. You were heard to call him Samuel. Where is he?"

And Mama stood frozen.

The woman fired her gun. Mama jerked back, clutching her left arm.

"I understand your reluctance," the woman said, "but I'm going to kill him either way, quick or slow. It's up to you. Where is the child?"

"Dead," Mama said, her voice shaking. Blood spilled around her fingers, dribbled down the silk of her sleeve. "Last December. From the Turn."

"How very fortunate for him. Any other progeny, my princess?"

"No," Mama choked out. "There were—complications. From the birth."

"Good," replied the woman, and pulled the trigger again.

But Mama was trickier than that, and rushed the woman. Sam tried to follow, yet she was thin and churning and couldn't manage to slide forward more than a few feet. Only Mama reached her. The gun fired again, and again, but Mama didn't fall; she and the woman were battling, fists and knees and guttural noises, and there were more people surrounding them now, more shadows and grunts and glowing eyes and the lump of them hit the table near the door. The oil lamp upon it smashed against the floor, and the rug was straightaway aflame.

The gun fired once more. The bullet tore through smoke-Sam to embed in the ceiling, and the tunnel it carved into her overtook the agony, sent her spiraling into black nausea. By the time she could pull herself free of it, the entire hotel suite was blazing, an orange-shimmering-scream that shook the world.

Where was Mama? Where was Papa? She heard people yelling and felt the thunder of running feet. Tasted, somehow, the sweaty panic of all the humans fleeing the hotel.

"Leave them," the woman shouted.

Samuele forced herself toward the voice.

"I said, *leave them*, now! We've done our job. They're dead, and everyone will think it was the fire."

A man coughed out, "Are you sure?"

"Damned sure. Follow the plan. Regroup at Far Perch, and we'll . . ."

That was all Sam could make out. She kept going though, lower, and there was Papa on the floor with his arms flung wide, his chest soaked in blood. She draped over him, useless as a wish. Flames danced along his feet.

Be me, Sam commanded herself, frantic. *Be me again! Me!*

But she remained smoke.

Someone moaned. It was Mama, also on the floor, closer to the windows. Ash from the burning curtains wafted up and down and around, blackening her face, her neck. A pool of crimson spread like opening wings beneath her back.

"Baby," she whispered, her eyes rolling. Her fingers quivered, and Sam pressed herself down to them, covered them, desperate to feel and be felt. Mama blinked hard, then focused on the cloud that was her daughter. More blood bubbled up between her lips. A tear cleared a path down her cheek.

"*Noia valenta . . .*"

(brave girl)

" . . . hide. Don't . . . don't return home. Hide."

Me, Samuele tried to roar. *Be me! Be me! Be me!*

"Fly away," sighed her mother, and closed her eyes.

She drew a shuddering, final breath.

Then the windows exploded, and the *drákon* smoke-child was sucked out into the night, whirling and wheeling.

Princess Réz of the Zaharen, née Honor Carlisle, did not plan for her ultimate breath to take in a slender, smoky fragment of her only offspring.

But that's what happened anyway.

And with that breath, she drew into herself her daughter's memory—just a strand of it. Just the girl's name, and her golden youth, and the violent passing of her parents.

Four days later, miles and miles away from the burned hulk of that hotel, a bedraggled child would be discovered wandering the streets of St. Giles. She would be rescued by a tinker, and then a constable, and then sent to an orphanage. She would be given a new name.

Given a new fate.

And then she would be given to me.

CHAPTER 37

HE TORE AFTER HER with a speed he hadn't known could exist, with a ferocity that felt like fire in his blood, or cocaine, or elation. He couldn't tell. All of his being, all of Armand's self had honed down to the fine-tipped apex of this moment. To this:

Save her.

Lora fell with her eyes open and her body limp. She wasn't reaching for him any longer; she seemed unconscious. The dark smear below her that had been background before became the crested peak of the forest in a nightmare rush.

Armand stretched. He was still new to this body, new to everything about it, but the golden claws that snagged in her hair *felt* like his own, and the way he pulled her up to him as they dropped—hair, arm, waist—*felt* like what he should do, an extension of his intent, his will. His desperation to rescue them both from the trees about to skewer them.

With Lora cradled to his chest he was able to open his wings and pull up not-quite-in-time; his back feet and tail struck a swath of pines, smarting his bones.

The trees shattered. It sounded like a barrage of gunfire going off in his wake.

He heard the sea, and human shouts, and the stars singing some wordless dirge. He heard a pod of seals screaming from below the cliffs, even more panicked than the humans.

A clearing came into view; he landed in it clumsily. It was actually more of a sideslip than a landing, with chunky streamers of grass and soil lobbed into the air behind him. It was, after all, his very first time.

As the grit settled, he laid Eleanore carefully upon the ground. Her eyes were still open. Her lips were parted. She did not move.

He opened his mouth, meaning to say her name, and before it had fully sunk in that he couldn't, he suddenly could: he was human again himself, crouched beside her. The air was pungent with the aroma of tilled earth.

"Lora. Lora."

He cupped her face in his palms. She had gone to wax, cool and lifeless. Three small holes dotted her ribcage where his talons had got her, but the holes didn't bleed.

"Eleanore Jones!"

His hands patted her cheeks, searched for a heartbeat in her chest. She wasn't—

"At your left, Lord Armand."

She wasn't—

Someone knelt beside him. A woman's hand pushed through the purple-gleam spill of Lora's hair to the side of her neck, pressed two fingers against her jugular. The woman sighed and eased back.

"No," Mandy said, bewildered, although no one had asked him anything.

The woman stood. Her feet were very pale against the dirt.

"Such a waste," she murmured.

ours, hummed the stars.

But Lora wasn't *bleeding.* She wasn't *hurt.* She wasn't even bruised, not that he could see, so why wasn't she breathing? Why were her eyes so glassy and her chest so still, why couldn't he feel her heart?

A man noted, dispassionate, "Those wounds to her ribs look too shallow for it."

"It must have been the work of the Time Weaver." The Alpha's bare feet shifted. "It must have been that girl somehow, before she Wove away."

Armand looked up. He was encircled by freshly shorn branches and ruined bracken and a handful of solemn, rapt *drákon.*

"I told her to step away," the Alpha said now. She wasn't speaking to Mandy at all, but to Chasen, yellow-eyed and two figures away. "I gave her fair warning. More than fair. I don't know why she didn't listen."

Mandy surged to his feet. He tackled Chasen hard enough that they both lost skin to the ground. He barely felt any of it, his blows, Chasen's, the hands and arms that yanked them apart and kept them that way. He went to smoke to escape them, poured himself back into human shape and was swinging his fist again, when the Alpha stepped in front of him and leveled him with a look.

"Your quarrel is with me, not my son."

Rage exploded through him, but her instincts were sound: he wouldn't strike a woman, not even her. He jerked free of whoever was struggling to restrain him and dropped back down beside Lora, gathered her to his chest.

It was Lora and not Lora. It was the empty shape of the girl he loved, a hollow husk pressed against his skin. The wind puffed and tendrils of her hair lifted with it, stroking his arm; the rage eating through him began a slow, horrific slide into something else.

She wasn't dead because she could *not* be dead.

She wasn't—

Her head rolled back against the crook of his arm. Her gaze fixed up at nothing.

"We must go now," said the Alpha.

Armand ducked his face to Lora's, closed his eyes against her cheek.

"All of us," the Alpha said. "This island is small and there are already men searching the woods. We caused a commotion. It's not safe to stay."

"Go, then," he said, without lifting his head. "Go, you bastards."

"All of us," she insisted.

"I will not leave her."

"No. And you cannot take her, either. We must give her to the sea."

A laugh escaped him, low and mirthless.

"Think," the marchioness said, more gently now. He heard her move to stand beside him, felt the barest pressure of her palm atop his shoulder. "She cannot be buried out here. There's no time for it, nor is there space. A grave on this isle will be discovered sooner rather than later. If we take her far out into the Channel, she becomes part of the waves. Part of the water. We are the pinnacle of nature's ambition, Lord Armand. It is fitting that we return to nature in the end. At Zaharen Yce, we leave our dead to the mountains. At Darkfrith, we become part of the vales. We must give Miss Jones to the sea. It's a more noble goodbye than anything that could happen to her here."

From a not-so-far distance, he heard twigs snapping. Men's voices. Footfalls trudging through the leaves and roots of the forest floor.

No, he thought, another answer to a question no one had asked.

No, this could not be real. No, he could not take her. No, he could not leave her. No, no, no, and Lora's long hair slipped once more along his arms, silken and teasing.

"Go," he repeated, but this time he lifted his head. The Alpha stroked her hand down his face; the tips of her fingers felt burning cold. She flicked away his tears.

"I'll do it," Armand said. "I'll take her out to sea. Alone."

Chasen began, "I want to—"

"Alone!" Armand snarled. "She was mine, not yours. I do this alone."

"You have no—"

"Everett," said the Alpha.

With a long, blazing look, Chasen backed down.

The marchioness returned her gaze to Armand. "We'll wait for you here as smoke."

"Don't bother."

"Lord Armand, despite your lies and your flagrant disobedience of my orders, you are of value to the tribe. You can Turn to dragon; too many of us can't. You can control the singing of stones, and I've never heard of another *drákon* with that Gift. From this night on, your life is no longer your own. If Miss Jones belonged to you, then you now belong to me, you and your brother both. My guard and I will await you here in this clearing, as smoke. When you return, we shall all fly to London tonight, to my residence there. And tomorrow we shall . . . hammer out the details, if you will, of our pact."

"Pact," Mandy echoed, flat.

"Provided we come to a mutual agreement, I believe your brother may be left in peace. You, however, will reside with us, and will choose a new mate from among our kind."

Lora's hair slipped and danced, brushed secrets across his skin. The men in the woods were tromping closer. A dog began to bay.

The Alpha gave his shoulder a final squeeze. "In time, you will understand this moment. You will recognize the wisdom of our ways, and you'll see how all will become well once again."

"Fuck you," Mandy said.

"One last thing. A small formality. Armand Louis, by the laws of the tribe, I hereby bind you. Do you yield to me, and to the will of the council?"

The dog got louder.

"Do you yield? Say yes."

"Yes."

"Take her now," the Alpha whispered, and Turned to smoke.

⊱ ⊰❖⊱ ⊰

SHE WAS A FEATHER in his fist. She weighed next to nothing, but at the same time, her body felt like a stone that had been lashed to his heart. Armand was certain that when he let her go, he would sink right along with her.

The Channel sloshed and splashed in silvery bursts; he was far enough out that he had no sense of land in any direction. The arc of the heavens had fallen silent. The stars still dazzled, but it seemed none of them had anything more to say.

Mandy concentrated on sailing lower, and lower still. He clutched his true love to his chest and let the water have them both.

A shock of cold. The bitter bite of salt. He Turned to boy and treaded water while still clutching her, and the stone-of-Eleanore tugged against his grip. Wanting to sink.

Mandy drew her closer instead. He brought his lips to hers. He'd done this once before, last summer, the first time they'd both tumbled into these waters and nearly drowned. But he'd kissed her then and had felt his world torch. He kissed her now and felt nothing.

There was nothing of Lora, nor his world, left.

His hands opened. She floated backward for a moment with both arms out; it was almost as if she treaded water, too. But the next wave washed over her face, and the next her head, and then all he could see of her were the glistening ends of her hair as the sea drew her down into oblivion.

Follow, commanded his dragon heart.

no, rise up, commanded the stars, animate again.

For a long while, Armand did neither. He pitched in place until his body grew numb and his pulse began to stutter.

up! demanded the stars.

In the end, his body decided for him. Without willing it, without not willing it, Mandy went to smoke, and let the winds push him where they wished.

What did it matter, anyway? What did anything matter anymore?

CHAPTER 38

T'S DARK. I INHALE, and smell the ocean.

"Isn't it funny," Jesse says, "to be offered all the time that spans eternity, and to have none of it left?"

"What?" I say, and open my eyes.

I'm seated at the edge of a cliff, my feet dangling over a drop that seems to have no end. I think it's one of the island cliffs, but I'm not certain. It looks right and not right: the edge is so sheer, and the beach below is so distant, and the colors of everything are so vibrant, ocher and azure and streaks of gold.

Jesse sits beside me, feet also dangling. He looks just as he did back in—

(what? what was it we had?)

—life. One of his hands clasps mine.

The air feels summery and soft. Clouds race above the faraway waves; I can see the curtains of rain that drape behind them, sky to sea, in blue slanted tails.

"Is this home?" I ask.

Jesse smiles. "Yes and no."

I glance around. The island greensward and trees behind us are not entirely themselves, either. They're wilder somehow, more supple. The beeches have leaves so lovely and perfect they nearly hurt my eyes. A breeze sighs along the ground, and all the blades of emerald grass swish and still.

Swish and still.

At the brink of the woods, a runner of wildflowers blooms in spiky magenta.

Jesse says, "I think this is the place that might have been home."

"I like it," I say.

"Me, too." He looks down at our feet, both of us kicking at the air. "So we have it for a little bit."

"What do you mean?" I'm frowning because I'm trying to remember something. It tickles me like the breeze, nudging and pushing.

"Time," he says again. "It's never really been our friend."

This, for some reason, makes me laugh, and then Jesse does too. He lifts our joined hands, turns them over so that our palms brush the sky.

"Lora-of-the-moon, you and I were promised this; we have this; we will have had it. Time can't steal away any of that. But we're not meant to linger. This is a temporary dream, a bridge between souls and desires. It can't last."

"Heaven!" I exclaim, because now I remember. "This isn't heaven?"

"No. This is our small moment that has been laid before it."

"I'm not . . ." I struggle to find the word. Why is it so hard? "Not . . . dead?"

"Oh, you are. You and I both. A bargain was struck, and you've honored it. Now I'm honoring mine."

Sugar dusts the royal blue sky, tiny sparkling grains that float lazily downward.

No, not sugar, I realize, watching them. Stars.

"But you already have," I say, pulling my hand free. "You did that. You gave your life for me, and for Armand, and the school, and everyone!"

"Human life," he acknowledges, lowering his lashes. "But I had something more to give."

I'm shaking my head. I want to say *no*, and *don't be absurd*, and *no one can give up their soul*, but the words won't free themselves from my tongue.

"Not my soul," he says, reading my thoughts. "Not that, beloved. The *other* life. The shining one."

The stars are falling, falling. Jesse points to a spot far out at sea.

"Look there, Fireheart. Do you see it?"

I squint against the sugar-stars and light. "See what?"

"Tilt your head some. Don't try so hard; it's there, waiting for you. That shimmer, that space—it's a glimpse into another universe."

And then I do see it. The sea and sky wink away; in their place is a room that looks like it belongs in a hotel, perhaps. There is a couple standing within it. There is a young girl with no-color hair, panting in a bed.

I watch their story unfold and feel my heart drop.

"Poor Honor," I say, and I mean it. "Poor prince and princess."

"Yes, the end of their mortal lives swept over them without mercy. But they considered their years together worth every sacrifice, and the ones spent with you their best of all. They showered you with love, and even though you never remembered, the gift of that love shaped who you became. Who you are, and how *you've* loved: fiercely, unbound and unfettered. Now, look over there."

He gestures to a new wink of space, a new shimmer.

"It's Armand?" I ask, but I don't know why I made it a question, because I can see that it's him.

He sits alone in shadow. His head is bowed. There are wraiths of people flitting rapidly around him, forming and dissolving, but he never moves.

"This is Armand without you," Jesse murmurs. "Because his love was also unbound. You taught him that."

I can't stand it. He seems gutted, a ghost trapped in a living shell.

"Can we help him?"

"We can."

Jesse climbs to his feet. I follow, and he gives me that slight, secret smile that always managed to steal my breath.

"Time is capricious, but love is life, and *that's* eternal. So although we're both dead, dragon-girl, at the same time, we're blessed with life." The breeze musses his hair, tossing it this way and that; sunlight gilds it into a corona. "Except . . . your life is going to continue on a rather more physical plane. Ready?"

"No," I protest, incredulous. "That isn't what I—"

"Go," he says, and steps backward off the cliff.

Like a grain of sugar, he falls and falls.

CHAPTER 39

I T WAS DARK. I inhaled, and breathed in the ocean.

As I convulsed, my body attempting simultaneously to rid itself of salt water while taking in oxygen—but there was no oxygen, only endless black water—I Turned to smoke, and was instantly crushed.

I was stunned into immobility. The ocean spread me thinner, and it was only when the black tar liquid surrounding me began to lighten that I realized I was rising. I didn't exactly burst free of it as much as I merely leaked free—atom by atom, it felt like.

I hovered where I was, trying to orient myself. Everything seemed strange and unfamiliar. Was this the Channel? How had I gotten here? Where . . . where was Jesse?

Above me spread a nighttime sky, a wan smear to my left of either dawn or sunset.

What's happened? I called to the stars.

a life for a life, they sang back. *our own for you.*

The heart of the sky held a faint blush of amethyst. A solitary star streaked across it, falling to earth: gold and green, blazing so bright that for the briefest, most magnificent moment, it changed the color of the world.

⊱ ⊰⊹⊱ ⊰

TWO DAYS SINCE.

Armand shuffled about his room, a sleepwalker determined not to wake. His eyes were bloodshot and his skin crackly and his feet dragged; he was building up a hell of a static charge from the rugs. He paused by the bronze Japanese incense burner on his desk (currently holding nothing but a few dry pens and dust) and touched his finger to its lip. The snap of electricity was palpable.

He hardly felt it.

He'd hardly felt anything in the past forty-eight hours, and that was fine by him. He'd flown to London and back, struck his deal with the devil and now he was packing. *Packing.* Because soon he'd be gone from Tranquility for-bloody-ever, and Aubrey would stay, and Mandy'd have to learn to be at peace with that, with all of that. Because that was all he had left.

Darkfrith. Zaharen Yce.

A *mate* (a painful word, an animal word, nothing subtle about it) who was not going to be Eleanore.

Even the fact that he could now fully Turn to dragon didn't stir him. All Mandy'd ever wanted was to soar at her side, wing to wing. Without Lora, what was the point?

From the shadows by the bed, blond and broken in his wheel-chair, Aubrey spoke.

"Don't . . . go back to them. Don't do as they wish. Do as you wish."

"How?" Armand responded, but without venom or even curios-ity; he meant it rhetorically. He already knew the answer to all the questions that mattered, because it was always the same answer no matter the question: *How do I stay? How do I live with myself? How will I survive the rest of my days?*

Very simply: there was no way.

Yet the Langfords were waiting for him in London. And he was going.

Don't. As if it were that easy.

Armand had declined food, wine, and the butler's offer to have the maids sort his belongings for him. But he was slow, and his trunk on the floor was only half-filled. He'd dumped in trousers and shirts and suspenders and socks, tossed the drawer of ascots atop all that— then fished out the ascots and stared down at them in his hands.

Why the hell would he need ascots? He couldn't even remember ever wearing them. They were holiday gifts, mostly, the sort sent by elderly aunts and great-aunts and godparents who couldn't be both-ered to learn anything personal about his soul. He was wholly certain that Lora would have never given him an ascot.

They gleamed up at him in sleek glossy folds, scented of money and expensive French balm.

He let them slither through his fingers.

"You're worried for me still," Aubrey said. "Even still. Don't be. I have . . . an idea about that."

Mandy made a small attempt to keep the despair from his tone. "Oh, an idea."

"A rather good one. I've been thinking about it ever . . . since you both left . . . for Zaharen Yce. I'll be fine, I promise you. I just . . . I cannot be the reason you're imprisoned."

Armand looked up, turned around. Aubrey was leaning forward in his chair, his gaze intent. The rasping hesitation that usually took his voice had vanished; for a moment he'd sounded exactly like his old self, deep and sure.

"You're my only brother. You're the only dragon alive who matters to me. You saved me from dying a miserable prisoner in that camp, and I won't be your jailer now, even by proxy."

Mandy closed his eyes, seeing the Alpha, seeing Chasen, seeing a future where he was pushed and prodded and molded into a puppet for the sake of his blood.

"I . . ." he began, but couldn't think of anything else to add.

"She's dead, and they're grasping at straws to control you." From the depths of the shadows, Aubrey's eyes flashed, silver-dragon-bright. "They *killed* her, and now they want you. And that will kill you *and* me, as sure as anything in this world. Man or myth, we're not meant to be caged. That's not who we are. That's not how I want to be, and it's the very last thing I want for you."

"Yes," Mandy agreed, his own voice a thread. "But—"

"Goddamn it, I *have* an idea." His brother pointed a shaking finger first to Armand, then to the ceiling. "So—I release you. Fly away. Be free."

Mandy tipped back his head, took a measured breath. He smelled silk and death and sea.

"I'll be right back," he lied, and went to smoke.

He was up the chimney and gone.

━━━ ❈ ━━━

I DRIFTED ABOVE THE waves, hoping I'd been wrong about Jesse, that it had been some other star, some other light extinguished, even though I realized it was foolish to hope. We'd had our moment before heaven. I knew, with all my soul, that I was never again to be given another like it. Jesse had always been a better person than I, nicer and gentler and wiser. Even as a star, he was the better person.

He was gone.

Eventually I found myself floating above Iverson. It had called to me, perhaps, just as it always did. The smear of light I'd glimpsed in the distance back at sea had been the remains of the sunset; I could tell that once I had the castle as my anchor. Plus, it was very dark now. Another night, a different night, I guessed, from the one of my death.

The universe would be forever a shade darker.

I was smoke above the castle's pitched roofs and limestone towers. I was smoke above the very tip-top of the fortress, where the blunt stone teeth that decorated its edges were missing a single merlon. However much time had passed, it seemed, had not been enough to repair the damage from Armand's battle with the marchioness.

A figure stood in that gap between the teeth, silhouetted against the rising moon. A boy, nude, lovely in poise and tension, balanced at the brink of the roof's edge. He had one hand on the merlon to his left, his fingers barely grazing it, the other lax at his side. A good sharp wind would whisk him right over into the surf.

He stood so taut and tall, like a sentinel. Like he watched for something only he could see.

At the sight of him, my confusion and sorrow melted away; a fine, sweet happiness expanded through me instead. Iverson had called, and now I was here, and Armand was here, and Jesse had handed me all this. Because of Jesse, I had been granted this darkly exquisite moment that I'd not asked for and done nothing to deserve—but I was taking it anyway. Jesse *was* the better person, but it would be a sin to throw away such a gift.

Every ounce of me, of this newly reborn me, needed to touch Armand. Needed to feel the weight of his body and the warmth of his kiss.

I materialized to his right.

"What are you doing?" I asked.

I had a half-second of his shocked face before he fell. I watched him plummet, watched him *not* Turn to smoke until the last second, alarming me enough that I smoked after him.

He shot above the crashing waves, wound upward again and came to me. We entwined; we rose; we fell once more together. As helices joined, we ended up at the window of my treasured tower.

I'd left it cracked, or Gladys had, or someone. The interior appeared untouched from my last moments there. Perhaps Westcliffe really did expect that I'd come back.

We Turned together, exactly timed. Before I could say anything, Mandy pulled me to him.

His kiss was better than warm. We were both flushed and breathless, and when I could bear it no longer I leaned back my head with my fingers still curled in his hair and sucked in the sea-chilled air.

He spoke swiftly, softly, a hushed garble against my neck. "This is real, you're real, you feel real, you smell real. I've gone mad but I think you're real."

I rocked him closer. "I am real."

"How can this be?" His body shook, as though he were either laughing or crying, or both. "I don't understand. Am I dead too?"

"No," I said, and then paused to consider it. "At least, I don't think so. I think we're both alive. Why else would this room be so bloody freezing?"

Armand lifted his head. He drew away enough to run his hands down my ribcage, his fingers light and searching.

"You were injured here. I punctured you *here* and *here* and *here* with my claws, and I thought that's what did it—that I'd killed you, even as I tried to save you."

I examined myself in the dim light: smooth skin, no holes. "I'm fine. I feel fine. You didn't kill me, Mandy. I have something to tell you, lots of somethings, but first come with me to the bed. My feet are so cold."

We buried ourselves under the blankets, pulling the top one over our heads to share our heat: a private little cave for two. With our bodies pressed together, with my hands on his cheeks, tracing his lips, the shape of his chin, those long lashes, I began my story. I spoke as quietly as I could, stopping every now and again to lift the top blanket and listen to the castle, to the crooning of the stones and mortar. The distant snuffles and sighs and rolling restlessness of a hundred sleeping girls within its walls.

I told him about my deal with the stars from last summer. I told him about how all my days since had been borrowed, and how Jesse had been waiting, and how I'd seen Honor and him from my place above . . . although, even as I recounted it, the memory stretched sparkly and thin, and the words I thought would describe how it'd been, how I'd felt, seemed so insufficient.

Jesse had claimed it wasn't heaven, but it had seemed like it was to me. Now that I was mortal again, I didn't know the language of heaven.

"Then I was alive once more," I finished. "Beneath the water, then above it. And I saw Jesse fall."

"I took you out to sea," Mandy said huskily. "After—after everything. I took you out there and let you go, because they told me to, and I—I couldn't think of what else to do. I'd planned to die with you."

"I'm glad you didn't. I'd be here in this bed all alone."

"Lora, my God, I . . ."

"I know."

I curled up against him, listening as he told me everything that had happened while I was gone. I rubbed my face against his chest, growing lost in his respiration, the cloud-spice fragrance of him. Satin skin and a hard beating heart.

As he spoke, his arms pulled me even nearer still.

Thank you, I thought to the stars, to Jesse, to the universe. To anyone or anything that might heed or care. *This isn't heaven, but it's life, my own real life. And right now it feels even better than heaven.*

I murmured aloud, "You told me once, ages past, that if you could Turn, you'd leave Tranquility and never come back. Remember?"

"Yes," he said. "I promised you."

"You promised," I agreed. I lifted myself up enough to touch the sandpaper of his cheek. "If Aubrey truly has found a way to protect himself—a *good* way—then let's do it. Let's leave and not come back. You and me, forever."

"Forever sounds about perfect," he said seriously, and I bent down again for his kiss.

↔ ✿ ↔

A GOOD WHILE LATER, as the sky was beginning to burn and the sun was breaking the stubborn line of the horizon, and all the posh princesses downstairs were rising from their beds to attack another innocent day, Mandy whispered, "This is the most astonishing dream I've ever had."

I tossed the blankets off us both so I could see him in this fresh new light, and so he could see my smile.

"Beautiful lordling, I think our dream is only just beginning."

CHAPTER 40

Letter from the Marquess of Sherborne,
at the Tranquility at Idylling Recovery Hospital,
in Wessex

To the Most Honourable Marchioness of Langford,
at Far Perch,
in Grosvenor Square,
in London

October 27, 1915

Madam,

I am writing to inform you that my brother, Lord Armand Louis, sends his regrets that he will not, after all, be joining you in London, or indeed anywhere else ever again for as long as he lives.

This news is, perhaps, somewhat distressing to

you. My sympathies.

I write also to inform you of a series of steps I have completed which may exert some influence upon your actions after you have finished reading this missive.

You will be interested to learn that I have recorded everything I know of you, of your family, and of our species, via a series of letters that currently rest in the hands of no less than a dozen trusted solicitors, peers, and soldiers across the Empire. In these letters I have included true names, locations, histories, activities, and any other details regarding your so-called tribe I could recollect.

The letters are signed, witnessed, and sealed. They will remain sealed until my death or the death of my brother, whereupon they will be immediately delivered to a list of editors in charge of publications both major and minor.

Allow me to clarify: Should I die, should my brother die, should any manner of unnatural misfortune or disappearance befall us, the letters will be delivered to their intended recipients.

You might be thinking that this is a risk you are willing to take. That, in fact, there is no man in the kingdom who would believe not only that dragons exist, but that they exist in the form of two of England's most noble and well-established families.

You might be right. However, I am quite certain

there is also no newspaper in the kingdom that will resist printing such a letter, preposterous as it may read, as it has been written by no less than the heir to the Duke of Idylling.

I feel confident I will survive the infamy of its publication. Will you?

(Oh, yes, and let's do include the death or disappearance of my father in my list of conditions, now that I'm thinking of it. Also Iverson and its inhabitants, as I was informed you toyed with the notion of knocking it into the sea.)

I perceive you to be a woman who appreciates frankness. As such, I wish to assure you of the depths of my sincerity. I expect both my brother and I to live long lives, unmolested by you or your tribe ever again. I trust you feel the same.

Most Candidly,
Aubrey Louis
M. of S.

EPILOGUE

YOU MIGHT THINK THE strangest moments for me would be Turning into a dragon. Or transforming into smoke from flesh, breaking free of gravity and mass to scale the bluest skies. You might think that the scruffy orphan who'd once been strapped to a lunatic asylum table and shocked and shocked until she'd bitten all the way through her lip would be utterly out of her depth as Lora-of-the-moon.

But you'd be wrong.

Blisshaven taught me that even everyday human decency could come with strings attached.

Moor Gate taught me that nearly anyone could turn out to be a monster, no matter their human face.

And Iverson taught me that all human girls are at least half-mad, all the time. (Put them together in a beehive of a school and shake them up, and see what happens.)

Becoming a dragon after surviving all of that was the most natural thing that could have ever happened to me, if that makes sense.

No, the strangest moments are the ones that still catch me by surprise, when I glance around and abruptly fathom that I live in a dreamworld of crystalline elegance: imported wine and teas; gold-trimmed dishes. Silken sheets and down mattresses. Servants and mansions and autos and people to fetch me whatever I wish, whenever I wish, at any time of the day or night. Dresses and shoes and lingerie designed just for me, made pretty for me, and only me.

Ostrich plumes and Spanish combs for my hair; jewels for my body that glimmer like stardust. Veils and hats and bottles of rare perfumes imported from the farthest corners of the world.

Who is that girl in that life? I never recognize her.

But then Armand comes. Always, always, and I can find myself again in his smile.

No matter where we are, or how far we roam, I am home.

And that is the fiercest joy of all.

IN THE YEAR FOLLOWING our escape, a series of seemingly unrelated events occurred:

Zaharen Yce ceased its screaming. Our clothing and knapsack, my golden cuff and engagement ring, all disappeared from the castle at the same time.

The moonless raids by German airships grew fewer and fewer,

possibly because they kept crashing after developing fatal gashes in their skins, no matter how thoroughly they were examined before their flights.

The Moor Gate Institute for Socially Afflicted Youth closed its doors forever after becoming swallowed by scandal. A pile of anonymous letters sent to the government—and the broadsheets—outlined its most egregious abuses, and included enough verifiable detail that there was no hope of salvaging it.

Doctor Vernon Becker was stripped of permission to practice medicine and forced to retire in disgrace to Cheapside.

Lady Chloe Pemington became engaged to one Lieutenant Laurence Clayworth, with the wedding to take place in a year, or two. Or three or four or five, depending on whether she could do better in the interim.

And, amid an appropriate amount of pomp and war-time restraint, the Iverson School for Girls graduated its eleventh-year class, minus a single ragamuffin scholarship girl.

❦

THEN, ONE BRIGHT AND orange-blossomed spring day, this happened:

"Eleanore? Eleanore Jones, is that you?"

I swiveled in my chair, searching the crowded Spanish coffee-house for the source of that very familiar voice.

"Sophia."

She wore billowing lilac chiffon and lace gloves and a wide-brimmed, flowered hat. She moved with her shark's grace around all the tables, narrowed eyes and an upsweep of platinum hair, her lips curved in a smile that could best be described as *hazardous*.

"And Armand, of course! It *is* you, both of you, here in Barcelona! Golly, what are the odds!"

Because we were in an extremely grand coffeehouse attached to an extremely grand hotel, and because it was daytime and people were staring (Sophia did have that effect on the general public), Mandy had no choice but to come to his feet and offer her a chair. She ignored it, holding out her hand to him instead. He accepted it, shook, and Sophia turned her smile to me. I swear I felt a chill.

"You wouldn't believe the rumors going around about you two. It's been—what?—two years or so since you vanished into thin air?"

"Or so," I agreed. Mandy gave up waiting for Sophia to sit and returned to his *café tallat*. His eyes met mine from above his cup.

Sophia planted a hand on her hip, her chin lifted, her gaze traveling the room. She spoke in a light, rapid staccato that I'd never heard her use before, but it did make her sound more grown-up, which was probably the point.

"Let's see. You were filthy spies for the kaiser, and murdered in your sleep. You were noble spies for His Majesty, and sent on a secret mission beyond the front. You found out that *other* charity girl, Honor Whosis, was a spy for either the Germans or the Allies, depending, and *you* murdered *her*. Oh, and you were desperate lovers determined to wed, no matter who didn't like it, and eloped to the Scottish hills."

"That last one was true," I said, and at last she looked at me, then sat down. "What are you doing here? Spain's rather far from the glamour of England's upper stratum."

"Isn't it, though?" Her face was shadowed beneath the brim of her hat. "Papa's chasing a filly for sale. An Arabian something-or-another, with a heart of gold and legs of fire. He's just outside, in fact, handling some tedious matter about our motorcar being out of petrol." She smoothed a ripple from the tablecloth with both hands. "I thought I'd come along, blow away some of the cobwebs of routine life."

"Well," I began, "It's nice to—"

"Chloe was invited as well, but it seems she's far too delicate for travel. Planning your wedding to the wrong fellow will do that, I suppose. And Aubrey . . ."

"Yes?"

Sophia looked up again, steely. "Aubrey hasn't said a bloody word about you two, except that he believes you to be alive and well."

I grinned. "Aubrey's a peach."

"I say, Eleanore—or Lady Jane, or whatever your name is now—"

"Lady Lora," Armand said.

"I have to admit that I hardly recognized you, you look so . . . clean."

"My." I sat back, marveling. "You *are* angry."

She drummed her fingers against the arm of her chair. "I thought we were friends."

"We are." I laughed a little. "You're my only friend, in fact, excepting Mandy and Aubrey. And since they're family now, they don't count."

Sophia leaned forward, stole my cup of hot chocolate from its saucer, and took a deep sip. "Then I want to know what actually happened to you."

Armand shook his head. "You don't."

Her mouth tightened.

"You do owe her a favor," I reminded them both.

"That's right," Sophia quickly agreed. "I kept your sordid secret about that summer, all this while."

Mandy gave the coffee in his cup a slow swirl with his spoon, then shrugged. He knew me well enough to recognize when my mind was made up. I turned to Sophia.

"Are you ready?"

She held me in a heavy-lidded look. "For what?"

"The truth."

"Finally!"

I smiled at Armand. He smiled back, wry, then reached across the table to hold my hand. We faced her together.

"Sophia," I said, "have you ever wondered what it's like to hunt the moon?"

"Or taste the clouds?" Mandy added.

She gazed at us, pampered and powdered and clever bright eyes.

With my free hand I took hers, linking us into three.

"Are you game to find out?"

About the Author

SHANA ABE LIVES IN Colorado with several rescued house rabbits, two loudly opinionated cats, about three dozen giant, surly goldfish—and a very handsome and patient husband.

www.shanaabe.com

Addendum

WHAT REALLY HAPPENED TO **Rue and Kit?** Who was their mysterious sixth child, ancestor of the dark and devoted Armand? Here's a glimpse into one of their many adventures beyond Darkfrith:

It is an acknowledged fact that dragons exist. For many ages they have girthed our clouds, burrowed through our mountains, and created great caverns of crystal with their breath. Water Dragons bring the rains, and Sea Dragons the tsunamis. Improper offerings to an Earth Dragon will cause it to writhe in anger, and the ground will shake violently. Villages have been swallowed whole by such a mistake.

Most recently we know of the Snow Dragon of Hokkaido and its noble defeat at the hands of the great warrior Kiyoshi. We know of the perfect pearl sliced from its throat by his blade . . .

—From *A Summary of Creatures*, by Imperial Court
Historian Akihiko, 1567

Edo, Japan
1784

SHE HAD HER BACK to them, deliberate, facing instead the delicate paper wall that defined the boxy shape of the room they'd been given, smoothing her hands down the silk that covered her thighs. Rue thought of all the reasons she should turn and face them: that Kit was right, that this was necessary, that agreeing to the shogun's plan to steal the gem might mean salvation for Ellery. A cure.

To their credit, they only waited for her to face them again, the pair of them as calm and still as the light from the lanterns was not.

Her two hearts. Her family—what was left of it—small and imperfect and beloved.

A moth batted the paper before her, hitting twice before settling against a shim. A faint golden sheen, *not* from the lanterns, spread across the entire panel, radiant enough to reveal the clever pattern of ginko leaves pressed into the fibers.

At night, surrounded by flame, Ellery gleamed like a fragment of the sunken sun.

She closed her eyes against it. Beyond the walls Rue perceived the muted workings of the palace, the guards shifting on their feet nearby, sequestered women sleeping in rooms unseen, smoke and sake and rain-fragrant wood. The hum of iron from the nails in the walls and floor was a gentle buzzing in her ears.

Outside, the winds nudged the clouds west, the midnight storm retreating.

I'm weary, she thought, surprised. *It's been so long for us now, all this running, and I'm weary of it. I never even realized.*

Rue turned about. Her husband and son regarded her with matching gravity, seated side by side on the bare tatami mat, their knees touching. She was struck anew by how much they were alike, and how much they truly were not: the same shape to their jaws, the same straight set to their shoulders and thick lashes and hair that had been left untrimmed for too long.

But, oh, everything else . . .

How was it possible that a child so beautiful could inspire such fear in mortal hearts?

"We should do it," she said.

Kit only raised a brow. The glass-green of his gaze had gone opaque.

"You want to," she said. "I know you do."

"Steal into a foreign fortress we've never been to before, a place no doubt armed to the rafters with insanely loyal men with swords and a taste for death, all for a ruby or pearl or what-have-you that might or might not be what we want?" His lips formed a slight, handsome smile. "Of course I do. It's what I live for."

She folded her arms. "You're beginning to sound a bit too much like me."

"All the better."

"I thought you lived for Rue," interjected Ellery, still grave.

Kit rose to his feet, holding out a hand to his son. "For Rue, for

you. We're all one. Tell me, which would you prefer this time, a diamond or a pearl?"

"A pearl," said Ellery instantly.

"Done," announced his father, hefting him up into his arms. It
was a movement and instinct Rue had seen a thousand times, and
felt a thousand more herself: with the upward sweep of his body,
Ellery's dragon wings at once lifted and curved, seeking air for flight
but forming instead a shield around both their faces, hiding them
from her view.

For that brief moment they were shrouded in gold, both of them,
shining and apart from her.

Then Kit lowered Ellery back to the floor, to the edge of the pillowy blankets of the futon. His gaze returned to hers; he shook a lock
of hair from his cheek.

"I cannot help but notice they've offered just a single chamber
for the three of us."

Rue nodded, striving to look impassive. The corners of his smile
grew more sensual.

"And I haven't yet glimpsed the moon tonight. Shall we explore
the sky a while, my lady?"

There was the futon and the guards and Christoff, looking at
her with his subtle bridled hunger, with the promise of dark release
in his eyes.

"Yes," she said. "Let's."

CPSIA information can be obtained
at www.ICGtesting.com
Printed in the USA
LVOW11s2144011117
554606LV00001B/77/P

9 780998 470221